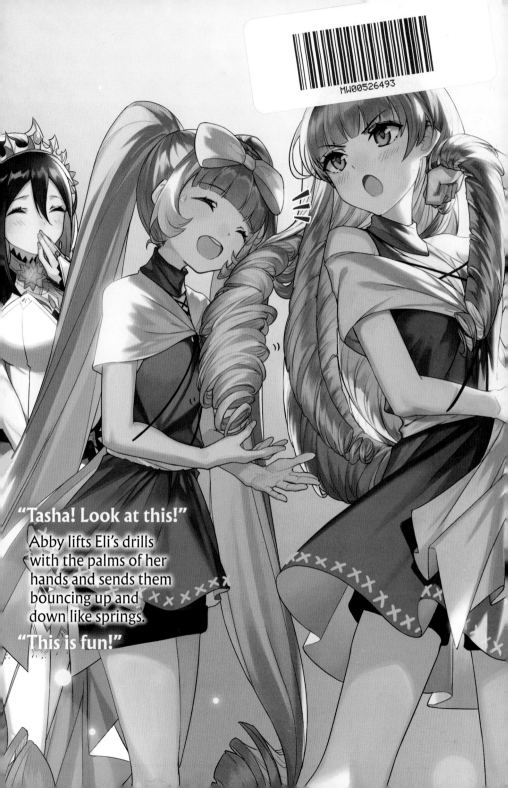

"Tasha! Look at this!"

Abby lifts Eli's drills with the palms of her hands and sends them bouncing up and down like springs.

"This is fun!"

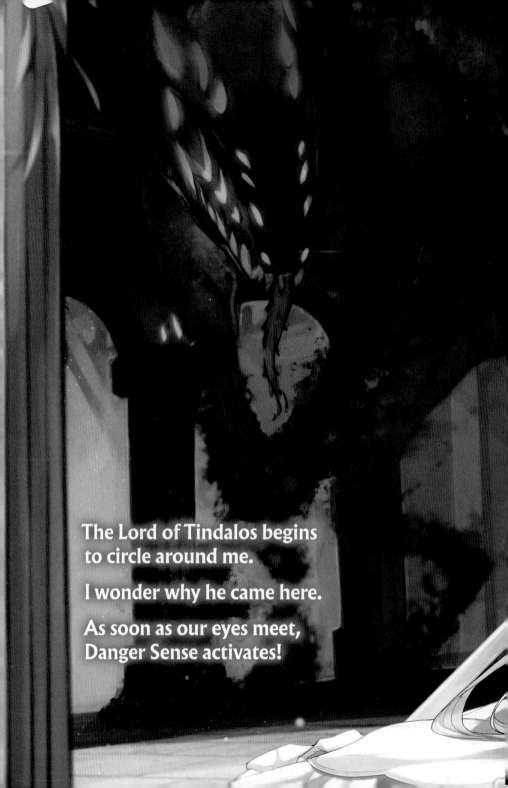

The Lord of Tindalos begins to circle around me.

I wonder why he came here.

As soon as our eyes meet, Danger Sense activates!

Wow... Regenerate deals six attacks at once? I'll certainly make use of it.

Free Life Fantasy Online
IMMORTAL PRINCESS

NOVEL 3

WRITTEN BY

AKISUZU NENOHI

ILLUSTRATED BY

SHERRY

Airship

Seven Seas Entertainment

Free Life Fantasy Online ~Immortal Princess, Hajimemashita ~ Vol. 3
© 2019 Akisuzu Nenohi. All rights reserved.
First published in Japan in 2019 by Kodansha Ltd., Tokyo.
Publication rights for this English edition arranged through Kodansha Ltd., Tokyo.

Seven Seas press and purchase enquiries can be sent to
Marketing Manager Lianne Sentar at press@gomanga.com.
Information regarding the distribution and purchase of
digital editions is available from Digital Manager CK Russell
at digital@gomanga.com.

Follow Seven Seas Entertainment online at
sevenseasentertainment.com.

TRANSLATION: Emma Schumacker
ADAPTATION: Renee Baumgartner
COVER DESIGN: M. A. Lewife
LOGO DESIGN: M. Lyn Hall
INTERIOR LAYOUT & DESIGN: Clay Gardner
COPY EDITOR: Jade Gardner
PROOFREADER: Meg van Huygen
LIGHT NOVEL EDITOR: Callum May
PREPRESS TECHNICIAN: Melanie Ujimori, Jules Valera
EDITOR-IN-CHIEF: Julie Davis
ASSOCIATE PUBLISHER: Adam Arnold
PUBLISHER: Jason DeAngelis

ISBN: 978-1-63858-925-9
Printed in Canada
First Printing: April 2023
10 9 8 7 6 5 4 3 2 1

TABLE OF CONTENTS

Character Introduction

Tsukishiro Kotone:
The main character. She enjoys a cup of tea while reading a good book, but she also likes to play video games with her little sister. Much like her mother, Kotone is stunningly beautiful. She has a healthy sleep cycle, waking up at 6 a.m. and going to bed at 10 p.m. every single day.

Tsukishiro Akina:
The main character's little sister. Her hobbies include video games and her big sister. To be frank, she probably loves her sister more than she loves eating three meals a day. Her sister gives her all the nourishment she needs. Akina loves games of any genre, both online and offline. She even plays TTRPGs.

Tsukishiro Ouka:
Their mother, Ouka, stands at around 170 centimeters tall. Refers to the main character as "Kotone" or "Tasha." Her looks would be described more as "beautiful" than "adorable." She keeps her age a secret, but she currently works as an actress and a model.

Bradford Clark Furnivall:
Their father is a British man who stands at 180 centimeters tall. He's relaxed and slender and would probably look good in a knight's uniform. Currently works as a fashion designer and was pursued relentlessly by Ouka.

Gozakura Tomohiro:
One of our heroine's two childhood friends. He's roughly 175 centimeters tall, intelligent, and wears glasses. Tomohiro has the personality of a caring older brother. IRL, he refers to the heroine as "Kotone," while in the game, he calls her "Stasia."

Horiai Suguru:
Our heroine's other childhood friend. He's just under 180 centimeters with a strong, muscular build. A tall and hearty individual.

Yanase Aina:
One of Akina's best friends. She's a bit shorter than Akina and has a relaxed and carefree personality.

Matsukane Karen:
Akina's other best friend who's about the same height as her. She's the more serious member of the group. You could say she knows when best to put a stop to things.

Elizabeth Ophelia Renfield:
Kotone's childhood friend and the daughter of a CEO. To be honest, she has the scary eyes of a villainess. She's a bit taller than the heroine and has a well-proportioned body. Refers to Kotone as "Tasha."

Colette Marcy Lane:
Elizabeth's personal attendant. You could call her a normal maid in a maid's uniform...but it's more accurate to call her a lady in waiting. She tutors Elizabeth as well, but since they've been together for so long, she's more like a big sister to her.

Silvester Noah Renfield:
The CEO of Kotone's mother's company. Elizabeth's father and Colette's boss.

Abigail Selina Lucraft:
A childhood friend of Akina and the daughter of a CEO. If Elizabeth is the villainess, then Abigail would be the heroine, at least as far as appearances go. She's the shortest out of all the friends and hates that fact, so she often lets her childish side spill out.

Dorothy Oriana Macy:
Abigail's personal attendant. She is both a work partner and friend of Colette's, since they see each other so often. They're allowed to wear whatever uniforms they want, so since a maid uniform fit the role, there were no complaints when she and Colette decided that would be their attire. It's not a bad thing; it just makes them stand out in a crowd.

Maximilian Louis Lucraft:
The CEO of Kotone's father's company. Abigail's father and Dorothy's boss.

KOTONE AND HER IRL FRIENDS/ACQUAINTANCES

Anastasia:
Kotone. A zombie character who wears a dress, and even though she wields a rapier, her main abilities are magic. Her current objective is to travel to the Nether, but she's not a high enough level to get there.

Akirina:
Akina. She plays as a plain and simple human. Her main weapon is a halberd, and she serves as a mobile attacker when partying up with other players.

Tomo:
Tomohiro. A pure magician who specializes in spells and just spells. His main weapons are books. As you'd expect, that's how he fights—with magic.

Sugu:
Suguru. A giant, powerful fighter. His main weapon is a two-handed hammer. With nothing but muscle for brains, he'll smash you with all his might if you get too close. That said, he still knows how to parry or block when attacked.

Nadia:
Yanase. A bard who delivers buffs over wide areas with her performances. Her main weapon is a ukulele. The songs she plays are quite effective, but her movements and ability to cast spells during a performance are limited.

Helen:
Matsukane. A scout for her party who mainly fights with a long bow. As a rabbit beastman, it's easy for her to detect enemies, as well as bait them with her archery.

Eli:
Elizabeth. A whip user who arrives during the second wave of players. She plays as a young rich girl with blonde hair drills, meaning acquiring a dress is her primary objective.

Letty:
Colette. She wields daggers as her main weapon. Her primary objective is getting a maid uniform.

Abby:
Abigail. A doll player who arrives during the second wave. Her current objectives are to find a dress and evolve from a demon to an angel.

Dory:
Dorothy. A brawler-type melee fighter. Her current objective is to get a maid uniform.

TOP GUILD PLAYERS

Cecil:
A knight straight out of a fairy tale! That said, he looks much more like a character from an otome game than someone from a fantasy game. He fights with two swords and loves to play aggressively. He's the guildmaster of The Knights of Dawn.

Kotatsu:
A young woman with cat ears. After upgrading her pitching skills, she fights by throwing items at her opponent. She's the guildmaster of The Critter Empire.

Musasabi:
He roleplays as a ninja, but by no means a historically accurate one—it also doesn't help that he fights as a slayer. You can tell exactly how much he enjoys FLFO, and as a top player, his skills are the real deal. He's the guildmaster of NINJA.

Lucebarm:
A bear. He's not playing like a bear—he is a bear! That's what happens when you max out your appearance after you choose the beastman race. But as a player, of course, he walks on two legs and talks like normal. He's the guildmaster of Furry Legion.

TOP PRODUCERS

Ertz:
One of the best at blacksmithing. He specializes in metalwork and roleplays as a hearty dwarf. All ores go to Ertz.

Dentelle:
One of the best at needlework. He specializes in fabrics and leather goods, even going so far as to create cosplay outfits. He'll give you a discount if you let him take a screenshot. All lace goes to Dentelle.

Primura:
One of the best at woodwork. She makes a wide range of items, from canes to bows to wooden utensils. IRL, she's in her second year of junior high and is always busy with crafting. Her name is a reference to the primula flower.

Salute:
One of the best at compounding. She makes potions and dresses like a scientist with a white coat and frameless glasses. Health = Salute

Nephrite:
One of the best at handcrafting. She mainly makes accessories, including the glasses that Salute wears. Nephrite means "jade."

TOP INHUMANS

Alfred:
AKA Alf. He began as living armor from the ghost race, but he then evolved into a Dullahan. He's also one of the players who joins the heroine's party, and he primarily wields a shield.

Honehone:
AKA Mr. Skelly. As his name suggests, Honehone's race is a skeleton. He's one of the players who joins the heroine's party and is surprisingly nimble.

Fairellen:
A wind fairy of the fairy race tree. Of the six elements, she has the highest aptitude for wind. Despite repeatedly dying while getting the hang of flying, she loves the sky.

Clementia:
Clementia plays as the rare plant race. Her third evolution is a sexy mandrake, which is like a lewd radish with different colors.

Cupid:
The first angel player who discovered how to evolve from a demon into an angel. She fights with a short bow. Cupid pierces hearts with her arrows (physical).

GODS

Supreme Deity, Creall:
The god of both creation and destruction. He created this world and its three pillars.

Goddess of Reincarnation, Stellura:
The goddess who governs light and darkness, life and death, time and fate, and contracts and judgment. She commands the undead and can take many forms.

Goddess of Love, Haventhys:
The goddess who governs water and earth, love and growth, and nature and rest. She commands all plant life.

Goddess of War, Sigrdrífa:
The goddess who governs fire and wind, and battle and victory. She commands animals.

RESIDENTS (NPCS)/GRANNY AND FRIENDS

Meghan:
The owner of a general store which you need a trigger to find, and the most powerful alchemist in the Starting Town area. She becomes the heroine's teacher.

Luciana:
An archbishop who takes care of things around Starting Town, although it's more accurate to call her a grand bishop. She's the third highest-ranking person in the church, but the heroine doesn't know this yet.

MANAGEMENT

Yamamoto Ittetsu:
A person in charge of FLFO. He livestreams when he's bored. He's a supervisor, but not an engineer himself. They say his stomach is made of a superalloy.

Kuon Mio:
A game master, often referred to as a GM. You can think of her as a member of management who also has an in-game character.

PROLOGUE

Mm... Oh, it's morning? This is the usual time I get up, so I might as well log in for a bit.

I stretch and check to see if I received any messages while I was asleep. All it takes is a glance at the icon to see if it's flashing, so it's easy enough to tell.

After that, I'll give my inventory a check and replace anything I'm running low on...but that probably won't be necessary.

I think I'll go for a stroll through town instead.

The real-life time in the world influences the in-game time, although it's not an exact mirror.

I usually wake up at six in the morning. At that point, it's dawn in the game too, and by 6:30 a.m., the game transitions to the afternoon. Morning, afternoon, evening, and nighttime follow a real-world pattern, while only weather is random.

Hmm. It looks like the rain came to pay a visit today... I guess I'll abandon my plans for a walk and pass the time until school starts. All I have to do at school today is help out with the cleaning

FREE LIFE FANTASY ONLINE

before our end-of-term ceremony, so we'll be done with that by the afternoon.

Dawn in the game comes again at noon. The weather will change then too, so I'll have to cross my fingers that I come home to sunny skies.

I finish getting ready and start to head to the front door, when...

"We'll be out on a date today, so take this and buy whatever you want for lunch!"

"What about tonight?"

"I'll buy you something," I tell my sister.

"Okay!"

It sounds like Mom and Dad are spending the day on a date. Akina *did* have Moreburger for lunch yesterday. But what about today? Sushi?

"Conveyor belt sushi? Or the regular kind?"

"Hmm...we have to clean before lunch today, so let's do conveyor belt sushi! I want quantity, not quality."

"Okay. Let's do that for lunch then."

"What about yakiniku instead?"

"But it'll take longer for us to get home."

"Grrr..."

I know the three pillars of my sister's life are meat, fish, and time for playing video games. I'm going to shower when I get home anyway, so I don't really care where we go to eat.

"Well, make up your mind by lunchtime."

"'Kay."

She still hasn't decided by the time we arrive at school, so I give up. I'll let her make the choice by this afternoon. If that's still not enough time to think, I'll decide for her. Why did this have to be such a vicious struggle in the first place?

"Ah! Morning!"

"Morning, Miss Kotone."

"Good morning."

My friends from elementary school always act a little "off" around me, so I make a point of ignoring them when they do.

As we chat, my childhood friends Tomohiro and Suguru show up to class, followed by our teacher soon after.

"Okay, people! Time to take attendance!"

Naturally, this is a big school. We have people who normally do the cleaning around campus too, so once our teacher divides us up and assigns us sections to clean, we chat amongst ourselves and finish up in no time at all.

I head back to the classroom. The other students gradually return once they've finished cleaning their own sections.

After some time, Tomohiro arrives, and he looks like he's in a good mood for some reason.

"Hey, Kotone."

"Hm?"

"Let's go on a date sometime."

Everyone else in the classroom turns to look at us, but I just ignore them. It's only a "date" because we're a boy and a girl, I'm sure.

"Where to?"

"The beach!"

"I don't know about that..."

"Ah, I mean in-game. Imbamunte in the south."

"Hm? Ah, I see. A safe zone?"

"It's super realistic there, and it's beautiful too. It doesn't cost any money, we don't need our parents' permission, and you don't have to worry about getting sunburned. We can just sit there and relax."

It's true that a beach trip is kind of a big deal for students. But that's not so much the case when the trip is in a video game.

"I'll have to get a bathing suit."

"I already have the materials. I was going to ask for Mr. Dentelle to make one. What kind do you want?"

"Hm... How about a bikini with a pareo?"

"The thing you wrap around your hips? What color?"

"Anything's fine."

"I guess Mr. Dentelle can take care of the color and design. I'm sure he'll be thrilled either way, and since it's a game, he won't need your measurements!"

If he's going to make me a bathing suit, I might as well just accept it. As for food, I'll be sure to prepare sandwiches or something of the sort.

"Oh, one other thing. Aside from our date, what say we have a barbecue too? We can invite the people in our parties along with our other friends."

"Hmm...I can prepare food, but I don't have the materials to make the sauces we'll need."

The charcoal cooker from my cooking kit would be a bit too small for a barbecue. I don't have anything like an iron plate to cook on, either... But most importantly, I have no barbecue sauce. It will probably taste plenty delicious with salt and pepper alone, but it's just not the same.

"Hm... Kotone, isn't it possible that because of your skills, you're the only one who can cook meat?"

"Ah... That seems likely to me."

"It's not gonna work, then. Making one person do all the grilling is no fun."

Having a barbecue with friends means everyone pitching in to grill the meat. That way, it becomes a fun group activity.

Our teacher returns.

"Great job, everyone! Since you worked so hard to clean up, I have a present for you all."

"Free juice!"

"Ha ha!" Our teacher pauses for a moment. "No, it's your homework."

"Awwww!"

"I told you yesterday that this was coming!"

He certainly did.

"It's a simple assignment to make sure you don't forget anything. It's not much, so get it over with quickly. All right. Dismissed! Don't be late tomorrow!"

It's still a bit before lunch. Did that sister of mine pick what she wants to eat yet?

What's this? Oh, my phone's ringing. It's Eli.

Elizabeth...the daughter of the person Mom works for. She's the real deal—the rich young daughter of a CEO. We're also the same age and have been friends since we were little. I guess I should answer the call. She'll want to speak English, but everyone knows I'm fluent in the language.

"Good day, Stasia."

"Good day, Eli. What's new?"

"Where are you right now?"

"At school. I'm about to eat lunch and then head home."

"Go straight home. I'll be there at noon."

I gather my thoughts for a moment. "You're here, aren't you?"

"I have Abby with me too."

"Abby" is short for Abigail, the daughter of the CEO my dad works for and my sister's childhood friend, since, like Akina, she's one year younger than me.

"So that's why Dad had a bad feeling about something."

"I'll bet he did! What were you planning to eat, by the way?"

"My sister's been trying to choose between sushi and yakiniku all morning."

"Let's make it sushi, then. I want some too. How about meat for dinner? Barbecue, right?"

"Ah, you haven't talked to my parents, have you?"

"Of course not!"

"I didn't think so. They're out on some sort of date right now, so I'll have to tell them not to bring us back dinner."

"Oh, they're not home? Hear that, Father? They're not home, so you can't give them a scare."

So they really *were* planning on scaring my parents. But it's just about time for lunch, and I'm starting to doubt if I'll have time for a shower. I need to get home fast.

We're probably going to need our lunch to be delivered instead.

"Let's head home, Tomohiro," I call out.

"Sure. Suguru! Let's go!"

"Fine."

We head for the gates and meet up with my sister and her friends.

"Big Sis! Let's go get some meat!"

"I'm so sorry, but we're going to have to wait until dinner for meat."

"Huh?! Why?!"

"Eli and Abby are coming over, so we have to head straight home. It's a surprise attack."

"An ambush from an army of rich girls?! So are the CEOs coming too?"

If the daughters will be there, so will the parents.

"Our lunch choices have been reduced, but the quality will be much higher."

"All right, I forgive you! Let's get going!"

It's the same members in our group as yesterday—Tomohiro and Suguru, as well as Akina's friends, Yanase and Matsukane.

We all head to my house, when two very conspicuous cars pass by us. Oh, wait, they're stopping just up ahead. A woman wearing a distinctive outfit steps out of the first car.

Yanase and Matsukane both gasp. "A maid?!"

"Oh, you two have never seen one, huh?" comments Tomohiro.

That made me realize Yanase and Matsukane never happened to be around when the girls showed up for a visit.

"It's been a while, hasn't it, all of you?" One of the maids approaches us. "Although, I haven't met you two before...have I? Please call me Colette."

"I'm Yanase."

"And I'm Matsukane."

"Would you like to join us in the cars?"

"Huh?!"

I head toward the car, since we won't all be able to walk together on the sidewalk.

All of us could fit between the two cars, but having Yanase and Matsukane take a car alone feels a little mean. Since Abby will be riding in the second car, my sister will choose that one.

"I can go with you two in Abby's car!" Akina offers.

"That sounds good. Tomohiro and Suguru can join me in the front car," I reply.

Those two have met our visitors several times already, so there shouldn't be any issues. We get straight inside the air-conditioned car and take off driving.

The occupants of the car include a kind-looking old man; Elizabeth, AKA Eli, in a light and simple dress; the driver; and

Colette, who stepped out of the car to talk to us earlier. Everyone inside is American, and they know me through Mom's work. The car behind us is full of British people who know Dad.

"Look at you! You're always so pretty!" says Eli's father.

"Thanks, I appreciate it. I'm glad to see you look well."

"I am! Although Japan's always so very hot at this time of year..."

I certainly agree with that. It's truly scorching here.

As we catch up, we arrive home in no time at all thanks to a quick car ride. I open the gates so that they can use our driveway, hand over my house key to Tomohiro, and walk over to my sister.

"Eli told me she'll have lunch with us, and she'll pay too."

"Then why don't you two join us?"

"Huh?!"

Akina drags Yanase and Matsukane into the house while I follow behind them. They both look rather stiff. That surely must be due to the overwhelming power of the limousine—a vehicle that anyone can tell is expensive at a single glance.

I wonder if those two will even be able to taste the delicious food we're about to eat? They just seem so nervous.

Since it sounds like everyone is spending the day here at our house, I'll order the food for delivery and then go take a shower. I'm sure they'll have no trouble making themselves at home. I don't need to show them where the parlor is... After all, they found my living room without any issues.

With my refreshing shower over, I head back to the living room.

Eli and Abby are both beautiful, but Eli has a "calm and cool" personality while Abby is perky and cute. Maybe it's simpler to call them the tsundere rich girl and the little bunny rich girl. Not that Eli is *actually* tsundere, but you get what I'm going for. Or maybe thinking of them as a villainess and heroine works better...

By the way, Eli's about one centimeter taller than me, while Abby is ten centimeters shorter.

"I haven't seen you in so long, Abby."

"It's good to see you again, Tasha! I'm still just so jealous of your boobs!"

Most of the younger girls in my life love to hug me, my little sister included.

I see two large bags sitting in a corner of the room. What could those be? Eli spots what I'm staring at, stands up straight in an intimidating stance, and declares in a loud voice, "Tasha, you have a fun game you play, right? It took so long for Father to get his hands on it!"

It's like our two hearts just became one.

My sister scoots over to the bags and peeks inside. "Whoa, it's FLFO. You're gonna play?"

"I'll be playing as a rich young girl with blonde hair drills."

"But isn't that what you *actually* are?"

"I could never get my hair that coiled in real life! By the way, we'll both be playing."

"What? You're going to have blonde hair spirals too, Abby?"

"Yes!"

FREE LIFE FANTASY ONLINE

"Ah, I see... But you have four consoles here?" my sister points out.

When I hear those words, I turn to look at the two CEOs.

"Sadly, it won't be us joining you... It's really too bad!"

"It's awful!"

They looked truly depressed. But that could only mean... I turn to look at the maids.

"Yes, the two of us will be joining them."

"We look forward to playing."

The girls were bringing their maids with them. Their names are Colette, AKA Letty, and Dorothy, AKA Dory. They choose to wear maid uniforms because they like them. The black-and-white long dresses are a proper uniform for that line of work, after all, so they say they're handy to wear.

Our height order starts with Letty, then goes to Eli, me, Dory, Rina, and Abby. Eli wears her wavy hair down just past her shoulders, Letty and Abby have shoulder-length hair, and Dory has hers up in a ponytail.

I remember the time I asked them if their maid outfits were too hot in the Japanese summer, but they just whipped out some ice packs wrapped in towels. The outfits allow them to hide things too, which, according to them, is a key benefit. They were quite insistent.

A real-life rich girl with blonde hair drills and a professional maid...or would she be called a lady-in-waiting? Regardless, there's even two of this exact pair... How intense.

"Will we be able to obtain maid outfits in the game?"

"This is the only outfit we feel comfortable in."

Is this the mark of a pro? Or an occupational sickness?

"Well...I'm sure you can find some...but we can at least have them made."

"Dentelle would be happy to make them, I'm certain. The only problem is that since he's the best, it'll cost you a lot."

Tomohiro is right. Mr. Dentelle will almost certainly make maid uniforms for them. He's the very best of the best. Since maid uniforms are so famous, I'll bet he's already stitched up one or two. I can't imagine there are many other people who go out of their way to seek them out as their outfit of choice.

The problem is probably going to be their own pickiness. In the end, they'll almost certainly order their own personal uniforms.

"What about fancy dresses?"

"He'll definitely be happy to make them, but I haven't found any silk yet."

"No silk? What about your outfit?"

"I was wondering about that too. Is it made of some kind of special in-game material?" Dad's company CEO joins the conversation. He's a designer, after all.

"That's right. Judging by the description, it's some kind of fantasy metal. It has that metallic luster."

"I see..."

But wait. Why do they know about that?

"I saw the video, of course. I figured that was you, so I looked through it carefully."

"I saw the commercial and the trailer too!" says Abby.

Ah, I get it now. They figured out who I am. That made them want to give the game a try, so they came to bother Dad, and now we're here. What were they thinking?

RIIING!

Oh, that's the doorbell. The food's finally here. I check outside and confirm the delivery.

Everyone swarms the food and carries it inside. I snap a picture of the group gathered around the table to send to Dad.

After a while, I hear a ringing from the connect board belonging to Mr. Louis, Dad's CEO. It's safe to assume that's Dad.

Mr. Louis checks the name of the caller and chuckles as he answers. As for me, I respond to a message from Mom and bring up the topic of dinner.

By the way, my family behaves the same way when we go to visit them, so it's really all fair in the end.

After finishing the delicious—and expensive—sushi delivery, I see our four friends off. They seemed to have calmed down enough to experience the taste properly, so I'm glad I didn't reveal our guests' true identities. But Akina will probably spoil it later. Tomohiro and Suguru already know who they are, so there's no need to worry about them.

As we chat, Akina races off to her room, letting me know she's going to stream. I stay behind in the living room to watch her stream on the TV.

The livestreams translate different languages automatically, but that's not necessary if you understand the language in the first place. Sometimes it mistranslates things too. It looks like she's turned off the automatic translation when it comes to English.

To Eli and the others, Japanese has a lot of words in it and the automatic translation seems fishy to them, so they really appreciate this. They also think it could bring in more viewers from the English-speaking world.

They're lounging around peacefully and watching the stream, which means it's all right for me to go play the game for myself. I log in too.

I'm going to go visit the old woman at the general store.

THURSDAY

I LOG IN, stretch, and head to the general store. The woman told me to come back when I'd raised my Alchemy skill to its second tier, and so here I am.

"Hello. I'm back today as an alchemist."

"Is that right? Then let me share this old soul's wisdom with you. Have a seat."

I sit down in the chair next to her, though I don't know why it's there in the first place.

"Let me first make sure you're ready to learn, because I'll start treating you like my pupil. You won't be able to learn from most other alchemists after this. Are you sure this old granny's the one for you?"

"I don't know any other alchemists, and the wisdom from a pioneer—or rather, from an older person—will be very valuable. I don't see a problem in choosing you."

"Good. Then let's start with the basics."

Granny teaches me all the things I can do as an alchemist. "You can use cores you get from monsters, create items, disassemble them, and control which attributes you get when you make a new substance. That's what it means to be an alchemist. What level are you now?"

"Right now, I'm...two."

Wait, how did it get there? Did my Dark Rituals count toward my Alchemy level?

"Hmm... Ah, I see. Do you know Darkness Magic?"

"I do."

"What about Necromantic Magic?"

"I learned that too. Is there a problem?"

"Is that right? No, that'll do. Now that you're an alchemist, learn Golem Training whenever you can."

"Golems? That sounds interesting."

"To put it simply, it's a worse version of Necromantic Magic."

"Oh..."

"Be sure to protect the secrets I'm about to share. If you don't, I won't recognize you as my pupil any longer."

"I understand."

"I'm going to tell you about Golem Training, Necromantic Magic, and how they relate to Chimera Creation."

Oh? Chimera Creation? This sounds interesting too. The word "chimera" makes it easy for me to imagine what this is going to be like.

Golem Training involves modified monster cores to create the core for a golem. These golems will only listen to the simplest of orders. They can fight in an unsophisticated manner, but any coordination from them will be difficult. If anything, they're great for straightforward tasks like carrying heavy objects, but alchemists throughout history have seen that behavior and researched whether it's practical to use the creatures for combat.

The problem with Golem Training is that golems aren't very smart. It's their only flaw, but it's also a fatal one. As long as they have mana, they can absorb materials around them so as to continue to function when their bodies break down. They're perfectly safe as long as their cores remain intact.

The best way to start would have been to upgrade Golem Training. I also could have used taming if I simply wanted to control monsters, but that has nothing to do with the Alchemy skill. That was how the taboo act of Chimera Creation came to be.

"You used Alchemy to control their bodies, right?"

"Exactly. But it didn't work out that well in the end, even if I did expect it."

Living beings who have their bodies manipulated won't listen to orders. Most alchemists end up killed by their chimeras. With the sudden changes to their bodies, it probably causes them pain when they're recreated over and over again.

The biggest problem is that once the alchemist is killed, the crazed chimera remains. After all, unlike golems, they were once living creatures.

These poor chimeras resort to violence and begin destroying everything in their paths—be it other monsters, trees, or anything else. Anyone who remains oversees cleaning up after them. Depending on what it was made from, the chimera's damage capabilities range from minimal to all kinds of extremes. They cause so much chaos that instead of being defeated by normal adventurers, it's far more common for them to meet their end at the hand of knights sent out by the government.

"But the next problem was the creation of undead. It's said that Stellura, the goddess of reincarnation, has full jurisdiction over the souls of the living. And that those of us here on the earth must never interfere. This was such a problem that the alchemists all came together, investigated, and quickly ruled that Chimera Creation was immoral."

To put it more accurately, it's not that they thought Chimera Creation was wrong in and of itself. It's the combination of souls, creating an undead, that's immoral.

"There's two ways to go about Chimera Creation. You can combine a living being with multiple fresh corpses or you combine a living being with multiple living sacrifices."

"I see. The latter isn't accepted because it involves a fusing of souls."

"That's right. They don't know how to function when the soul is fused to a different body. So in that case, all you have to do is fuse parts from the same kind of body...or so they say. People are always coming up with ridiculous ideas like that."

Humans never know when to give up. After this, they turned their attention to the Summoning Spell, curious to learn the principles behind it. This eventually resulted in the discovery of Necromantic Magic.

However, engaging in true necromancy would make this another act of meddling with the undead. That wasn't something anyone was interested in. Despite it being called Necromantic Magic, it's more like the head of Summoning Spell fused with the body of Alchemy. Summoning Spell creates a growing brain, while Golem Training from Alchemy creates a physical body.

At that point, the rest came down to trial and error. That was when they found that using the powers of Darkness Magic was the most efficient way to utilize a monster's flesh and bones as a catalyst.

"That's why we combine these forms of magic to create a golem powered by something completely unlike the soul of a living being. Its brain doesn't devolve even if it's defeated, and you don't have to worry about it being injured. Well...there's still the problem of having to compensate it with flesh and blood, and considering the materials, it will never be anything other than undead in the end. That's where the name Necromantic Magic comes from too."

In other words, alchemists went off fundamentals and AI to use Summoning Spell, then added in Darkness Magic and Alchemy to use a monster's flesh and blood, and finished off with the art of Golem Training to produce a body that could serve as a vessel.

Darkness Magic and Alchemy are combined for this act, which means Dark Ritual probably raises both skills at the same time.

"These days, Chimera Creation is still taboo, especially now that we have Necromantic Magic. Although that's certainly not a bad thing."

Now I understand the backstory here. I decide to ignore the question that was raised of whether skills were truly things brought about by gods. To be honest, I don't really care. I think I'm going to ignore that mystery entirely.

Still, it doesn't seem like there's any value in attempting Chimera Creation. After all, you end up fighting the chimera you created yourself, and I'd be making an enemy of a fellow undead at the same time. If you beat the chimera, you must face an undead. If you lose, then the knights are deployed to exterminate it, right? Then the government will be after me too. And Granny will drop me as a pupil. I'd probably be making an enemy of every alchemist in the land as well. There's just no upside.

I'm definitely fine just sticking with the Secret Art of Necromancy.

"Very well. It doesn't sound like it has any merits, so I won't be resorting to Chimera Creation."

"But it's a quick way to get a very strong servant."

"Can you really call it a servant if it doesn't obey you?"

"Hmm. Good point."

"I'm an undead too, after all. I can't be making my comrades into my enemies."

She paused for a moment. "What's that? Oh, that's right, you're an outsider. Hmm..."

"Ah, that reminds me...do you know of an entrance to the Nether?"

"Well, I'd like to say I don't, but..."

"So, you *do* know?"

I only asked her on a whim, since it seemed like an old lady might know that sort of thing. But despite being the one to ask the abrupt question, I'm the one left feeling startled. It's not every day that you meet someone who knows about an entrance to the Nether, you know?

"I don't know for sure, but there's a place I have my suspicions about. There's a woman who works at the town church. She probably knows more than I do about it."

"A church...?"

"You look like you're at a pretty high level, huh?"

"Yes, I'm a High Undead. You can tell just by looking at me?"

"Undead who barely look different from the living are usually high-level zombies of some sort. I'd be more surprised if you *weren't* at a high level. You have Purification Resistance, right?"

"I do."

"That'll be a big help, even at its low tier. Mid-tier will be enough for you to safely enter churches. Go pay them a visit, and feel free to say that Meghan ordered you to speak with Luciana."

"Ms. Luciana, is it? I guess I'll head over there after this..."

"Ah, that's right, since you're undead, I have something that will probably help you... Wait a second, I'll go get it."

This was the first time I'd ever heard her name: Granny Meghan. She strolls away briskly, unlike the slow shuffle I expected, and returns a minute later carrying a book.

"Let's see... Here we are. Memorize this passage."

"Oh...I was wondering how I was going to do this. I really appreciate it."

> You have learned basic Alchemy recipe: Parts

The Parts recipe is a way of repairing bodily damage. It looks like it's the combination of core stones with living flesh (mid-level or higher). There's a note written down as well... Quality reduces the penalty time that comes with a repair. A+ and higher quality lowers the vulnerability of the part after death? I'm so glad I know this now.

"Thank you very much."

"I'm just getting started. Read all these too."

My log fills up with a bunch of recipes again.

"These are the absolute basics. In other words, anyone on this path must know these recipes. If something doesn't make any sense to you, come see me. I may or may not teach you more, depending on what you're asking for. It's important not to forget how to research things yourself, or your future will end up bleak."

"I understand what you mean, but don't you think that's pretty harsh?"

"I don't take a pupil in the first place if I don't think they can keep up."

"I see. What else should I know about, aside from Chimera Creation?"

"Let's see... Have you used Alchemy Circle, the one you get at level 30?"

"No, not yet."

"You start by looking at the cloth and tracing the circle with mana. But that's only the beginning. You'll be able to start using things you can't place on the cloth."

"Could that be the same as Chimera Creation?"

"Alchemy Circle is one way to do special circles like that. But don't try anything crazy that you don't know about yet. Remember that Alchemy is a convenient skill, but it comes with dangers too."

"I understand."

I decide to ask her for advice about Necromantic Magic while I'm at it.

"Necromantic Magic starts you out with a baby, basically. The creation will be slow-witted before it begins to learn. How it grows up depends on how you raise it. You can use it as a meat shield, sure, but what's important is to not forget your feelings of love for it. Try praising the creation after a battle and be sure to remember what the skill has in common with Summoning Spell."

"Got it. Thank you so much."

"All right. Get going."

She taught me all those recipes and the origins of skills like Necromantic Magic, so I feel like I got a lot out of this visit. I exit Granny Meghan's shop.

Special requirements fulfilled. You've unlocked "Title: Alchemist's Pupil."

> **ALCHEMIST'S PUPIL**
> Become a student of Meghan from Starting Town.

That was simple enough.

I guess I should head to the church now. It's somewhere northwest of the plaza in Starting Town. I've avoided it until now, but I'm beginning to sense the same thing I felt in Imbamunte. I ignore it and enter inside.

The church looks like...a normal place of worship. It's a room with four statues and long pews. There appears to be another player here, praying in front of the statues. But suddenly, light envelopes them.

I've seen that light before... It wasn't me, but Mr. Alf and Mr. Skelly who experienced it.

A woman with a pair of white wings emerges from the light.

"Yes!! I get to be an angel now!"

"Congratulations."

"Wha?! Ah...Princess?"

"Good day. It looks like I just so happened to arrive at the moment of your evolution. The two of us are enemies, aren't we?"

"No way, no way, no...way? Um...I guess I'll upgrade my light magic."

"So we *are* enemies."

"Four times damage multiplier against dark attribute..."

"It sounds like we're an even match."

She pauses for a moment before responding, "Ah, I'm Cupid."

"My name is Anastasia. Please feel free to call me whatever you like."

"Certainly, Princess."

I knew she'd say that...

We part ways so that the angel can go report this information on the forums. I have a feeling we'll be seeing even more angels in the future.

I ask a nearby church worker if Ms. Luciana is around.

"Is there a person here named Ms. Luciana? Ms. Meghan asked me to meet with her."

"Lady Luciana, you say? Please wait just a moment."

The title of "Lady" must mean she's important, right? But I still get to meet with her like normal... Well, it's also possible that mentioning Ms. Meghan's name has some sort of weight to it.

After I wait for a while, an old woman returns alongside the church worker. The old woman's disciple robes are quite fancy and eye-catching.

"Oh my, what a pretty young visitor we have."

"My name is Anastasia."

"I thought so. Women who wear gray dresses are famous for being mild-mannered."

"I've never heard that before."

"That's what they say in this town. So, what's this about Meghan?"

"I'm an undead, you see, and I'm looking for an entrance to the Nether."

"I see. So that's why you came to pay me a visit?"

After a moment of thought, she points at a nearby chair, and I take a seat.

"I don't actually know of it myself, but I'm at least aware of a place where you might be able to find it. I just don't know for sure what state it's in right now. After all, only Undead can see the entrance to the Nether."

"This is the only lead I have right now, so a potential location alone is plenty."

"Hmm...I see... All right. I'll tell you where it is if you'll do me a favor."

"A...favor? I don't mind, as long as it's something I can do."

"Can you use Laundry yet?"

"Yes, I can."

"Then it's absolutely something you're capable of. What I need your help with is cleaning."

"Cleaning?"

"Exactly. The place where I think the entrance can be found is to the northeast of this town, past the currently unused catacombs. I want you to clean up Stellura's former temple—her place of worship."

"There used to be a temple past the catacombs?"

"It's been abandoned for a very long time. I'm sure it's all run down by now...but it's likely that the area around the statue, the church itself, is still intact. Clean it as well as you're able to while you're searching for the entrance, and that will be fine."

Quest added: "Clean the Abandoned Temple" is now
available.

CLEAN THE ABANDONED TEMPLE
Travel to Stellura's former temple to the northeast of
Starting Town and tidy up her place of worship.
Quest giver: Luciana
Reward: ???

Since I accepted the request in exchange for information, I imagine Ms. Luciana won't have any other reward for me... which must mean the game will provide me with something else. It sounds like there might be some kind of secret to discover.

"I don't particularly care how long it takes, so just be safe out there. It's been a long time since the area was inhabited. These days, you might not even be able to navigate through it."

"Have you heard any reports of monsters in the area?"

"I'm guessing there will be the undead types out there, but I'm not sure. Try asking Belstead's adventurers' union about it."

She explains that a single statue of Stellura can be swarmed by the undead, which is why the old temple ended up abandoned. The current church now has statues of Stellura at all four pillars to prevent such an outcome. It's one of those little bits of trivia you find throughout the game.

"But isn't there a single statue of Stellura in the town square?"

"That one's a little special because of how it was built and what materials it was made with. It's a representation of the faces of space, time, and fate, but it also serves as a barrier for our very town. The statue in the town square has a different presence and color than the ones here in the church."

"I see. So they're not all 'statues' in the same sense of the word?"

The statue in the town square and the ones in the church really *are* different colors.

Ms. Luciana tells me she has to return to work, so I thank her and exit the church. I guess I'll head back to the town square. The church is still working to purify me while I'm within its walls.

Catacombs to the northeast of Starting Town...that must be my home. The temple is supposed to be even farther past that, which probably means it's in the forest to the north of Belstead, right? If that's the case, it probably *would* be safe to get information from their adventurers' union.

All righty. It looks like I've finished up everything I want to do. What next? Mr. Skelly isn't around at this time of day, so I'll have to tell him about things later.

Hmm...since I don't have anything else to do, why not head to Belstead? There's no time limit on the quest, but I'm still curious about that secret reward. I think I'll go for it.

I watch a few members of the demon race heading for the church as I teleport to Belstead from the statue of Stellura. Then I head to the adventurers' union.

"Welcome. How can I help you today?"

"Do you have any information about what lies past the forest to the north?"

"I really don't recommend visiting that area...but I do have information."

"It's important to me. Could you tell me about the enemies there? A person from the church told me there would be undead..."

"You'll find undead there, certainly. These are mid-tier classes of undead. They won't be very intelligent, of course, since they're not immortals, but as wild creatures, their instincts will be intense."

"What does that mean, exactly?"

"Packs of armored skeleton wolves and the like will attack you together."

The instincts of "wild creatures"? As an undead, that's a bit insulting. But sure, let's go with that.

Setting that aside, armored skeleton wolves? I've never heard of them before. They'll be in packs too? That must mean they're linked together. Hmm...Light Burst will hurt me as well, so dealing with them will be tricky.

For now, I take the information on the enemies.

ARMORED SKELETON
These skeletons are dressed in chain mail, making them more resistant to blunt force attacks.
Armored skeletons may wield either swords or bows and arrows.

ARMORED SKELETON WOLF
An armored skeleton in wolf form. Be wary of sudden Shadow Magic attacks.

REVENANT

A type of zombie without Decomposing Body. A tough foe with normal movement capabilities.

FOREST WOLF ZOMBIE

A northern forest wolf in zombie form. Forest wolf zombies also lack Decomposing Body.

FLYING SKULL

A skull that flies through the air, attacking those below with Dark Magic.

PHANTOM KNIGHT

A living armor foe who is extremely resistant to damage.

"Do you already have Identify?"

"I do."

"Then be very cautious if you spot a leader or general. They'll have command skills, which makes them much harder to defeat than normal."

"Is there a chance I'll run into them?"

"Definitely. If you plan to go there, you'll need light magic, but learning Holy Magic would be even better."

Holy Magic, you say? I could easily get hit by that too... I can probably ignore revenants, since we're the same race. But if they link up with the others and attack me anyway, I might just

FREE LIFE FANTASY ONLINE

crumple into a ball and cry. The wolf zombies sound intriguing. They're fellow zombies, but will I really be able to ignore them as well?

I thank the receptionist woman and start toward the door, but I decide to retrieve some equipment before I go. I choose the iron equipment I earned when we defended Starting Town: a sword, spear, axe, dagger, greatsword, helmet, armor, gloves, and boots. I can use these for my Secret Art of Necromancy, so they won't take up inventory space. I'll take some monster cores along too.

I won't know how strong the enemies are until I go there and see for myself, so I may as well start heading that way. I have over 40,000 gold on hand. I suppose I'll buy some more veggies and pork intestines as well. That leaves me with a bit over 10,000 gold left.

Since I have 39 capacity now, I could do a summoning if I wanted to...but suddenly starting off in the second area like this seems like it will be tough for them. It's still worth a try though. As for weapons...I'll give them an axe and no armor for now.

In order to summon something, you must pick a spot and include key phrases of a summoning command and what kind of thing you're calling for. But does it matter what order you say them in? Hmm...since it's essentially calling for a servant to obey you, it's probably best to use the imperative form?

As for the site of the summoning...that seems a little harder. I take out my rapier and point it at the ground in front of me. This makes it official, right? It seems like it takes a bit of practice to set the site of a summoning ritual.

"Come forth to me, skeleton!"

The Dark Ritual summoning circle...or maybe it's an alchemy circle, since it uses Alchemy? Well, whatever. A black circle appears on the ground where I point my rapier, and I watch as a skeleton emerges. I see that it has an iron axe on its back and everything. From the outside, it looks like a normal skeleton—just a bunch of bones. I couldn't really say it looks like something that can fight in the second area.

Should I arm it with iron equipment instead? Hmm...what about using a monster core or something? I take out the goblin core to show it, but I get what feels like a "no thank you." The two of us can understand each other, it seems.

"Is that axe the only weapon you need?"

CLACK

Its neck made a little rattling noise as it cocked its head. Is it just me, or is this skeleton actually pretty cute? Wait, no, it's still only level 1. I must question the skeleton in ways that are simple enough for its slow mind.

"Do you want a sword?"

CLICK

That was a nod. I also felt like it was saying "yes," so that must mean it wants a sword, right? Well, maybe it's too soon to know for sure.

"Do you want a spear?"

CLICK

"Do you want an axe?"

CLICK

Actually... "You're fine with using any weapon?"

CLICK

Yep. Um... "You'll learn to use whatever you're given, so anything's fine?"

CLACK CLACK CLACK

It's very honest. What a proper servant.

It looks like my skeleton is very capable of responding. By the way, all I'm hearing is the rattling of its head when it moves. I can only kind of discern things through the secondary voice.

But I haven't asked the important questions yet. It feels strange to ask the skeleton directly, but I'll see what I can get out of it.

"Do you need a name?"

CLACK CLACK

That's...a no.

"If I summon more of you, would you share a soul?"

CLICK CLACK CLACK CLACK

So it's like a soul shared on the cloud? I see. That explains why it has to learn new items you give it from square one.

"You need time to get accustomed to things when you're in a new body?"

CLICK

Of course, of course. It'll take time for it to gain experience with any new weapon I give it now. But that also applies to its physical body. If I customize it, I think it will need to learn how to handle its weaknesses.

I thought for a moment about my next question. "Do you need monster cores?"

CLICK

"You do? So you won't last in this state?"

CLICK

In that case, I should use Core Processing with my Alchemy skill. My goblin cores turn into monster cores (extra small). Then my elite goblin cores become monster cores (small), my troll cores become monster cores (medium), and my goblin general core becomes monster core (large). Now I have eighteen stones in total.

"Here, you can use these."

CLICK

"All right...let's give you a medium core."

CLACK CLACK CLACK

I hand a monster core (medium) to the skeleton, and as soon as it sticks the stone in its mouth, the stone dissolves and disappears.

> Servant's level has increased.

Servant's level...I think I get it. That seems to be a way of expressing the strength of my servants. Well, considering it's at base level, this must mean the AI level went up. So that rises when you feed it monster cores? The skeleton went up four levels and is now at level 5.

If monster cores work, then what about orbs?

"How about this? Can you use these?"

CLACK CLACK CLACK

That was an intense rattle. "Here, take it."

> Servant's level has increased.

Whaaat? Something's not right here! My skeleton passed level 30?! Um, I need to call a GM... No, I'll just send a normal message to Support.

I write up a question, asking if they can please confirm the amount of EXP my Secret Art of Necromancy servant just gained when I gave it an orb and if it was a bug or not.

I take my skeleton and its newfound power for a test of battle skills with a pigg.

"All right, show me what you've got!"

CLACK CLACK CLACK

It jumps up and strikes the pigg with a one-handed axe. I feel like I should also give it a shield, but the pigg's actual attacks are easy to dodge. The skeleton's having no problems. I'm sure its stats must not be that high due to its low skill level, but its AI level sure shot up. I'm not sure if that's a bug or what, exactly. Maybe it was an increase in processing ability? Well, I don't have anything to compare it to before the skeleton leveled up, so who knows.

"Oiiink!"

CLACK CLACK CLACK

Watching a cute cartoonish piggy engaged in battle with a skeleton feels surreal.

As I watch from the side, I see a message arrive from management.

So it really *was* a bug! I knew that was too many levels all at once. Let's see...they say they'll message me when they're ready, so I need to log out, wait for their next message, and log in again.

The skeleton managed to defeat the pigg without any trouble, so I end the summoning, dismantle the pigg without absorbing it, and log out once I reach the town.

I do my stretches in the real world and log back in when I see another message has arrived.

The message informs me that my orbs will be refunded, and my servant's level is being rolled back.

"Hi there, Anastasia. I'm GM Kuon."

Oh, a GM showed up.

"We apologize for the bug you encountered and appreciate the report you sent in. In return, please select one gift from the following list."

I have the choice of either 50,000 gold, a set of combat consumables (potions, etc.), a set of production consumables (materials, etc.), a one-hour skill EXP boost ticket (must be used within one day), and 3 SP.

The combat consumables set may as well be garbage for me...

"May I ask what the material set contains and how I retrieve it?"

"If you choose the production set, you'll be able to pick which skill you want to use your items for. However, the items you're given depend on your own skill levels. They're not available to trade, of course."

I see. So I can't have someone with higher skill levels than me activate the gift and give me the contents. The admin explains

FREE LIFE FANTASY ONLINE

that the combat set provides a different rank depending on my base level.

I have to be careful, since the EXP ticket disappears after a day if I don't use it. It doesn't say how much it will rise, but the increase depends on the skill. Maybe it would work well for first-tier skills? But at the same time, leveling those quickly isn't too impressive.

"I'll take the 3 SP, please," I finally answered.

"The SP... You're sure? You won't be able to change your choice later."

"I'm sure."

"Very well. I'll transfer you 3 SP."

"Thank you."

"Of course. Could you please confirm that you've received it?"

I check and see that I have three more SP than before. I got my orbs back too, and my servant's level is now at 7 instead of 5. What's with that?

"Is my servant supposed to be at level 7?"

"It looks like the EXP from the pigg battle is contributing to that."

"Oh, I see. I only gave that a try because I thought you'd reset the level anyway."

"Feel free to think of it as a small bonus. Do you need anything else from me today?"

"No, I'm all right."

"Understood. I hope you continue to enjoy your FLFO experience."

Kuon disappears into the air after that.

I summon my skeleton again. For some reason, Unit One is more slumped over than before. Is it because his levels were rolled back? There was nothing either of us could do about that. I give him one orb, three monster cores (medium), and five monster cores (small).

My servant gobbles them down and grows to level 23. Now he's an adequate fighter for this area...or so I'd like to think, but the only thing that's really grown is his AI level. I need Unit One to put in a lot more work.

Since he's still ten levels lower than he was before the reset, I have him do some more pigg battling.

I feel like he's reacting slower than before. He's making decisions slower too, I think. There really must be some sort of effect on his processing power. Hmm...it seems like he's got to put in a lot more work when his AI level is lower. Maybe I should be feeding him monster cores whenever I get them, since that's what bumps his level up. That makes the orbs I regularly get much more convenient. It's not like I use Libertà very much.

CLACK CLACK CLACK

It looks like he defeated the pigg. I'll have him keep fighting as we head north.

Superior Magic Assist is now level 5.
You've acquired Overspell from Superior Magic Assist.

That came out of nowhere, considering I'm not even fighting.

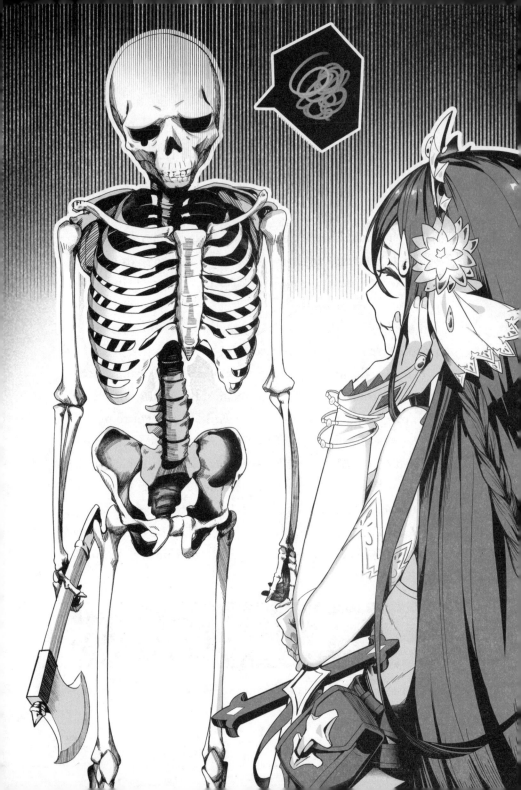

This must be my servant's doing, since Space Magic is level 3 now too.

> **OVERSPELL**
> Doubles both the cost and effect of your next chant.

I see. That's a pretty standard ability. I can already think of situations where I can make good use of it, like when I go hunting, for instance.

I enter the northern forest. It feels pretty much the same as the one to the south—not impossible to walk through at all.

I stop for a moment. Wait, what? Did I show up at a bad time? It's almost night now. Well, I guess it doesn't matter. I'll get stronger just like the enemies will. In fact, as a High Undead myself, my modifiers are even stronger than the enemies. But I suppose that depends on whether I'm restricted by my base level.

Now that I'm thinking about it, I was so focused on what was past the forest, I forgot to ask about what I might run into *inside* of it.

Before me is a forest wolf—the kind that hasn't turned into a zombie yet. Forest wolves are a type of dog that stand about a meter tall, with a bit of a green tinge to them. Wait, does this game include an active sense of smell? The answer to that question must be what determines dog races. Maybe there's information about that on the forums.

Anyway, since it's in my path, I need to deal with this wolf. I start by striking with my Dark Lance and then have Unit One stand at my side. I could have him protect me from the front if he only had a shield. But maybe it's better to give him a greatsword instead of a one-handed axe so he can be a real attacker? Then again, we're in a forest right now. I'm worried about how to maneuver... Maybe it's not such a bad idea to have him do nothing but jumping slashes for now.

I tell Unit One to wait until the enemy is targeting me and use that opportunity to attack. He's currently attacking a foe from behind. But the wolf, clearly irritated by all the hits, kicks backward like a horse, sending Unit One's health straight into the red zone.

"Unit One!" I cry out.

In a normal game, the area around an enemy would be safe, so long as they weren't using an AoE attack, but that doesn't seem to be the case in this game.

Now that I know Unit One can't be directly behind an enemy, I decide to place him diagonally behind enemies in the future. It might be smart to equip him with a spear to put some distance between them... This is tough.

I defeat the wolf while Unit One regains HP by resting.

"Let's change up your equipment, Unit One."

CLACK

I resummon him because of his low HP. I also try absorbing the forest wolf and go for a 2× summoning, since a 3× costs too much for me. This should raise his stats a little more. Unit One reappears with the Sword skill and a greatsword on his back.

I like having Unit One along with me, since he raises my Secret Art of Necromancy, Undead Unifier, Undying Royalty, and Royal Privilege skills. I'll be sure my servant puts a lot of effort in.

"You're going to stand diagonally behind the next wolf, Unit One. Understand? Once you attack, get away from it."

CLACK CLACK CLACK

Good. We continue onward.

I want more capacity, but I'm also curious about what a forest wolf drops. Drop information..."forest wolf"...there it is. They drop pelts, fangs, and wolf meat? Yeah, I don't need any of that. I can definitely just absorb it. If I want wolf meat, I'll go hunting for it later. Wolves give one capacity, and forest wolves give three.

While I have the BBS up, I take a look at enemy information.

The other enemy is...aquilegia? They say it's a plant monster with skeletal appendages hanging from it, and its weaknesses are slashing attacks and fire. Since they don't move, they're very easy to defeat. Their one annoying move is to suddenly wrap around you if you get too close, but we can just ignore them.

We press onward, continuing to defeat forest wolves. I spot several aquilegia along the way, but the information I read about them seems perfectly accurate, so I just pass them by.

Unit One, with his brand-new fighting style, is performing well as an attacker. That's a good thing. I do see him miss the occasional attack, but since he's up against wolves, that's to be expected. I'm sure his stats aren't very strong yet, so as long as he doesn't die, I'm happy. I don't have any extra capacity right now, after all.

That reminds me. When I use Dark Ritual, my Dark Magic

and Alchemy skills go up, but Discern and Dismantle aren't affected, right? This is tricky.

We arrive in the next area, so I recall Unit One. The enemies up ahead will be one grade higher than the ones in the last area, so I doubt my servant can keep up.

The area containing the ancient temple is still within a forest, although this one is much denser. I don't expect there to be much light from the sun or moon in this place. It's an unnerving forest full of the undead, where the living dares not enter.

That thing up ahead must be a revenant. It doesn't have Decomposing Body either, so it kind of resembles a person if I ignore the tattered rags it's wearing. Its gait is a little stiff too. Fortunately, revenants shouldn't target me at all.

Suddenly, a diagonal red line tags me from above! I dodge it like my life depends on it. I look up to see a flying skull. Whew, that was close! Hmm...if it was using Dark Magic, then I guess I didn't need to dodge its attack. Still, I guess it's not a good idea to just let it hit me.

Just then, the revenant links up with the flying skull. It's not attacking me, but I can still see the link marker. I'll keep an eye on it, but for now, there isn't anything for me to do about it.

I start up a battle of spells with the skull above me in the air. Of course, I use light magic, while the enemy uses Dark Magic. The main problem is that the skull just won't stop flying. I'll have to calculate the angle to shoot it from. The target preview line does appear when I start to chant a spell, but it only shows where the spell will land if I fire it at the exact same speed and angle. Changing either factor could mean I'll just graze the enemy or miss altogether. That risk only goes up when the battle is being fought in the air instead of on land.

I use Royal Defense to handle the skull's spells and fire back with Light Arrow and Light Lance. The lance works best against the enemy's slow spells. It looks like two hits are enough to defeat it. The flying skull lacks durability and dies in only a hit and a half's worth of damage or so. That's not very good, huh? The other enemies require three whole strikes.

A few seconds after I defeat the flying skull, its link disappears, returning the revenant to a normal status. I can ignore the revenant now, so long as I don't hit it with any of my attacks.

I undo my Inventory Expansion art from Space Magic because I need my MP back. I want to be able to use Boundary Control if I need to.

I see a quest marker in the center of this area, so that must be the ancient temple. I'll head straight for it.

When I listen a little more closely to the nearby noises, it's easy to hear a flying skull, since the only other sounds coming from above me are the rustle of leaves.

Maybe the enemy respawn rate here is pretty low? I *think* I'm the only one around. While I do have night vision, visibility still isn't all that great here in the forest anyway.

Hmm...something's here. That must have been my Instinct just now. There's no way I imagined it...right?

Suddenly, my Danger Sense activates! Enemies jump out at me from three directions at once!

My Danger Sense shows me which directions I can dodge to avoid getting hit. Waltz is really putting in work. Danger Sense uses red lines to show the area of attack like in a traditional MMO, and I'm sure the accuracy only increases with its skill level. I would call this not just convenient for a solo player, but a necessity.

So these are armored skeleton wolves? They just used Shadow Magic to launch their surprise attack, and it was a closer call than I would have liked. I'm in a bad position, pinned down from three directions like this. Light Burst would probably get me out of this pinch, but I don't want the light magic to take me out along with my enemies.

The wolves circle around me—or rather, they "triangle" around me, since there are just three. Ha ha! No, I can't panic. I have to counter their formation.

I send Light Lance shooting out of the tip of my rapier and strike each of the wolves as they leap at me. Then I keep them away with a barrage of Light Ball and Light Arrow. I need to be sure they can't find the right timing to attack me. Next, I change things up with Dark Burst. The wolves have some resistance to it, but my own Dark Magic is buffed. They can't absorb or ignore it. When I see them flinch from the hits, I know it's affecting them.

This is going better than I thought it would. Well, actually, they're still grazing me quite a bit and whittling down my HP.

I'll need my automatic recovery skills to put up a fight. I'm at 60% HP already, so I'll use my Dark Heal to recover. Now I'm at 80%.

> Your race level has reached level 20. New race skills are now available.

Yes! These higher ranks are a nice treat. But now's not the time to be checking over my skills. I make a note to look them over later.

Leveling up fully restores my health too. That's much appreciated.

In front of me is a link between an armored skeleton soldier, an armored skeleton archer, and a phantom knight. They have a burst sword, a small bow, a mace, and a large shield between them. This won't be fun.

Huh?! The archer spotted me! Aaaah, he's running for me! He's got a bow, so I can use Royal Counter and Royal Defense for any normal attacks. Arts allow you to easily repel attacks, but the regular parries are very hard to use, although not impossible. Danger Sense helps too, since it shows the paths where the attacks will land.

I shoot off spells at the archer until all the enemies reach me. I think I'll stick with Boundary Control and Light Lance. How do you like that?!

Hmph, still hanging on? That's level 36 enemies for you.

Phantom knights sure are slow, although I guess they're still faster than me. The one attacking me uses Arrow Line...and misses entirely, hitting one of the trees instead. Ha ha ha! Bested by the power of trees! Undead aren't smart enough to choose arts that suit the map they're in. Is that the end for one such annoying art, here under the cover of branches?

Boundary Control has a longer cooldown, and the soldier with the sword is coming at me, so I shoot Light Arrow at the archer.

Now that I think about it, my fighting skills aren't particularly suited for battles against skeletons. My main weapon is my magic, and my actual weapon is a rapier.

I use Break Parry to escape the oncoming soldier's attack before jumping up into the air and firing off Light Lance while the enemy's off-balance. Then I go in for a slash attack. Since he's staggered, he'll receive double damage for three seconds. But I still can't kill him! He clearly has the right modifiers.

The phantom knight joins the battle. This is going to be annoying. He's weak to blunt attacks and light magic. I can use the Penetrate art from Rapier, but that's not strong against undead.

I'm still getting pelted with arrows, the phantom knight is blocking my path with his large shield right in front of me, and the soldier's attacks are genuinely dangerous... Is this impossible after all? I'm pretty sure these are the main enemies that appear in this area...and they probably always spawn in this same combination. In other words, I'll have to struggle through these fights if I want to continue onward. If only they were a cluster of three wolves instead! Then I could do it!

I block two incoming hits with Rapid Shoot, dodge a mace blow, jump to avoid the sword again, and farewell, soldier! Next is the archer, who's on his last sliver of HP.

I have 60% HP remaining, so I need to heal when I get the chance. But first, I'll hit the archer with Light Arrow... Hmm?! Wait, hang on! There's a skeleton dog coming at me! There, there... good doggy... Argh! Hey!

I'll just have to finish off the archer once and for all...if only this skeleton dog would please stop chomping on my arm! The phantom knight swings his mace down at me, so I use the skeleton dog attached to my arm as a shield.

I cast Dark Burst, then Light Arrow. Finally, I managed to kill the archer.

A canine arm shield is a pretty good defense against the mace. Farewell, skeleton dog. But farewell to me as well, as the mace is a blunt weapon. May I do a better job on the battlefield in my next life...

Oof.

Hello, new me. I'm home, in Starting Town.

> Death Penalty: All stats temporarily reduced, lowered
>   EXP gain rate, half of gold on hand removed.
> You have lost your left arm.

Farewell, left arm. The left one again, huh? I seem to lose that one all the time. Well, perhaps that's an exaggeration.

"Ah! Hey, Sis!"

"Huh? Oh, Rina."

"Sis! Where's your arm?!"

"I lost it. Please congratulate me."

"That's not really worth congratulating..."

Time to use some parts. I select dark parts and then go to the left arm section. When I press the new arm that appears into the missing spot, it fuses back into my body. For the next three hours, my left arm won't be as responsive when I use it.

I place the ring and vambrace in my inventory back on my arm, and then I'm good as new.

"Sis is back from the dead... Where'd you die?"

"The third area. It was too much for me, both in level and in location."

"Ah...next to the second area, then. You die if you get surrounded there, right?"

"Yeah. I couldn't make it out alive once reinforcements showed up."

"You went solo?"

"I just wanted to check the place out."

I use Inventory Expansion from Space Magic again.

It's almost time for dinner IRL. I'm sure Mom and Dad are home already, and I may as well log out while my death penalties are active. I say goodbye to my sister, head to the inn, and log out.

Mom and Dad are in the living room when I arrive...but why are they drinking already? The drivers are drinking too. I guess our guests have no intention of leaving anytime soon...not that I expected them to leave in the first place. I don't see the maids around, though.

I grab a juice and tune in to Akina's livestream. She has over 10,000 viewers right now. That's even more eyes on her than the principal gets during a school-wide assembly. It looks like Akina's escorting Ms. Primura while she goes out to gather supplies in Imbamunte.

Ms. Primura does carpentry, so Rina would normally be with Mr. Ertz, the blacksmith, but I guess her party must have needed Ms. Primura's help. Ms. Nadia and Ms. Helen do carpentry too, as I recall.

Ms. Nadia and Ms. Helen show up to help out along the way.

"Those are the two girls who ate lunch with us here. Ms. Yanase is Nadia, with the ukulele; and Ms. Matsukane is Helen, with the bow," I explain to my parents.

"Oh, so that's who they are."

I watch the stream while I steal the snacks that are meant to go along with the adults' alcohol. Meanwhile, the maids return. It looks like they were out shopping...in their maid uniforms. They bring us ingredients for dinner, snacks, liquor, and juice.

Dinner prep ends up involving nothing more than setting up the grill in the garden. Dad is preparing the meat as a main dish while the maids take the job of skewering it. I suppose I should call Rina down via chat comment. *"Dinner's ready, Rina."*

The purple text goes passing by. It looks like she chose that color for my comments in advance.

"Yay! It's meat time!"

"Come out to the garden."

"We're really having a barbecue, aren't we?"

"Barbecue...in the garden?!" A bunch of chat comments expressing their shock get posted all at once, but I'll leave my sister to handle them.

I light the grill, prepare water, and begin to cook.

"Meat!"

"Here's your tofu."

"Tofu...? Oh, soybeans—meat of the earth. Well, at least you didn't just hand me plain soybeans."

"And here's your soy sauce."

Tofu makes for a wonderful palate cleanser, although I suppose I made her eat it before she had anything else. All I did was find it in the fridge.

I take out the meat Dad had prepared and salted.

Then I change it up a little in a way that most families probably don't do for a barbecue. I apply a spice rub of sugar and other seasonings to the meat and smoke it at a low temperature.

All that's left is to let it cook now. I coat it with a little sauce and fire up the grill.

Along with the sounds of the sizzling meat, I can also hear a conversation between Mom and her boss, Mr. Noah.

"So why'd you come all the way here?" Mom asks him.

"Because I wanted to try something new, of course."

"What do you mean?"

"Companies with special patents are currently in negotiations with Future Software. Maybe not as a friend but as a CEO...I want to scout little Tasha!"

Huh? I know Mom already told him not to scout me, since I get to decide my own future...but now he wants me as a CEO? Did something happen that I'm forgetting about?

Mom is now jokingly strangling him.

"Do you know what he's talking about, Eli?"

"Mm...I haven't asked him directly, but I have a general idea."

"Hmm?"

"Do you like fantasy stuff, Tasha?"

"I suppose I don't hate it."

"You'd never play that game if you hated it."

"That's true."

She's nodding her head like this pleases her, but I still have no idea what we're talking about.

"Father. Explain it to her, please," Eli requested.

"Right... But first...Tasha, could you...get your mother to...let me go?"

Mom's still got a grip on him? Well, it sounds like Mr. Noah is ready to tell me about it now.

"Oof... Ah, I have to keep it quiet for a while still. It's a state secret!"

"Liar. This is company business, right?"

"Well, to put it as simply as possible, it's about VR idols."

"Idols?"

How is Mom even capable of a growl like that?

"Was that too simple?"

"Father...an idol refers to something else, you know."

"Then maybe 'VR actress' would be more accurate?"

I decide to ask for more details, since this is about my future, and I learn that new FDVR technology is being used to make movies.

In other words, once Mr. Noah saw how realistic Future Software's commercials, trailers, and livestreams were, he theorized that the content could be recorded and turned into movies.

The only problem is that an FDVR movie would have to consist entirely of stuntmen, essentially. It's nothing more than having a flashy playstyle, which makes things hard on the actress. But if you replace the actress with a stuntwoman, then you need to dub over the whole thing, making this no easy endeavor.

"To me that sounds impossible," I say.

"Yeah...it is." Mom doesn't play video games, after all.

Since this would all take place in VR, you could give someone the same avatar to perform as another person, but that replacement would have to be well versed in FDVR, acting, and combat to top it all off. Besides, it's much better to have the main character of a movie be consistent.

Using a hyper-realistic medium like FDVR means you don't want it to feel unrealistic in any other way. You want it to feel as seamless as possible.

"Also, wouldn't it generate more buzz if you really had the

same person doing everything, considering it's a brand-new use of technology?"

"Well, I'm sure it would be more interesting than if you used a stand-in..." I replied.

"It's a game, so the battles can be as eye-catching as you want! Send spells flying back and forth! And *they're* in charge of all the fantasy costumes." Mr. Louis is flashing the peace sign.

Now I see his plan. In other words, he wants to use FDVR to create an incredibly realistic fantasy movie.

"Won't it be too gory...?"

"But FLFO already has settings for gore. Can't we play with that to get by?"

I see... Well, I'm sure he'll think of something, since he's a professional.

"Filming a realistic game to make a movie... Of course, you'll have to adjust the angles and effects, right?"

"Of course."

"And you'll be coming up with a story?"

"Naturally."

My sister speaks up. "I wanna see that!"

"You do, don't you?!"

Mr. Noah and my sister are getting all excited, but...hmm...

Even livestreams of the game are pretty hype-inducing, and the official trailers and such gather huge amounts of views too. They could get rid of the Japanese server requirements and allow connections from overseas as well... Well, it sounds like they're still thinking about it.

"This is still a ways off, right?" I ask.

"Right. Like I said, we're in the negotiation stage, so it might not end up going anywhere. But my instincts tell me this would be a box-office hit. I think Future Software will go for it too. Still, it'll be two more years at the very earliest, I think."

"Make your own choice. I'll support you if this is what you want, but if it's not, I'll make him back down," says Eli.

"Feel free to take some time to think about it. Ah, but be careful of things like VR idol contracts. If you sign one of those, it'll be harder to join our company in the future."

I'd use the word "impossible" myself.

"But, Tasha, if you become a VR idol, you'll never get to show off your real body."

"That's true. I don't like the sound of that, but I'm not interested in being an idol in the first place."

I watched my mom work, after all. She's an actress, not an idol. I don't want to go on silly variety shows. But aside from that...looking at this realistically, I just got scouted by one of the most famous CEOs in the world, right here in my own backyard.

Think about the money...

"Do VR actresses get to show their IRL bodies?"

"Ha ha! Is that what you think of my company? Of course they can show them off! If you go for the same path as your mother, you'll be walking the red carpet someday down the line!"

"Also, Tasha!" Abby chimes in. "Everyone will be so surprised to see the VR character IRL!"

Does she have a point there?

"That's true, Sis. VR players rarely make public appearances. You've gotta go for it!"

"If you want to join her, Rina, then put a little more work into your RP! I know your personality and background, and I know you're great at full-dive games, so that just leaves the acting part! We're professionals, so we won't compromise in that regard. It's really important when you're just starting out!"

Yeah, they wouldn't scout every top player just for the heck of it. Some of them already have jobs, or maybe they're students, or maybe their personalities and backgrounds aren't easy to figure out. A bunch of research would have to go into a player they really want to scout.

"Aside from my movements, I'm not exactly roleplaying at all… although I did go kind of crazy during the events. I had lines prepared for me and everything."

"If you want it, then go for it!"

In other words, I'm supposed to do more roleplaying in the game as practice? I'm sure it's faster to learn acting when you're enjoying yourself, so I suppose I get it…

Well, it's still two years away at the earliest, so I'll be able to graduate high school, at least. I'll take some time and think about it.

We chat some more as we eat, take our baths, and then the four of us girls have what basically amounts to a slumber party before bed. I mentally apologize to Mr. Skelly…but then I remember I can simply send him a message to explain the situation.

2
FRIDAY—THE DAY BEFORE SUMMER BREAK

I WAKE UP in the morning, prepare for the day ahead, and glance out at the garden. There I see Eli elegantly sipping from a cup of tea, so I head straight for her.

"Is Abby still asleep?" I ask.

"I assume she'll be up soon."

It's almost 7 a.m. I imagine she can't sleep much longer.

Letty hands me a cup of black tea. I spend a few peaceful moments with Eli until Abby shows up.

"Good morning."

"Morning, Abby."

"Did you sleep well?"

"I sure did!"

Abby joins us, becoming the third member of our breakfast party.

We kill time at our own pace, as my sister and I will be driven to school together today.

"It's too early for it to be this scorching. We won't be able to enjoy any tea once it gets even hotter than this," says Eli.

"It's usually better to stay inside during the summer."

"How do you ever get by?"

"We stay close to the air conditioner."

"I see..."

It's impossible to relax unless the temperature is tolerable. Heat alone is hard enough to bear, but the humidity only makes it even more torturous.

Shortly before school begins, one of the drivers steps forward and heads off to the car. Abby's maid, Dory, arrives with Akina, and the three of us leave for school. Eli and Abby stay at home, of course. The inside of the car is nice and cool—the driver must have turned the AC on in advance.

We arrive at school in the limousine, and the driver drops us off in the staff parking lot.

"Shall I wait here until you're ready to return home?"

"Well...they said it's just one ceremony, and then we get our report cards and leave, but I don't know how long the ceremony itself will last."

"I imagine it won't be more than two hours. I'll wait here for your return."

I'm sure I don't have to worry about the driver breaking that promise. I exit the limousine and head to class.

"Mornin'!"

"Morning!"

"Good morning."

"I haven't seen that car in a while!"

"But you've actually seen it?"

"Yeah, a while back, though."

The people I went to elementary and junior high school with certainly might have seen a limo before. I was dropped off in one many times over the years.

Mom and Dad don't currently have the slightest interest in cars, so the one we have at home is entirely normal. They said all that really matters is that it can drive. They prefer things like cosmetics and electronics.

I chat with my classmates while everyone else shows up to class. Eventually, the bell rings.

"All right, kids!" our teacher calls out. "Get to your seats for attendance... Oh, you're all here, huh?"

All it took was one glance to determine that, apparently.

"There was some sort of crazy car parked out back. I almost jumped out of my skin when I saw it! Whose is that?"

"That would be Kotone's."

"It belongs to a friend who's staying at my house."

"Ah...I see. Well, that explains it. All right, let's get to today's schedule. We'll do the ceremony first, then I'll give you your report cards, and you're free to leave after that. The exact length of the ceremony comes down to how long the principal talks for, so pray he keeps it quick."

I don't think our principal will drag it out too much. The driver probably won't have to wait very long.

We head out to the ceremony. It ends up finishing so quickly, we don't even have time to zone out before the principal wraps up. I think that was a good choice. He hit all the important points instead of rattling on, which meant he kept our attention to the end.

Then we return to the classroom, receive our report cards, and prepare to go back home.

"We couldn't do this yesterday?"

"The grown-ups at the school had something to do with that. In fact, they wanted your last day to fall on their last day."

"Whaaaat?!"

"My vacation starts today too! I don't know how many of you in this class are joining tomorrow's FLFO patch, but don't forget your homework! Hey, don't make a fuss; just do the work if you don't want to get in trouble. Like the principal said, be really careful if you're gonna vacation at any spots like rivers or the beach. Okay, that's it for me. Dismissed!"

"I'm glad that didn't take long, but now it's like...why the hell did we have to come here for this?"

"Pipe down, Suguru. I'm sure we're all thinking that."

"I'm just glad Ms. Dory and the driver didn't have to wait too long."

"Oh, they're still waiting? Let's get going, then."

Suguru, Tomohiro, and I head to the car to see that my sister and her two friends are already inside. We head home without any further delay.

Our friends go their separate ways once the car arrives at home. It's still early in the afternoon, which means they'll surely be logging into the game soon. I hope they have a safe trip back.

"We're home," my sister and I say in unison.

"Welcome back. You're early today."

We hand over our report cards to our parents, change clothes, and return to the living room.

"Looks like, as usual, there's nothing here we need to address."

I got all 5s, while Rina got half 4s and half 5s. Mom's right— this is exactly how our grades have always been. The consistency is a good thing.

We chat for about half an hour until the CEOs and their families have to leave, so I see them off.

"See you in the game, Tasha, Rina."

"Until next time!"

"Yes, see you soon."

"Remember to think it over, Tasha!"

"I'll try to keep roleplaying on the brain from time to time."

"Exactly. See ya!"

Abby, who's holding my sister's hand, bounces up in the air with her before getting in the car. What was that all about?

Eli leaves with a "Good day" before joining them in the car. "Good day" is truly a phrase that works in any situation—not that many people still use it.

It sounds like Mom and Dad are going out on another date now that the guests are gone. Akina says goodbye and rushes back to her room for some gaming. I suppose I'll do the same.

When I log in, I'm at the central plaza of Starting Town.

A message from Mr. Skelly says, *"I've taken up Alchemy. I'll report my findings on the BBS."* Yeah, I knew about that. I'll leave things up to him.

Let's see... Ah, that's right. I unlocked some new race skills, didn't I? These look the most interesting from what I've seen.

> **LUST FOR LIFE**
>
> *Grants a small chance of revival when defeated in battle.*

> **LIFE ABSORPTION**
>
> *Absorbs enemy HP during close-quarters battles. Amount of HP absorbed is relative to skill level.*

> **AUTOMATIC MP REGEN**
>
> *Regain MP relative to skill level.*

> **SPECIAL AUTOMATIC REGEN**
>
> *Increases the effect of automatic regen skills. Become a specialist in the art of resurrection.*

I definitely want Automatic MP Regen...but it wants 3 SP for each of these race skills. I'll have 9 left if I take them all. To make sure I get the right skills, I'll ignore that strange Lust for Life skill for now and take the other 3. That leaves 12 SP.

Next, I change Unit One's Physical Immunity to Life Absorption. His Physical Immunity level is just too low to make any difference. Although, that's the fault of my own Secret Art of

Necromancy skill being low. I add Special Automatic Regen too, since my Undying Royalty skill is at 20 now.

This would be a good time to go buy some new equipment for Unit One, but Mr. Ertz probably isn't around right now. I'll sell some things at the shop, buy a mace, and head north. It looks like it's finally time to acquire Mine. I'll sacrifice the rest of my SP for it.

If I remember correctly, the weapons shop is next to the adventurers' union.

Is it just me, or is metal equipment really expensive? Now I don't know what to buy. I want something for blunt strikes during this trip north, but it's hard to commit 30,000 gold for something I'm going to swap out after no time at all. Maybe I'll go for copper instead of bronze, and I'll also buy a round shield while I'm at it. The cost comes out to 8,000 gold.

Without any further delay, I set up Unit One's equipment. The mace falls into the Polearm category instead of Sword. But he's still not at the right skill level for Defend. Unless he raises it soon, the shield will be little more than a decoration.

Time to head to the northern city of Welshtead... Actually, I'll sign up for some hunting quests from the union first. I end up with orders for rabbit, wolf, stone caterpillar, and stone turtle culls, which I'll leave up to Unit One.

I summon him at the northern gates. He's equipped with a copper mace and a round shield now.

"All right, Unit One. Take out any rabbits that approach us."

CLACK

I watch as Unit One handles the rabbits, and I stick my dismantling knife into their bodies once they're dead. I should probably repair this knife soon. I'll ask Mr. Ertz to take care of it later.

Once Unit One's health falls below 60%, I cast Dark Heal on him as I follow along from behind. My Life Absorption level is pretty low, but I don't really know how it works either, so it's hard to relax at the moment.

I dismantle the wolves and rabbits for their meat, since it always comes in handy. When I finish up the quests from the union, we head north. I don't personally need any drops from the caterpillars and turtles, so I'll absorb them for rituals. It's always important to increase my capacity.

The path north starts to get more and more sloped as we go, while the plains grow less grassy. In its place, I can see the soil now. We are yet to reach the rocky terrain we're heading for.

The enemies change along with the environment, meaning I now see stone caterpillars and stone turtles spawning. The caterpillars have rugged, rocky backs, while the turtles are essentially just walking around with boulders for shells.

In other words, they're slower but have better defense. Blunt attacks and magic will be very effective on them, and therefore, this area of the map is suited for players starting out with those two weapon types. It's easy to take in my surroundings from this spot, and I even see a few other players around.

"Go ahead, Unit One."

CLACK CLACK

He swings his mace down hard against the sluggish turtle. With each powerful blow, the sound of metal against stone rings out.

All I do is stand and watch. Secret Art of Necromancy won't level up at all unless Unit One puts in the work. I need him to raise it high enough for me to be able to take him along wherever I go.

I'm sure my combat skills won't rise very much here in the starting area anyway. The combat skills I have are already at their second tiers.

Secret Art of Necromancy is now level 5.
Secret Art of Necromancy has unlocked Life Assignment.

LIFE ASSIGNMENT
This skill can only be used at half stamina or more.
   Transfer 1% of your HP at a time to any servant. Skill ceases when the servant is fully recovered, you cancel the skill, or your stamina falls to below half capacity.
If the player has multiple servants, 1% of player HP will transfer to each servant.

It may be a second-tier skill, but it still levels up quickly in the beginning. How nice.

So this is an art for servant HP recovery? At most, my own HP will decrease in increments of 6%. I can use this and

Dark Heal together, along with automatic HP regen skills...and Life Absorption too? Wow, Undead really do have it good, as long as we don't run into any light magic types.

I use the ritual to absorb the corpses that keep piling up while I'm busy checking on skills. How sad that they still only give a capacity of one.

My Unit One has a number of buffs that allow him to function with ease in this beginner's area with all its beginner's costs. He also managed to get by in the second-tier area where the costs were doubled, so I'll make him the attacker when we encounter bosses.

"I'm going to resummon you, Unit One."

CLACK CLACK CLACK

I think I'll do a max summoning this time at three times the base cost in order to raise my hunting efficiency. Summoning at the base cost is more than enough to do some good hunting, but the stronger my servant, the more my numbers go up.

It may be a good idea to summon one of the fast skeleton wolves to grind quickly, but they're not suited hunting grounds. I'll keep Unit One as a skeleton for now. I summon him again and follow from behind.

I remember the northern boss being a rock golem, but now that it's been defeated, it supposedly appears as a weaker mini-rock golem. I wonder if I can use Dark Ritual on it. Since I might be able to get golem blueprints, I've got to try absorbing it.

The turtles that previously took four shots to defeat now only take two. I absorb their bodies and press onward to reach the boss.

Hmm...should I take on the boss once my Secret Art of

Necromancy is at level 10? At that point, I'll be able to summon a Unit Two. I'll also earn more base skills to set them up with. What if I could summon a red skeleton? All right, let's raise this skill.

> Secret Art of Necromancy is now level 10. You have earned 1 skill point.
> You have earned Necromancy through Secret Art of Necromancy.

> **NECROMANCY**
> Attach undead attributes to any target.

So that means I can make things more vulnerable to light and holy magic? I bet I can purify them too. But the enemies will also become more resistant to Dark Magic, so I'll have to only use this one in parties. I doubt I'll find any use for it on my own.

Wait, hang on a minute... Can I use it on party members so that my buffs will affect them too? This requires further testing. If I can use it on party members, it will be a good idea to— wait, no. There's a problem with regeneration restrictions. I'm sure they don't have Special Automatic Regen, so this will just hurt them in the end. Hmm...

Well, either way, I reached my goal, so it's time to give Unit One Defend.

I resummon Unit One with a 3× cost, leaving me with 40 capacity, so I can summon a Unit Two at a 2× cost. However, since I don't know much about the golem, maybe it's better to

FREE LIFE FANTASY ONLINE

keep my costs down for the moment. I'll go with Unit One alone instead. I'm at the point where I can summon him as a red skeleton or high zombie, but I can't stomach those high costs.

"Unit One, when the enemy strikes at the ground, you have to jump."

CLACK

"Also, try not to be behind it."

CLACK

"You'll be facing an enemy who uses blunt attacks, so your life depends on how you dodge them. Prioritize evasion instead of getting damage in."

CLACK

"Let's get going, then."

CLACK CLACK CLACK

I use Dark Enchant to raise my own intelligence stat. With that, we head on in.

The look of the area is generally the same as the rest of the place, but there're now large rolling boulders. There's a different color on the map to indicate that we're in a boss area.

The system takes control of my body, showing me how one of the tumbling boulders rolls all the way down to the golem.

It stands on two teardrop-shaped legs, has an elliptical torso, and sports two round arms. Its appendages seem to be floating around the creature, as I can't see any joints. It also spins its arms sometimes.

A real golem is supposed to tower over you, but this mini-golem is really only as tall as an adult man.

It swings its arms back, howls at the sky, and with that, the battle begins. This isn't the first game where I've had this thought... but how does a thing like that have a voice?

Putting that thought aside, I get straight to the task at hand. I use Magia Amp and Overspell to shoot a bulkier Dark Lance at the golem.

Oh, that took off over 20% of its health already. That makes sense, considering that it's a low rank, it's already been weakened by its first defeat, and it has a weakness to magic. I don't think this will be a hard fight at all.

It stomps toward me, its legs planted wide apart, but I send the creature off with a gift of Light Lance before it can get too close. It hits, but the golem swings its right arm down all the same. I crouch, hold my rapier up to receive the blow, and see that Unit One is hitting the golem's left leg from the side.

The golem doesn't have many attack patterns, and it's easy to see what's coming based on its telegraphed animations. It swings its arm at you, rolls around if you get behind it, stomps when its stamina is low, and punches with its left arm.

The right arm swings. The left arm punches. The cry it let out during the intro cutscene is for when it's about to roll. When it raises the right arm up, it's time for a stomp.

The biggest headache is that left straight punch. It never even does the rolling move if you don't go behind it. As for the stomp, well, you just jump up in the air. Arm swings can be stopped with a blade.

The main problem is that, even as a mini-golem, its arms are still bigger than me. They're practically impossible to parry... meaning its attack knocks me off my feet. I guess you can say that size matters in a time like this. Although it can be a curse as much as it is a blessing, depending on the situation...

I feel like jumping to escape the blows might be my best option when fighting a huge monster like this. In real life, my bones would definitely snap, but in the game, the hits send you flying. That would be a problem when you're in a party, but you can just use the Heavy Stand art with a large shield to stand your ground.

That's the only real problem, though. If I continue using Overspell to shoot Dark Lance and Light Lance whenever I get the chance, I should be able to win just fine.

"Time to jump, Unit One."

CLACK CLACK CLACK

Oh, the boss lifted up its right arm. As soon as it slams it down into the ground, we see an effect activate, which Unit One and I both jump to avoid. Considering how close we are, we end up jumping the exact moment the arm touches the ground.

The stomping animation is really dramatic, but the golem can barely defend itself at all after using that move, so that's our time to strike. Then I shoot more spells at it while Unit One and I both get in some good hits.

We jump to perfectly dodge the second stomp, and finally, Unit One delivers the finishing blow to its leg. The golem collapses and dissolves into pieces.

> Darkness Magic is now level 5.
> You have learned Nox Shot through Darkness Magic.
> Your servant level has increased.
> Defeating the northern boss has allowed you access to the north. You also receive 3 SP for your successful battle.

CLACK CLACK CLACK

"We got some good skill grinding in, so I'm happy with this."

So I know Nox Shot now? It's a powerful and fast chant, but its range is dreadfully short. It's more like a shotgun spell.

Now it's time for the Dark Ritual.

> Your Dark Ritual grants you the materials for a Mini Golem.
> Dark Ritual increases your capacity by 3.

Hmm... So now I can make a skeleton mini-golem and a minigolem zombie? They're small, but once they evolve, they become a medium-sized golem. I just don't have enough capacity for that...

Time to head to the town. I'll summon Unit Two while I'm at it. He'll have Sword...and I think I'll give him Footwork or Strength Boost too. As for how something without muscle can gain strength, well, it's best not to think about it too hard.

FREE LIFE FANTASY ONLINE

Since I'll be giving him a greatsword, I think I'll set him up with Balance Control. I also decide to keep the race skills the same, and commence the summoning!

"...You're both Unit One, aren't you?"

CLACK

"Well, I'll call the first one I summoned Unit One, and the next one will be Unit Two. You've used a greatsword before, so you know what to do, right?"

CLACK

"All right. Let's get going."

We leave the boss area and head onward. For now, my goal is to unlock the portal, but hunting can wait until later. I also need to find out where I can mine ore.

There's still so much to do, but that's a good thing.

This second area where Welshtead lies isn't so different. The whole place is covered in rock caterpillars and turtles instead of the stone ones we were fighting.

But they're a lot bigger, huh? Out of the corner of my eye, I watch Unit One and Unit Two beat up a turtle while I look around.

Both the Starting Town and eastern regions are made up of plains and woods. The south lines a large ocean, while this area to the north has plenty of mountains. They must be where I'll find those ores. The mountains look entirely brown.

I perform the ritual and absorb the enemies that Units One and Two defeated, then head to town. Striking those armored enemies with a greatsword only damaged it a little faster than

86

normal. But since the one mace is the sole blunt weapon I have, it's really my only option.

Should I really turn Unit Two into a golem? Punches are the same as blunt strikes, I'm sure. The only problem is that a golem costs 400 capacity. I really don't have enough to cover it, and a mini-golem is no different from a skeleton, so I may as well stick with what I have.

Fighting in the second area increased my capacity, so I might be able to change after defeating a few more enemies. I receive 15 capacity in exchange for those victories.

"I'm going to resummon you, Unit Two."

CLACK

This time, he's coming back as a skeleton mini-golem. We'll start with a base skill of Fist. The new Unit Two looks like the boss mini-golem but with an outer shell of bones, which isn't very protective.

"Punch any turtles you see, Unit Two."

The light shell of bones allows him to nimbly creep up and deliver a straight right punch. Then I hear a surprisingly loud crunch and immediately come to notice a fatal flaw.

It feels like I fell into a trap... "Unit One, swap places with Unit Two."

CLACK CLACK CLACK

I make them swap places again after Unit One attacks. Skeleton golems certainly have some problems, huh? Golems fight bare-handed, while skeletons are more easily damaged by blunt hits. Therefore, I'm now in this ridiculous situation where Unit Two is taking damage from the recoil of its own strikes.

I'll resummon him as a mini-golem zombie instead. That will give him some meat on those bones.

This is trickier than I thought. Skeletons can use weapons, but they can hardly withstand body blows, even from something as weak as rabbits. But what if I give him custom arms? I could put arms on his back to hold weapons, which might make him more powerful against the quick-footed wolves.

Well, with all this customization available, I can probably do whatever I want. I don't know how to judge any of it without information in advance, so there's no choice but to try it out.

"Let's try that again, Unit Two."

The sound his attack produced this time wasn't as striking, but it dealt plenty of damage. His stamina still looks fine too. Golems really do work best as zombies. The problem is Decomposing Body. I doubt he'll be able to get rid of it any time soon. It's a matter of skill level and capacity.

We press onward, defeating enemies along the way, and once I spot the town, I recall my servants.

"Welcome to Welshtead, a humble mining town!" the gatekeeper greets me.

I say hello back and head inside.

There's a lot of smoke coming from one corner of the city, which makes sense considering the mining work they do here. That must be a street for craftsmen. Judging by the passing residents, this area seems to have a lot of dwarves.

It's by no means a small town. I get the sense that there're lots of blacksmiths, miners, and even adventurers here. Metallic

FREE LIFE FANTASY ONLINE

gear looks cheap here too, and I'll bet that's because they gather the materials themselves. Lots of the adventurers are residents, of course, but I also see plenty of players around too.

I sightsee just a little bit before unlocking the portal.

"Oh? Yo, Stasia. Didn't expect to find you here."

"Hey, Sugu. I'm glad I found you."

"What's up?"

"Do you know where I can mine some iron ore?"

"You can do that in pretty much any of the mountains in this area...well, except those ones. Over there, that's where you can mine."

"There're mountains that don't have ores?"

"It's part of the game's story. The townspeople are currently using those. But since the ones over there are already pretty stripped of resources, they're free to use. The idea is to make your choice but be ready for the consequences."

"I see. So you'll cause trouble for the townspeople if you mine without their permission."

"You can't even enter the mine shafts that they're using, so if you find a hole that lets you go in, it means you can use it."

"That's nice. It makes it easy to tell the difference."

"By the way, there will be enemies there too, of course. Ants, ants, and ants."

"There're three kinds of ants?"

"Ants with spears, fighting ants, and ants that shoot acid at you. You'll just need light... Actually, I guess not."

"I have my night vision, so I'll be fine."

I could picture the townsfolk ending a hard day's work in the mines, only to be met with ants... Maybe they don't mind us mining in certain mountains if it means we'll defeat ants for them at the same time? It saves both time and work for them.

"The enemies themselves aren't too strong, but there are a ton of them. You'll have to fight two or three at once in those mine shafts, and they keep coming at you for a while."

"So they're the kinds of enemies that come in waves?"

"You'll be able to excavate more the further down you go, but there'll be more ants there too. Right now, you can get iron, nickel, and cobalt."

Supposedly, we can't use nickel or cobalt right now. We're mostly looking for iron, with steel still being down the line a bit. Hang in there, Mr. Ertz.

Without any firepower, the endless attacks from the ants will probably make mining a real pain in the ass.

Sugu will be in the north for a while with his party to craft some new equipment.

"Oh? Hey, you two."

"Ah, hi there, Cecil," Sugu responds.

"Long time no see," I say.

"Yeah, I've been in the west lately. But I heard I could get steel soon, so I came here for upgrades. Believe it or not, my party still uses bronze!"

Oh, so they're on the verge of an upgrade? Then maybe I should work on providing my servants with steel equipment too. I ask him about the prices.

"I made pretty decent profits, and we've gained new members as well, so I decided to change things up."

"I made good money during the tournament too."

"Yeah, I remember the line outside your booth."

We chat for a while, but lunchtime arrives IRL, so I log out. Once I'm finished eating, I log right back in again.

I check to make sure the bronze pickaxe I bought from Mr. Ertz is still in my inventory, and finally, it's time to head to the mountains. I use 3 SP to acquire Mine while I'm at it.

I head to one of the mountains Sugu specified and spot a good few entrances to mine shafts. Standing there and staring at them won't help me decide, so I enter more than one and take a look around each.

The mine shafts barely seem wide enough for a mini-golem to move around in, but I think a skeleton with a mace, shield, and greatsword might fit.

I need to raise my hunting efficiency in this area... I need to be sure I don't get killed too, so I summon my servants with a 3× cost multiplier. That should give them a 1.5 stat multiplier to their stats like before. I wonder if that applies to bone density too...

Ignoring that question for now, we travel straight through into the mine shaft. The pathway is wider than I expected inside, probably to haul out ores and such. A more meta reason for the size might be so that we can properly battle in here.

The shaft starts to branch off after a while, making this trip more complicated. But my mini-map is updating automatically, so there's no need to hesitate. It's a game, after all, so we shouldn't have to walk around with a pen and paper in hand the whole time.

We continue into the mine shaft until I spot a light shining from the wall. Well, that's quite handy, isn't it? I take out my pickaxe and begin to swing.

Mining in this game simply means that you can obtain the item you see in front of you. It isn't a flashy graphic in the game, and it's similar to how I can actually pick any medicinal herbs and mushrooms that I come across. These stones enter my inventory the moment I pick them up.

Of course, since this is a game, the materials will respawn after some time. There's also no need to feel guilty about gathering from these spawn points, as they are unique to each player. Sure, it's not realistic, but it's better than getting into fights over hoarding, I'm sure. That said, gathering materials depends on a player's skills and equipment, so it's not guaranteed that everyone can collect everything they're looking for in the first place.

Just like in most games, this light on the wall is telling me that I can gather materials here. However, the light in FLFO also tells me how many times I can dig and how many ores I'll receive. The players refer to this as a god-tier mechanic. Apparently, there are random places within the game area where the materials also respawn automatically. In other words, if you take lumber from a special tree, another tree in the same area starts to give the same bonuses as the first.

All players share the same bonus spots, but it's not too appealing when you think about having to compete over who gets to gather from them. It sounds like there're multiple spots in each area, and once harvested, they transfer to another random location, so the whole thing isn't very productive.

I continue swinging my pickaxe into the wall, causing the *clang* of each blow to echo throughout the mine shaft. Units One and Two are standing guard nearby.

The pieces that come off the wall include iron and copper ore. Well, it's all going to Mr. Ertz anyway, so I don't care what I get. Maybe the reason I'm mostly finding copper is because it's still too early before I can mine anything else. Either way, I'll head to the next spot now.

Oh, here come some enemies. Those are definitely the kinds of ants you only see in games: a little cartoonish, with hands gripping a spear. This must mean the empty-handed ants are the ones that fight with their fists. There're two ant lancers and one ant fighter, but I don't see any of the acid-throwing kind yet. My servants can handle the lancers.

"Unit One, take out the two with the spears."

CLACK

Spears are stabbing weapons, so the servants should be able to handle them. Meanwhile, since there's only one, I'll take care of the ant fighter and its blunt attacks. This dark mine shaft hidden

94

away from the sun makes for a perfect hunting ground. I doubt they can sneak up on us in these tunnels.

The fighter ant holds up its fists and charges at me on its multiple legs, while the lancer runs at me with its spear at the ready. These creatures are actually pretty speedy.

I cast Light Lance at the approaching fighter to draw him my way. Unit One and Unit Two stand in front of the lancers.

The fighter had gathered momentum into its straight right punch, but I manage to dodge it anyway and slash to my left to hit its undefended side. I then dispatch Nox Shot and begin to chant Light Lance. The fighter ant recoils from Nox Shot, causing it to miss its next punch, and then I dispatch the spell.

It looks like the ants' joints are their weak points, so I aim for them with my rapier and spells. I glance to my side and see that despite Unit One having a spear stuck in his rib cage, he still manages to smack his mace into the ant's head. So the skeleton doesn't take any damage in that empty space, huh... The bones are hard to stab into, and even when the blow lands, they don't take much damage from it. Of course, if the enemy had a hammer or something, it would be game over.

I use Break Parry to jump up and dodge the punches, slash into the ant's weak spots, and cast another Nox Shot. This finishes off the ant for good.

Projectile spells are most convenient, although, people who play this game with spells alone probably have difficulty aiming them. They fly over ten meters away, after all. These spells are probably priceless to those who specialize in magic and weaponry together. I really want to get Lumen Shot soon, so I'll focus on using light magic for a while. It doesn't pack as much of a punch, but that's not important.

As for Unit One and Unit Two... I'll go take out Unit Two's opponent first. I jump in front of the lancer and use the rapier art Penetrate on its weak spot. The rapier glows red with the art, and once I'm aiming at the right point, what looks like a laser shoots out of the tip and pierces the lancer's body, producing an eye-catching visual effect. The game is acknowledging that I hit the ant's weak spot.

With its side cut open, the lancer stumbles, and Unit Two uses the opportunity to strike it with his greatsword, sending the foe to the grave.

I send Unit Two back to help Unit One and absorb the ant with Dark Ritual. It looks like they managed to defeat the other lancer with a full swing of a greatsword from the side, then another full swing of a mace to its head when it stumbled. They both called out their moves, so it sounds like they're perfectly synchronized.

I'm seeing that individual enemies on their own aren't very strong. These may be ants, but they're large ones, so I receive 3 capacity for each kill. Now that's what I'm looking for. This was a difficult fight for the servants, so I restore their health. Maybe I can leave small amounts of damage to auto-regen. If things get bad, then I can resort to Life Assignment.

I continue forward, mining from the walls occasionally, when I hear the sounds of combat from up ahead. Other people must

FRIDAY—THE DAY BEFORE SUMMER BREAK

be here. The further I go, the more the path branches off, so I might actually be heading toward another entrance to the mine. The maze-like paths here make it feel like a dungeon, although it's no different from any other map in the game.

As I head down the straight path, I start to hear loud voices, and eventually I see the distant figures of people... Hmm, I hear a lot of "my liege"s there. It must be Mr. Musasabi's party.

"Why, if it isn't the princess! I don't see you here very often... Oh? Does that yellow marker mean you have servants?"

"Good day. Funny running into you here. These two are with me to help gather materials for new equipment. I believe Mr. Skelly has posted about it on the BBS already, but this is the result of Necromantic Magic."

"Oh, so you really have become a necromancer, my liege!"

"It's a complicated thing, and not just anyone can become a necromancer..."

"So it's out of our reach. Well, let us carry on."

Mr. Musasabi explains that the plan is to take turns fighting enemies if we run into another party, then split up again once we reach a fork in the road. First-wavers really do seem like a peaceful group.

"A war of words does nothing but waste time. Everyone wants to have fun, do they not? Besides, forks in the road come quickly here!"

This is also a party of top players...meaning that anyone at the top levels really isn't that different from one another. Their IRL circumstances, be it work or school, will allow for a fixed cycle of play. In other words, you'll start to find anyone who plays for the same amount of time as you in the same hunting grounds, and you'll start to develop a relationship with them. It also seems harder to start fights in a game as realistic as FDVR.

"Most of the people in this area are top players, my liege. There's a high probability that we will be fighting alongside each other in future raids."

Five enemies appear along the way as we walk and chat. I let the players go ahead to challenge them.

"Of course, my liege."

"Onward, onward!"

Mr. Musasabi is in a party of six. They're easy to spot, as they're all dressed in ninja outfits. I can tell how their friendship started at a glance.

"Hiyaaah!"

"Hiyah! Hiyah!"

So this is what I heard earlier? They scream with every attack. At least you can tell they're top players by their movements.

"Hacchah!"

"Hiyah!"

They traded places to protect an injured member... They really do know what they're doing.

"Farewell!"

"Depart, beasts!"

Oh, it's over? These ninjas aren't even close to historically accurate. You can tell they're all slayers.

"Well, I can certainly tell how much fun you're having."

"Indeed. It's incredible."

"It's the best of fun, my liege!"

We continue on our path again, only to run into four enemies next: two lancers, one fighter, and one shooter. The Ant Shooter must be the one who shoots poison. I'll leave the lancers to them and handle the other two.

"Unit One, take out your spear."

CLACK

I bait the fighter with a Light Lance like before, then shoot a Light Arrow at the shooter to draw its attention. My rapier can't attack as frequently, but I'll just have to accept that. I tell my servants to go mess with the lancers.

I'm about to deal with the fighter like before, but the shooter suddenly sends something yellow flying at me. I block it with Royal Counter. I see that the poison is being registered as a long-distance physical attack like an arrow, not a spell.

To be honest, my rapier is more like a shield to me than a weapon. My spells use the tip as a magical catalyst, unless I put in the conscious effort to change that. In other words, if I focus, it doesn't matter where I point the rapier. I use it to block hits and attack with my spells. This is my combat style—I focus on magic and land a rapier attack only when the opportunity presents itself.

I continue to assault the fighter with Nox Shot and Light Lance while I keep the shooter occupied with my Light Arrow. I can't let these two high-level enemies focus on my servants, or I'll lose out on capacity. Since I see them as equal to me, I take on the enemies myself.

My Nox Shot pierces the fighter, leaving me to deal with the shooter. I block the incoming poison volleys, fire off spells, and close the distance between us since my spells work best at close range.

The fighter had the highest stamina of them all, followed by the lancers, then the shooter, whom I finish off in no time at all.

After that, I help Unit Two take out the enemy he was handling, and finally, I get to absorb all four enemies with my ritual.

"Your Parry is most impressive as always, my liege. What is that stylish ritual of yours, exactly?"

"It's my Dark Ritual. I absorb these to gain capacity, which I use to summon servants."

"I see... Is this Necromantic Magic? I understand why not all can accomplish it. What becomes of the drops?"

"They despawn, of course."

"Ah, I see... Although, I hear that ant armor can be used to make light armor."

"Grr...but I want my capacity..."

Right now, only Unit One is wearing the armor I earned when we defended Starting Town. Unit Two, as well as the future Unit Three, need armor too...

Mr. Musasabi's party defeats the rest of the approaching enemies, and once we reach a fork a bit further up, it's time to part ways.

"I'll be going now."

"I bid thee farewell!"

I continue on, defeating any ant that crosses my path and gathering whatever ores I can, ending up with copper, iron, nickel, and cobalt. I stopped finding copper once I reached the area where nickel spawned, but most of what I found after that was iron, with only a bit of nickel and cobalt along the way.

It seems like you really do have to go quite deep into the tunnels. The enemies started at level 23 or so, going up to level 26 deeper in.

The middle of the mine shaft was like a giant plaza. It was also a safe area, so I was able to keep mining while also finding time to log out and eat dinner. I came out with large numbers of ore, capacity, and even a few ant materials. It's still early, but maybe I should go to bed. No, I can't. I never delivered my potions. I'll hand them over before going to bed. The event ends today, and since holding on to them won't do me any good, I can only hope someone will take them off my hands.

I warp to Starting Town via portal and decide to go pay Granny Meghan a visit. Since you need permission to sell at her store, I'm not sure if she'll take them or not, but I suppose it doesn't hurt to ask. I head straight to her shop.

"Hello. Do you take potions, by any chance?"

"Are those for the new outsiders? Go take them to the pharmacy next to the adventurers' union," Granny Meghan answers.

"Now that I think of it, I never even looked into what places sell potions."

"Well, I know you have no use for them. I'm sure the pharmacy's dying for the supply, so head on over."

I leave the store and head to the pharmacy next to the union. It looks like the adventurers' union has the weapons shop to the left and the pharmacy to the right. I've passed by it so many times too, but somehow, I have no memories of the place whatsoever. It must have simply not caught my interest before.

"Good day," I greet the clerk on duty.

"Welcome. Can I help you find something?"

"No, I'm actually here to give you some potions."

"Thank you so much! Come right along then."

To be technical, the pharmacy here is more like a compounding pharmacy. I take in the rows of potions on display, as well as the smell of the place, which reminds me of an IRL hospital. Although, unlike an IRL hospital, there's also the scent of magical herbs. It's not the minty freshness you might expect, but more like the scent you get when you grind leaves together.

Well, it doesn't exactly matter, since it fits the setting so perfectly. I take my potions out of my pouch and place them on the counter. There're twenty-five HP Potions and 366 Beginner's HP Potions.

"I actually have leftover bottles too. Do you need them?"

"Certainly, if they're a quality of C or higher."

I end up handing over my 297 bottles as well. Even though this was a donation quest, the clerk ends up paying me approximately 17,000 gold for the lot. And to think these were just the byproduct of my attempt to raise my Alchemy skill. I'm happy to see they'll buy the potions for a slightly lower price than what they would be sold for. I'll never use any potions for myself, and if anything, I'm glad they'll stop taking up space in my inventory now.

I think I'll leave the shop and go to bed now.

Tomorrow is the update patch. The second wave of players is finally joining. As soon as the maintenance is over, I need to go see Mr. Ertz.

UPDATE—THE SECOND WAVE

I DECIDE TO USE the maintenance downtime as an opportunity to spend a few hours doing homework in the morning. Just before lunchtime, Akina shows up to talk to me.

"Sis! An FLFO dev is going to do a livestream this afternoon!"

"What...? During the maintenance?"

"The title is 'Yamamoto Ittetsu's Time-Killing Stream.'"

"He said that working things out is his job. Should he really be killing time while on the clock?"

"Who knows?"

I was going to do my homework until the maintenance finished up...but I guess I can watch the stream at the same time.

"We're live, Mr. Yamamoto."

"Ah, so I didn't make it in time?"

Now that it was afternoon, the stream starts up with Mr. Yamamoto eating lunch in the cafeteria.

"Howdy, folks! It's me, a higher-up!"

"It doesn't sound like you're taking this very seriously..."

"But it's my own personal stream. I'm gonna eat my lunch and talk about the new patch notes, so until then, enjoy watching an old man stuff his face on stream."

"Did you lose a dare or something?"

Akina and I are also eating our lunches as we watch. Today we made soumen noodles—a nice and easy dish.

"Ooooh, what could it be? Let's check the notes... They're adding new daily, weekly, monthly, and biannual quests? Changing the drop rate for meat... Oh, and they're adding guilds too..."

"There're new dailies now?"

"It looks like it."

"I'm curious to see what the new meat drop rates are like."

It's the first update since the game was released, so it sounds like it's going to be a big one, full of things like new items, bug fixes, and changes to mechanics.

Mr. Yamamoto says that he's eating a katsudon lunch set from the cafeteria. It comes with miso soup and pickled veggies. It certainly sounds like a filling lunch.

"Phew, that was great! All right, shall we get back to the update?"

Now that he's finished eating, he heads into another room and takes out a controller.

"First of all, the biggest change with this update is the second wave of player sign-ups. The total player count in the game is going from approximately 20,000 to 60,000 players. Next up are the daily quests. We'll be adding new login bonuses and dailies. The daily quests will offer rewards that you can think of as pocket money, weeklies give consumables that you might enjoy getting, monthlies

offer fancier versions of weekly rewards, and biannual quests give you 10 whole SP each!"

So they're not the kind of login bonuses you have to collect daily or else you lose your login streak—according to Mr. Yamamoto, they come from the total number of daily quests you complete. If you clear half a year's worth of quests, you're guaranteed to get the final prize. He says this should be a relief to those of us who can't play for certain periods of time, like if we have business trips.

"The game does have 'life' in the title, after all. Living in that world for half a year should come with some newly learned skills, don't you think?"

The daily quests are all a little different, so we'll be able to choose which of the dailies we want to complete each day. This is supposed to prevent those feelings of obligation, like *"Aw man, I've gotta do my dailies first..."*

"Plow X fields." "Collect X vegetables." "Create X potions." "Defeat X monsters." "Read X books." There's going to be all kinds of things like that.

"If you think up any dailies that would really suit your own personal playstyle, try sending them in to the devs. I think you'll be able to see most of them added to the game."

The consumables you can choose to receive from the weekly quests are the same gifts I was offered after my bug report...except for the SP. There's a combat consumables set (potions, etc.), production consumables set (materials, etc.), and a one-hour skill EXP boost ticket (must be used within seven days).

"Oh, about that EXP boost...you'll be able to raise your first-tier skills a whole lot with that one. For second-tiers, well, it should help a bit? If you're planning to use it to level third-tiers, you may as well rip it up."

Potions and materials received will depend on the level of the person claiming them.

Monthly quests will offer money along with the same selections as weekly quests, but with more items included.

By the way, these quest times are determined by IRL time and not the four in-game days that go by during one real day. The quests reset at four in the morning to account for workers who come home late at night or for those who get called away on urgent business.

"Next up... We're adding a dungeon to Starting Town!"

"No way! A dungeon!"

"Okay, sorry for the exaggeration...but it's a place that the first wave of players won't have any need for."

"Oh... Oh no..."

My sister's excitement just went out the window. Mr. Yamamoto must be talking about a way to deal with the traffic in town, right?

"We made Starting Town a pretty big place, but since the hunting grounds rely on random spawns, this dungeon will give you whatever you need. Head there if you feel like the hunting grounds are too crowded."

It sounds like, with no bosses to speak of, it's really just a simple measure to prevent overcrowding.

The enemies come from the northern mountains, eastern forests, western forests, southern forests, and areas around town.

Besides the fact that you can select which enemies you fight, it's otherwise a normal dungeon in terms of mechanics. Those of us from the first wave are allowed to go test it out, but we won't get much out of it. It *does* seem like a way to farm rabbit and wolf meat, though.

The map of the dungeon will change each time you enter. It contains a base level of plains, then caves, and then a forest.

Mr. Yamamoto also says it's supposed to stay around for a while. I'm sure we'll be seeing a third wave at some point too.

"Let's see. Next up..."

He continues to give simple explanations about each new addition while snacking on ice cream and sweets. Since he's streaming from his personal account, he clearly doesn't care about putting on a show.

"What else... Ah, how about this? We're adding a new public board to find people to play with. You can find it behind the Stellura statue in each town's center, as well as next to the quest board in the adventurers' union. If you're interested in full immersion or RP, be sure to check it out. But if you don't care about that stuff, you can also bring it up in the UI at any point. It's not easy to get by in an MMO without this sort of thing."

Now that I'm thinking about it, we've always had an official BBS but never a feature for finding parties and such. This should make it easier to find random players to team up with.

"The board will have tags, like for hunting, production, and trading, so don't forget to use them if you're looking to join up with people."

You start the search process by choosing a hunting, production, trade, or skill tag. If you select hunting, you'll be shown boxes for location, time, level, roles, and comments, which you can fill out as needed.

"The location is to specify which hunting grounds. Time is for how long you want to play, level is for what level range you want to team up with, and comments are a free space to add a message of up to 200 characters. As for role...we made it so you can choose from things like tank, melee, ranged, combat magic, support magic, healing, and performance. I'll give you an example..."

Ex.
Location: North of Starting Town
Time: Until midnight
Level: 10 or higher
Role: Melee, attack magic
Comments: Melee fighters, please use blunt weapons! Any magic attribute is fine!

"That'll do it. By the way, the 'healing' label is for people with Holy Magic or those who can throw potions. Though I doubt you'll find many potion throwers out in the wild."

Potion throwers...wasn't there a Pitching system in the game?

"Right, you can get Potion Pitch under Stone Throw. Is that what he means?"

"There's no point in getting it if you're on your own. You might as well be throwing your money away."

"It would be better if there was someone who could return all those materials back to you. A solo player has no hope of making them back up again."

That's just the way it's got to be. I imagine that most people with Potion Pitch who might join a team as a healer are making their own potions, and for that, they'll need materials.

You have to throw a potion at a teammate to heal them or at an enemy to inflict status ailments on them. It's a unique combat style. I could see them playing as doctors, alchemists, or maybe even witches, depending on the person.

"Those interested in production can also leave a location, time, level, skill, and comments. The role section is replaced by skills where you can select from Gather, Mine, Logging, and of course, Fishing too."

Ex.

Location: Volcano

Time: Leave at 8 p.m. and finish by midnight

Level: High enough to fight

Roles: Gather, Mine

Comments: "Let's go mining. Prepare your own heat-resistance measures." or "Leader has Heat-Resistant Magic."

"By the way, crafting requests fall under trades, not production. Let me explain trade requests. The categories fall under buying, selling, creation, and exchange. Once you choose one, you can fill out each of the boxes."

Ex.
Selling: Iron sword
Asking: 15k
Quality: B
Comments: Secondhand crafted item. Slightly damaged.
Contact me on whisper chat.

Buying: HP Potions
Offer: See comments
Quality: See comments
Comments: C+=500, B-=600, B=700

Creation: Red undergarment
Seeking: Needlework Knowledge
Materials: Bring your own
Reward: Consult
Comments: It's gotta be red.

"*As for exchanges, you just tell 'em what you've got and what you want for it, then take things to whispers. I guess you can throw in bonuses too, or just let them leave it in the log if you want to go to bed. We'll also have whisper chat and party request buttons for the shared boards. Feel free to chat with whichever you prefer.*"

The price changes based on quality, just like with HP potions, and you can use the comments to specify if you want multiples.

As for why he used red undergarments as an example item...

I won't even bother questioning it. I doubt it has a deep meaning. He probably just thought of it off the top of his head. Those potion prices aren't accurate to the current game, either.

"As for skills, I honestly don't know if you guys will use this or not... but maybe it'll be useful for performers? You choose a skill to raise and search for people who will level up with you or give you a hand. I think performers could use it to find people to help put on a concert. Well, it's there for you now, so feel free to use it."

Skills don't level up unless you use them or participate in some kind of related event. Anyway, I'll make a mental note of these new recruiting boards.

It's now been almost five hours since the start of the stream. Maintenance should be just about over soon.

"Mr. Yamamoto!"

"What?!"

"Everything's going according to schedule."

"All right, then we'll be back up at 5 p.m. just like we announced."

"Roger that!"

"Okay, folks. Have you downloaded the patch already? Are you ready to log in? There should be lots of beginner's equipment coming to Starting Town!"

I bet it's going to be really crowded for a while. I want to avoid that sort of thing, but I do have business with Mr. Ertz. I won't be able to escape Eli and Abby's arrival with the second wave of players, either. I *did* log out in Starting Town yesterday.

All right, I've made some good progress on my homework. I think that's enough for today. The livestream's over too, so I'll go queue up to log in.

> Standing by to log in. Please wait. You are number 1,052 in line.

...Ah, okay. I'll keep an eye on it and wait for the number to go down. It only takes another minute or so before I manage to log in.

There's a blinking icon on the right side of my vision. That must be my daily quest. What's on the menu today? Let's see... Improve an existing skill, cook any item, use Alchemy to produce an item, harvest a resource... There's quite a lot.

Combat...production...harvest...other... Oh, there's a quest for reading a book too. That must be for Language Learning.

All right, I'll get cooking then. Mr. Ertz isn't around yet, so I'll make some jerky and give it to the consignment seller.

As for a smoking liquid... I'll make a brine by dissolving salt and sugar in water, then soak some wolf meat slices in it. Next up is Fast Reaction...although I don't have enough MP, apparently. I undo Inventory Expansion, wait for it to recover, and use the spell.

I take the meat out after it's soaked for two days and remove some of the salt. Then I dry it with Humidity Control and place it in the smoker.

Once it's ready, I take the meat out and leave it to rest for the day.

Let's see...I'll do this over again five more times. One piece of meat makes sixty strips of jerky. One person can stave off hunger with a few strips, so this can probably feed twelve people. Five pieces of meat will make 300 strips.

While I'm waiting for my MP to regenerate, Mr. Ertz logs in. I'll head to the trade union when I'm done and hand over the jerky, then visit the usual spot.

I receive 1,000 gold for my daily quest reward. That's really only pocket change. Oh well. I'll just go to Mr. Ertz's place.

I thank the innkeeper and head outside where I spot a group of people wearing matching outfits. I don't see anyone with blonde hair drills, so I continue onward to visit Mr. Ertz. I can contact the others IRL when I want to meet them.

I thought it was going to be difficult to walk around town, but people are actually clearing paths for me. That's very nice of them. I'll take bold and elegant steps in that case. With that, I arrive at the shop.

"You're like, what's that guy's name? Moses?" jokes Mr. Ertz.

"I was able to get here pretty easily thanks to them doing that. Anyway, I got some ore for you, so I'd like to sell it and have some crafting done too."

"Oh, I can do that for you. What do you want crafted?"

"A one-handed hammer, one-handed sword, two-handed sword, small shield, and a large shield. Can you do that?"

"That's a tall order. Is this for your Necromantic Magic?"

"Yes, it is."

I wonder if they can use bows too. That request would have to go to Ms. Primura, though.

"How much will it cost?"

"Let's see... If you want the highest quality, it'll be about 850,000 gold, but if you want them one grade lower, then it's 600,000. It depends on what you want to sacrifice."

"Iron is the highest quality?"

"No, that's steel now. I'm looking for more ways to raise the quality. If you're fine with C quality, then I have some made already."

"Hmm... How far have you gotten?"

"I can get up to B at the moment, but if you want a full set, that'll cost you over a million gold."

"I can do that. I saved up a lot of gold during the tournament."

"Ah, I see. All right... I also have one-handed swords, two-handed swords, and large shields that are above a B grade."

One-handed and two-handed swords are both popular and essential, so he ends up making them a lot. People only buy large shields occasionally. I'll ask him to contact me whenever he makes the rest of my order at over a B grade.

"I'm finally gonna be able to buy a shop!" said Ertz.

"Oh, it's about time."

"A million gold will be plenty for that. What say we settle on that exact amount? That would be...twenty-three one-handed swords, twenty-five two-handed swords and large shields, fifteen small shields, and twelve hammers."

One-handed weapons are popular, as are two-handed swords, although he needs materials for them. The same goes for large shields. He's willing to discount the small shields and hammers a bit. It all sounds good to me, so I put in the official request.

Oh, that's right. I need my dismantling knife repaired, and I need to buy two more pickaxes too. I'll have Mr. Ertz buy the iron ore and ant drops from my list. That will be a return of 90,000 gold or so.

After that, I go to the union and withdraw my remaining 650,000 gold, then pick up my steel one-handed swords, two-handed swords, large shields, and two steel pickaxes. The weapons cost 730,000 gold, while my repairs and pickaxes cost 4,200 on top of that.

"Thanks a bunch! You'll have to wait a while longer for the one-handed hammers and small shields. Do you have any preference for the type of hammers?"

"I'm fine with maces. My servants may not be able to use anything too complicated."

"Simple's always best. Leave it to me."

"Oh, that's right. Do you buy the iron equipment drops from the war?" I asked.

"I do, so I can break them down. The price depends on the piece."

I have him buy my iron sword, spear, axe, dagger, and greatsword for 9,000 gold, while I keep the mace for myself. I also keep the small shield I bought, since it isn't iron. I don't have any substitute for that one yet.

Now it's time to give my new steel equipment away via Secret Art of Necromancy.

Oh yeah, when you equip items that are too advanced for your stats, there's supposed to be a bit of a penalty or something. I hope that's not going to be a problem for my servants.

"I summon you, skeletons."

It'll be quicker to just try it out myself.

"Oh, check out the bones," comments Mr. Ertz.

"Does this new equipment work for you, Unit One?"

The two servants pause for a moment before nodding their heads, so it looks like there's no trouble. Maybe the penalty doesn't apply to servants? Or maybe the skills are giving them a boost.

"They say it's all right."

"Yeah? That's great. I still don't have a good handle on the penalties this stuff will give."

"Unit Two can use two-handed swords, so I think his stats must be pretty high."

"A pure magician with no Strength at all won't be able to raise those stats!"

"He can fight in the second area, so I think he's stronger than second-wave players, at least? Although I don't know what'll happen if someone uses Light Magic against him."

"Is Necromantic Magic pretty strong?"

"I'm not entirely sure. Some of my own buffs are affecting them."

I can't make a solid judgment with nothing to compare it to. Their AI level seems higher than my own base, but that shouldn't affect their stats at all.

"By the way, if you've got any food, c'mon and sell it to me!"

"Um...I do have bear soup," I answer.

"Yeah? That works for me."

"How many do you want?"

"Can I have six?"

"Sure thing. That'll be 800 gold per soup, for 4,800 total."

"No problem at all."

I sold most of them off during the tournament, so I'm pretty empty-handed now, but thanks to that, my inventory is pretty free. Though it's hard to say how open the remaining nine slots really are.

Now...I think I'll cook. I'll make some rump steaks and sandwiches. I have baguettes I can cut up for sandwich bread.

"Hey there!"

"Hi."

"Good day, Ms. Primura."

Ms. Primura slips through the crowd and starts setting up her stand next to Mr. Ertz. As always, I set up my own cooking set a bit behind them.

I use my Fast Reaction on my baguettes while I grill up the rump steaks. Since I don't have any lettuce, the sandwich can have cabbage, and I can use roast beef in place of ham. But the roast beef will require the stone oven, so I'll start with the bread.

The bread is made with my art—starting off with natural yeast to form a dough that I knead, let rest, and repeat to mass produce the bread until my MP runs out.

Once I'm out, I put the dough in the oven and handle the steak next. I cook it with beef fat and garlic, and I make sure it's grilled well on both sides. Then I pour in brandy to create a flambé. Finally, I extinguish the flames and set it on a plate where I keep it warm, flip the bread over, and get to work on another steak. By the time that one is finished, the bread is ready to come out.

"I haven't seen such mouth-watering cooking in a week now!"

"No fair! Sell me some steak!"

"Sure, if you want one."

"Me too!"

"Are they...1,000 gold each?"

"Twelve hundred. The buffs depend on the quality...but please wait just a little longer."

"Sure thing."

I grill up another steak and take the bread out of the oven. For now, I'm done with cooking and can sell my products to the two of them.

Oh, they came out with buffs. I collect the bread and note the results. Rump steak, garlic, and brandy results in an increase to Dexterity.

"It's B+ quality and comes with a Dexterity buff of 5% for five hours. That'll be 3,000 gold."

"I'll take it!"

"I'll take it!"

"Looks like we'll have to rely on a dice roll."

The five-hour time limit is IRL time. One day in the game is six IRL hours, so for those who engage in production, it's a real treat of a buffed meal.

We roll 1d100 with the winner being whoever gets the higher number. They both pick the dice roll from the menu, select the type, and see the die appear in midair as an item. It's big enough for a child to carry it in their arms.

"Victory is mine!"

"Victory is mine!"

I wait for their violently thrown die to settle. It looks like dice have no collision detection, so we can't kick them to change the outcome or something like that. They phase through other players too.

A pop-up display appears above the die once it falls still, as well as above the player who threw it.

"Woo-hooooo!"

"Grrrrrr!"

Looks like Ms. Primura wins.

All right, now I can get back to cooking. The next Dexterity buff I manage to create will go to Mr. Ertz.

I take out my freshly baked baguette and cut into its side to create three even pieces of bread, then I chop the cabbage up into thin strips. I place down a layer of chopped cabbage on the bread, followed by a layer of roast beef. I sprinkle some fried onion slices on top, then pour some gravy over the rest of the fillings...and with that, it's complete.

Now that I think of it, I haven't made any deep-fried foods, have I? For a sandwich filling, chicken katsu probably works better than fried chicken. Maybe beef katsu would be good too... I have both flour and potato starch on hand, so I can definitely do that. Honestly, I should probably try making soft bread as well, instead of just the French style.

"Would either of you buy sandwiches if I had some ready?"

"Well, this is a game, so I'd buy them...but wouldn't combat players appreciate sandwiches more?"

"There were quite a few people who had monsters show up while they were eating, and they got really upset about dropping the food made by the princess."

"Of course, people told them to just eat in the safe zones..."

"Some were just blinded by the delicious jerky. It's surprisingly rare."

That must mean that some people eat with one hand the whole time they're on hunting trips.

"I remember Cecil having jerky in one hand and a meal in the other. He eats while he takes breaks but also while he's focused on hunting."

"Ever since the martial arts tournament, the consignment sellers have had lots of meat. The people from the cooking board were so happy they were finally able to cook it, and after selling meals to people, they had enough money to buy some more food for themselves."

The chefs must have realized that they could buy meat, cook it up, and sell it for profit once they learned that meat was something people wanted to buy. Thanks to that development, people on the cooking board obtained Fast Reaction and upgraded it to a second-tier skill, allowing their production rates to increase a bit. But it's probably not any faster because of its MP usage.

They also apparently learned about developing flavors from things like hot dogs, which increase MP consumption...so it's still going to be a while before they catch up to me.

Anyway, let's move on to deep-fried foods. Wolf meat... No, the softer rabbit meat will be easier to use. But that's for later! Right now, I need to focus on baguettes and steaks.

The steaks result in Strength and Dexterity boosts. Sandwiches only give Stamina. Strangely, freshly baked baguettes offer no buffs at all. Maybe they're too simple? I wonder if croissants give anything. I have butter, so I could try making some now.

I set the topic of croissants aside for the moment and get straight to working on the items I had planned. I end up with fifty steaks and forty baguettes. Next, I lower the heat in my stone oven so I can finish up the roast beef.

```
[COOKING] HANDMADE SANDWICH
   Rarity: NO          Quality: B
   Satiety +30
   Bonus effect: Stamina +5%
   Time limit: 4 hours 30 minutes
   Chef: Anastasia
```

Continuing along with the baguettes I have leftover in my inventory, it comes out to a total of 123 sandwiches. I made a bit too much roast beef, though, and have two leftover helpings. Oh well. I can just keep them on hand.

FREE LIFE FANTASY ONLINE

"If you have anything with Dexterity, then I'll take another two or three."

"Me too!"

"Sure thing."

I end up selling four of each to the both of them. The buff meals come out to a total of 24,000 gold. A delicious profit for me.

"Oh, that's right. Do you have any bows for beginners, Ms. Primura?"

"Hmm? I only have ones that are one level higher than beginners' bows."

"Would it be possible to borrow one?"

"For what?"

"I want my Unit One to carry it and see if he can use it or not."

"Ah! Your mass-produced skeleton, right? Go ahead!"

"Thank you."

Mass-produced skeleton...? Well, I'll ignore that comment. I recall the two servants, who had been out all this time, change up their skills and equipment, and then summon Unit One again.

"Well? Think you can use it?"

CLACK CLACK

No good? I wonder what the issue is.

"You don't know how to use it?"

CLICK

I see... It's a stat issue. So if he can use swords and shields like normal, I can safely assume this is a problem with his low AI level? He could probably learn to use a bow if I taught it to him from square one. Yeah, that sounds annoying. I say goodbye to my skeleton archer and return the bow to Ms. Primura.

"It looks like it's going to be a while before he can use a bow. I don't have much need for stabbing or long-distance weapons right now, so that's fine with me."

"I'm sure it would be hard to get equipment for a humanoid servant..." she comments.

"But there aren't really any humanoid servants available right now."

Summoning Spell and Necromantic Magic function differently, so even summoning the same type of skeleton will result in quite a difference. Which is the better skeleton will be based on the person doing the summoning, but for undead, the order of value, from best to worse, goes Secret Art of Necromancy, Necromantic Magic, and Summoning Spell. Any other order would be trouble for us undead.

I log out for dinner, eat, take a bath, and then log back into the game.

"You picked the perfect time to come back," says Mr. Ertz. "I just finished your maces and shields."

"Oh? You're done already? I'll go get my money then."

"That'll be 270,000 gold."

I head to the trade union and retrieve my jerky profits. After the fees, it comes out to a bit over 110,000 gold, so I withdraw enough to cover the rest of the costs. Let's see...I'll take 100,000 more gold, so I have 3.4 million gold remaining in the account.

Armor is going to deplete that quickly, so I'll save it for later. I go back to the stand to purchase my items.

"Here you are."

"Thanks as always!"

I change Unit One's equipment to a steel mace and large shield. Unit Two can keep his two-handed sword for now, and I'll also keep Unit One's previous mace around for him. Yes, this should be perfect.

"Hey there, everyone!"

"Yo!"

"Hey."

"Good day, Mr. Dentelle."

Mr. Dentelle sets up his stand opposite of Ms. Primura, on the other side of Mr. Ertz.

At the same time, Ms. Salute, the Compounding user, and Ms. Nephrite, the Handicraft user, arrive next. Ms. Salute sets up next to Ms. Primura, while Ms. Nephrite sets up next to Mr. Dentelle.

The five of them begin to talk about their future shops. It sounds like they ideally want their shops as close to each other as possible.

I wonder what I should busy myself with until it's time for bed...

"I see Tasha!"

"We finally found you, Tasha!"

Oh, I know those voices... Well, actually, there're only two people in the world who would be calling me "Tasha." I turn around and see the two girls, who—wait... Ha ha! Aha ha ha ha!

"Don't you think it's rude to laugh when you look at someone's face?"

"Well, you went a bit overboard, didn't you? Look at those incredible drills."

"Aren't they lovely?"

She tugs at them with her hands, and they immediately bounce back to their perfect drill shapes. Eli's drills are extremely tightly wound, while Abby's more subdued drills are more like pigtails that curl up at the ends.

Eli's hair really does uncoil nicely when tugged. It's fun to watch them curl back up into the perfect drills each time.

"Tasha! Look at this!"

Abby lifts Eli's drills with the palms of her hands and sends them bouncing up and down like springs.

"Hee hee hee…"

"This is fun!" Abby exclaims.

"Could you *please* stop using my hair as your plaything?!"

Abby ignores Eli's glares and tries to leap forward and hug me…but the game's unwanted contact defenses send her away. I can tell she's shocked, so I decide to add her to my whitelist. She lunges at me again, and I stroke her hair while she wraps her arms around me.

"You two are humans, aren't you, Eli and Letty? Abby and Dorothy are…demons?"

"That's right. Abby's going for the angel route and is focusing on Doll Magic."

"What about you, Eli?"

127

"I think I'm going to focus on using whips."

"Is that...because you're looking for that kind of aesthetic?"

"Exactly."

"Holding a whip turns you from a young lady into a queen, so you might not want to go with that."

Letty's suggestion is ignored with a huff. "How rude."

Eli's going to do whatever she makes up her mind about, of course. I'm sure Letty understands that well.

For now, I add all four of them to my friends list.

"Ah, that's right. You can have these, Eli. Please share them with the others."

"Potions?"

"They're garbage."

"Hey!"

"They're low-quality garbage from before I raised my skill levels. But they restore more stats than the Beginner's Potions do, so please use them early in the game. The residents won't buy them unless they're quality C or higher, and I can't use them because of my race. I've been wondering what I should do with them."

Eli hesitated for a moment. "I'm not sure about how you're phrasing it, but very well. I'll take them."

Yay! Free inventory space! My only option until now was to throw them away, but these four will find some use from them. Ah, this is actually the perfect opportunity to show them the stand that's set up next to me.

"You can ask this man for dresses and maid uniforms. He's the best needleworker here, although his prices are somewhat high."

"Oh? Dresses and maid uniforms?" Mr. Dentelle speaks up. "I'll cut the prices if you model the clothes for me and let me take screenshots. I'll also pay you if you model some of my other wares too...but I'm getting ahead of myself. Where's my silk? I know I have some..."

Mr. Dentelle sure jumped on that suggestion. Are dresses and maid uniforms so appealing? We still don't know what their base materials consist of. I haven't found any bosses in the second area yet, but the enemies are too strong for me to make any more progress. That will still take some time.

I'll introduce them to the others here too. I don't know when these IRL friends of mine will be able to use the shops, however, due to the prices. Just one weapon costs somewhere in the range of 200,000 gold—and that's not getting into all the pieces of armor and accessories they'll need.

Well, I fulfilled my role of introducing them, so that's all I can do right now. The next step is up to them and their wallets.

"By the way, Tasha, do they have tea leaves here?"

"I've been quietly looking for them myself, but I haven't found any yet. I'm sure they exist, since this world has royalty and nobility in it...but it might be more of a problem with the trade routes than anything else."

"Hmm... Well, our first step should be to familiarize ourselves with the game while we raise our levels, right?"

Right. They'll never be able to search for tea leaves unless they get that out of the way first.

If only my dress colors were a little nicer, I could go straight to a company myself... Well, that's one option, at least. For now, I'm ignoring the matter of the missing tea leaves.

We end up chatting all the way up to bedtime. But that sort of thing is fine from time to time. It's all part of the charm of MMO games.

THE WESTERN BOSS

SINCE IT'S SUMMER VACATION, I'm in no rush to do my morning stretches and such. Once I'm all set, I log in to the game—wait, no, I have to upload my homework first. I load up the data onto my VR device and link it to FLFO. There, all set. Now I can do it at any point.

I log in for real this time.

I arrive in a room at the inn in Starting Town, stretch some more, and head outside. Since it's both summer holidays and nine in the morning on a Sunday, the town is already packed with people.

I haven't really decided what to do today. Hmm...I suppose there's that quest to clean the ancient temple. I guess that's my most pressing goal right now, so I'll need to level up. The enemies there are around level 35, so I should get closer to 30 before I head back to take revenge.

Yeah, I already hunted living dead that were around level 30. So what? But this won't be the same as fighting at my "home." They didn't have weapons back then, and I got the jump on them

FREE LIFE FANTASY ONLINE

every single time. Plus, they couldn't really move around properly, and I always fought one on one. I definitely went into those fights with a clear advantage.

I could take Mr. Alf and Mr. Skelly with me, but the enemy links are probably still going to be a headache for us. Since there's no time limit on that temple quest, I'll go slow and solo for now.

Space Magic has reached level 5.
You have acquired Raum Escudo through Space Magic.

RAUM ESCUDO
Sets an invisible shield in front of the user to block long-range attacks. The shield's strength scales with user's Intelligence and Spirit.
Success rate depends on user's skill level.

Ah, okay. This could be good, depending on the time it lasts and the MP cost. I'll give it a try... Oh, I don't have enough MP? I undo Inventory Expansion, wait for the MP to regenerate, and try again.

Thirty percent? I won't have enough for it. But I see a new icon with a small number "1" on it. That must mean that it will block the next attack. Looks like it lasts for 360 hours total at this rate. One day in the game is six hours IRL. The number of attacks this art will block seems to go up as you increase your skill level, so I'll probably be able to ignore the MP consumption someday. It'll be something to use when I have extra MP. Although I don't know how many attacks it will block in the future, and it's not something I can test out at the moment.

In conclusion, this is a spell I just need to raise my skill level for. It only blocks attacks from the front, but considering what I know about game design, I bet it will block from other directions and even protect my party members once I level it up.

My inventory is getting fuller, but the amount of MP an expansion costs remains unchanged. I can't wait to get it to level 10.

I'd like to do some combat today, but where? I could go to the hunting grounds, but there's a good chance of me dying there and losing all the XP I'll earn. Maybe I can do some simple hunting in an easier part of the third area.

Another option is for me to conquer the path to the west that I haven't yet unlocked. I could get some SP from that too, and it would be nice to have access to its portal.

I also want to check out the new dungeon to the northwest of Starting Town, and I have my homework waiting for me at the library as well. There're lots of options on the table.

I decide to open up the western area. I don't think it will be difficult, and I already made progress on my homework yesterday. There's no need to rush to the dungeon, either. It'll be around for a while in order to prevent overcrowding. I head straight to the western gate and see that, as usual, people are clearing the way for me.

"Ah, if it isn't the princess! Heya!"

"Oh, Ms. Fairellen. Good day."

Being a fairy allowed her to fly down from above my head. I'll bet the sky is just as free as before, even with the new wave of players.

"Nice to see you there, Moses! It's easy to tell it's you when I'm watching from above."

"I still don't know why people are clearing paths for me, but at least it makes it easier to walk around."

"I doubt very many people could stroll so majestically through the middle of the road like that."

"But I didn't ask them to do it. I have to walk along the paths they make whether I want to or not."

"Ah...I guess I see."

It's fine by me, honestly. Regardless of why they do it, it's convenient and really does nothing but benefit me.

Ms. Fairellen apparently just wanted to say hi after spotting me. She flies back up and away with a "See ya!"

Once I exit the western gates, I see lots of second-wave players fighting outside. They're defeating enemies as soon as they spawn, so my trip through the forest should be an easy one.

Solo players are, of course, being watched over by their first-wave friends. Others are gathered in small parties to fight.

The saddest thing I see is wolf players being mistaken for enemies and attacked. I suppose that was inevitable. There'd also a horse, a fox...oh, and a goblin too? It looks like the four creatures are actually in a party together. That must be an easy way to group up. Maybe they have the right idea.

Anyway, I stride past them all and head straight for the forest.

It's my first time coming to the western forest, but I've heard that it's full of insect enemies like the fighting ants I'd encountered in the northern mountains—only here, they must be one level lower. There're also forest spiders, forest snakes, and forest owls. The rest are just normal spiders, snakes, and owls.

The west will be tricky to navigate without burst attacks. Having those will make the trip more pleasant. Without them, I'll be stuck in a hell where I'm constantly swarmed by realistic-looking bugs, even if they're a bit cartoonish in style.

To be honest, I'm already at such a high level, with Physical Immunity to boot, that I can probably just press onward and ignore the enemies.

I slash any that approach, absorb them with Dark Ritual, and make use of Dark Burst to send clusters of them flying before I then absorb them. With a capacity of 1 each, I want to get to the boss quickly. The benefits of this process are getting lackluster.

I've absorbed skeleton and zombie ant materials from the north already, so now it's time to pick up snake and spider bodies. I have owl parts too. I'll check over everything when I get to town.

"Aaah!"

What? That voice sounds like it's fairly close to me... Oh, a forest owl is clutching some kind of yellow carrot player and flying off with her. I can't imagine that plant races really enjoy being in the sky.

I activate Overspell and shoot a Dark Arrow spell at the owl.

"Aaah?! Oof!"

The carrot goes tumbling through the air and hits the ground. That seemed to work. She gets up and runs over to me on her stubby legs.

"It's the princess! Thank you!"

"It's no trouble. I just happened to be in the area."

"My name is Clementia. I'm the second evolution of the sexy radish race—a sexy mandrake."

"I'm Anastasia. I'm the second tier of the extra zombie race, an Immortal Princess."

"Are you gathering materials, Princess?"

"No, I came to unlock the western region."

"Oooh! Can I come with you? Those owls are really giving me a headache... Getting nabbed by them doesn't kill me, but I can't get to the boss like this!"

"Sure, I don't mind."

"Thanks!"

The sexy mandrake sure is cute. The leaves sprouting from her head sway back and forth, and the base of her body is split into legs. She even has short little arms. I remember making the tough decision to continue playing as a zombie. The sexy radishes were the cutest plant race, but zombies still resembled humans in appearance. Cuteness doesn't matter if you can't see it, and this game is exclusively played in first-person.

Anyway, I send a party request to Ms. Clementia and head forward with her.

"Ms. Clementia, what's your fighting style like?"

"I focus on monster skills. I'd say I usually use Wood Magic."

"Those are long-distance spells, right? Depending on the situation, I'll be the one to stand out in front."

"Okaaay!"

Plant races start out with combined Wood Magic spells as part of their race skills, so she must be at a pretty high level.

Since my goal is to unlock the western region, not gather materials or raise my level, we both turn off our Dissection and fire off spells at enemies along our way to the boss area.

I undo Inventory Expansion so that I don't run out of MP.

"There's going to be a lot of mobs around the boss."

"There will be clusters of small worker bees that come our way, but I hear they won't have poison now!"

"Poison doesn't matter to me anyway, so I'll take on the boss myself."

"Got it. I have the perfect skill to clean up all the small fries at once."

Mandrakes have the unique spell Rejection Shout, which knocks out all the enemies around them.

"I'll take my position in front of you, Princess, so please aim your spells at the boss."

"Will do."

We finalize our plan and head to the boss area. The game takes control of our bodies once we reach the spot to make sure we watch as a buzzing massive bee greets us. There're lots of smaller ones around it—or rather, maybe they're only small in comparison to the boss.

Ms. Clementia totters forward as promised while I shoot my Dark Lance with Boundary Control at the boss. Just then, the smaller guard bees gather up to form three separate swarms. They fly up past the boss.

Once she's set up in front of me, Ms. Clementia finds the right moment to cast Rejection Shout. The spell flies out of her in an even wider radius than a burst attack. In the blink of an eye, the three swarms around us go crashing to the ground. Then, my Nox Explosion and Ms. Clementia's Frons Burst rip into them. An explosion of darkness and green-colored membrane envelops them, wiping out all the swarms at once.

Now that the guards are dealt with, it's time to focus on the boss. Bees' joints are their weak spot.

You see, bees don't have very many attack patterns. It seems like everything inhuman is the same in that matter. Bees have body blows, circular thrusts, and stinger attacks.

I block the stinger attack with Royal Counter, try out Counter Parry when it's time for a body slam, and fly straight at the bee for a stab when it circles me—that's when it lets its guard down.

"Counter Parry isn't so bad..."

"Frons Bind! Frons Entangle!"

As we test out our arts, a vine starts to grow out of the ground, wrapping around the boss and squeezing it for continuous damage. Ms. Clementia continues to attack.

"Snipe Seed! Parasite!"

She fires seeds at the bee, causing plants to grow where they strike its body. The new icon that appears indicates even more continuous damage being dealt over time.

I step in to hit the boss before Frons Bind wears off. Maybe I should use Libertà more often. I activate it and cast Penetrate on

the bee's weak spot, which gives off a flashy effect as it takes out a chunk of the boss's HP.

"Oh ho! The princess has some firepower!"

"That can only be used a few times."

The boss's HP is already in the red zone by the time it breaks free of the Frons Bind. Another round of worker bees shows up, but Ms. Clementia's Rejection Shout knocks them out of the sky. The two of us finish them off with our burst attacks.

Our magic also manages to hit the boss, sending its HP down to the 10% mark. All it takes is a few more shots to knock it out for good.

> Your race level has increased.
> Rapier has reached level 10. You have earned 1 SP.
> You have gained the art of Assault Pierce through Rapier.
> Eloquent Princess-style Protection has reached level 10.
>   You have earned 1 SP.
> The subjugation of the western boss has unlocked the
>   western area. As a bonus for your triumph, you receive
>   3 SP.

Oh...it looks like I got more arts.

> **ASSAULT PIERCE**
> Based on agility level, rush forward and deliver a speedy jab.

> **ROYAL STOLZ**
> Attack power increases with each successful use of
>   Defend or Parry.

I see. So I get a rush move and a buff. The latter sounds like a passive art.

"Great job! Let's go see the town now!" said Clementia.

"Thanks for your help. I'd like to get that portal unlocked."

"I guess the boss drops will give us a little pocket change."

"Really? That's all?"

"Yeah, that's all these weakened versions are worth."

Ms. Clementia and I head toward the town as we chat.

The other towns were built in wide-open spaces, but the western town is supposedly within the forest itself.

"The town's right at the end of this road!"

"They must need these proper roads since carriages are the main forms of travel in this world."

"Yeah, exactly."

It looks perfectly normal to me, since it must have been used frequently before the boss showed up. I don't even think they'll need to do any repairs, although who knows if that's part of the game system at all.

"I hear the western enemies are really strong. Or rather, I guess it's the status ailments that make them so annoying."

"Ah, so that's how the western enemies fight?"

"Well, you also find materials to heal yourself, since the enemies are bugs and plants. They do poison, paralysis, and binding. That sort of stuff."

Binding does work on me. Binding, freezing, and turning to stone all render you immobile. Depending on the type of status ailment, they still work on players without flesh.

"Hm? Horses? Maybe it's a carriage..."

Just as Ms. Clementia says that, a carriage comes toward us from the opposite direction, so we clear the road for it before walking again.

"It wasn't that you heard it coming, right? Was it your race's instincts?"

"I guess so, in a way? I think I can sense the vibrations in the ground. It's pretty handy, but it doesn't really work in the air."

"Ah, I see. That does make sense for a plant race."

She tells me that she unlocked the skill at level 20. Other races, like snakes, also have similar instincts through means such as heat detection.

"I was wondering something. Can your hands hold items?"

"Hmm? Oh, not at all. I use my vines! They do the trick once you know how to use them."

She wiggles the multiple vines sprouting from the leaf portion of her head. I guess she has control of them.

"I can only move these four tiny little limbs a little, but they don't help me at all."

"So you don't get that mysterious game mechanic where a character can hold things, even when it defies all logic."

"Sadly, no. I have to get my vines moving to use things as small as a dismantling knife. It's definitely a necessary skill."

"Ah...but on the other hand, that means you have the ability to hold weapons too, right?"

"I tried that, but the metal's so heavy that it really hurts! I went with magical catalysts after that, but I didn't feel like they did anything. This race has to have hidden stats or something."

"Magical catalysts are generally wooden staves."

"Yeah. I'm thinking that my whole body might be a magical catalyst, in that case."

This game has lots of masked data behind it. It's rarer to see the stats and skill explanations written out than not.

But the entire backstory of this world is secretive too, since to the people who live in it, it's just common sense. Playing as a horse is said to result in kind treatment from the residents, especially traders. You can't talk, but you're still a person, so horse players have high intelligence. There're even supposed to be special requests from traders if you play as a horse. They'll ask you to pull carriages or let them practice their horseback riding skills.

I haven't seen any of that sort of thing as an undead, but maybe that will change when I get to the Nether.

"I got my own special quest from a farmer."

"Is that because you're a plant race? You must have some kind of relevant skill."

"I've got one called Plant Knowledge. It makes it so I know how to grow things and even check on how crops are doing. If I want to communicate, I can write out letters on the ground with my vines."

Farmers are probably plenty happy just to know that they're doing things correctly when they try something new with a crop, but it's even better that they can tell if something's wrong with their existing plants. It sounds like residents are starting to understand how outsiders do things now, and I'm sure outsiders will take up their requests if they come in the form of in-game quests.

"Welcome to Brayerich!"

After chatting and walking some more, we arrive at the western forest town of Brayerich. The northern town was mostly brown in color, but this one is completely green. We head straight to the town square to unlock the portal.

"They're growing quite a few monster plants there," I point out.

"Oh, you can tell they're monster plants?"

"My Magia Trace shows me."

"Ah, that makes sense. I didn't know about that!"

It allows my vision to see magia, plain and simple. As potion ingredients, monster plants possess magia, so it's easy to tell which plants are monsters. But the skill stops at revealing anything more than that. The rest is up to Appraisal.

After unlocking the portal, we look around to see what we should do next, when I spot something familiar. I've got to take another look at that.

"Are those...lavender and roses?"

"Where? Oh, looks like it!"

"I bet I could make herbal tea, if they're for sale."

I go to look at the resident's store, but the items are far more expensive than I expected.

Lavender, chamomile, peppermint, eucalyptus, rose, rosemary... They sell all sorts of herbs, but none of them are cheap.

"Pretty pricey, huh?"

"Indeed..."

As Ms. Clementia and I fret over the prices...

"Ha ha! Of course they're expensive," the shopkeeper says. "They're materials for potions."

Yeah, that much is true. "Would you say that the parts that go in potions are the best parts of the plants?"

"I sure would. That's where you'll find the most magia."

"What happens to the rest of the plants?"

"The parts that don't become potions? Nothing, I suppose."

In other words, they leave them and use them for seeds or fertilizer? So they're not being sold? The sellers probably don't even think of using potion materials for something like herbal tea. After all, potions are medicine with reliable results, while drinking herbal tea doesn't guarantee any effects at all.

"May I buy some seeds, then?"

"We don't sell seeds, but you can get 'em over there."

"That shop? Thanks for your help."

"Sure thing."

The store I'm directed to sells all kinds of monster plants as well as seeds.

"Are you going to do some farming, Princess?"

"That's the problem. I have nowhere to plant these seeds if I buy them. All I want is to make herbal tea, but I suppose I could sell the more valuable parts of the plants to others..."

"Time doesn't pass for things stored in your inventory, so maybe you could walk around holding onto a flowerpot?"

As Ms. Clementia and I discuss options, a shopkeeper arrives to speak with us, so I explain my situation.

"Uh-huh. So what you're looking for are parts of the plant that have a strong scent but aren't used in potions?"

"Exactly."

"If you'll wait just a moment, I'd be happy to sell to you."

My goal of acquiring herbs was successful. I purchase an herb set for 5,000 gold. It looks like these items also have a use limit on them, just like salt and other things I've bought before. I'm able to take any herbs from it to sell, which makes this a very convenient package for me.

"Thank you very much."

"Of course. I'm just happy I was able to sell the parts we weren't using."

"By the way, do you know of any area where tea leaves are produced?"

"You can find tea leaves in the Chrichston Kingdom, but they're not exactly available around here. It's usually the nobles who consume the stuff. They're easier to find if you head to any royal capital, and they'll sell for quite a price if you bring them back to this region."

"Chrichston Kingdom? I see."

"You'll find it if you head south from here."

So that's where they make tea leaves. I'm so glad I stumbled across this information.

I've also heard that the water from this area is particularly delicious. That must be part of the reason they grow monster plants here.

We leave the shop and head to the well the shopkeeper pointed us to. I can use this in my cooking. I've been using my Drinking Water art to produce water for it so far, but cooking with tasty water will probably have some kind of good result too.

Water can also affect hunger, so even Ms. Clementia, a member of the plant race, is excited about this discovery.

Photosynthesis also reduces hunger by consuming water. We undead have the unexplained system of Automatic HP Regen, although we also take damage in the sun, which is the downside.

Ms. Clementia easily scoops up the water with the vines from her head. But then, she dives right into the bucket.

"Ahhhhh! It's filling me uuup!"

Now she's shrieking and banging her head. Water's getting everywhere, but more importantly, this seems like quite the change of character, doesn't it?

"Phew..."

Ah, this must be the post-soak clarity I've heard of. It seems like her leaves and skin are even glossier now. She takes another scoop of water, places it in a container, and stores it away in her inventory. It has an even higher restoration stat than Drinking Water.

I take a few scoops of water myself. It looks like this is B-quality water, and it also has a limited number of uses as an item.

I add Ms. Clementia to my friends list, log off, and have a late lunch.

I spend the afternoon relaxing a bit before I log back in at 3 p.m. It's evening during the game now. What should I do next...? For now, I'll head back to Starting Town.

"Oh, hey there, Princess! What a coincidence."

"Good day, Mr. Skelly."

"Here, I have something for you. Oh, and by the way, are you free right now?"

"They're parts? Thank you very much. I was actually just thinking about what I should do next."

"Then come help me with some necromancy research!"

"Oh, sure."

He gives me three parts for physical damage repair. I really appreciate this present, since I have no way of knowing when I'm going to next lose a limb.

We head out the north gate, since it doesn't matter which one we choose, and exit the town. The two of us form a party off the road so we don't get in anyone's way. With that, we begin the research.

Mr. Skelly has Secret Art of Necromancy too, so we'll be able to compare and share information.

"By the way, did you learn Undead Unifier?"

"Huh? I haven't even seen the option..."

"That must mean it comes from my race...or my evolution? You're still at the lower tier, right, Mr. Skelly?"

"Yep, I'm Low Undead. Maybe that means I'm too low to unify any other undead."

We can figure it out if Mr. Skelly evolves, so we'll put the question on hold for now. We won't get an answer until he gets to that point.

The idea is to follow the same rules so that we can get a look at the summoning costs. We both summon skeletons at the base cost and then try making them fight without any weapons.

"Hmm... What's your AI level, Princess?"

"Right now, it's at 25."

"Huh. So your servants' responses are at a totally different level than mine. I'm still in the single digits."

"It seems like a more important stat than I first thought. I fed mine monster cores to raise their level, so I don't know what the beginner's levels really look like."

We test the AI some more, but Mr. Skelly's skeleton doesn't listen at all—or rather, it doesn't seem to understand him. It only knows Fight, Return, and Wait, by the looks of it. I'm sure that means it's smarter than a baby...perhaps it's more like a trained dog?

From there, we test them out on rabbits and learn that Mr. Skelly's servant does little damage with a sword. I didn't observe any issues with mine. I can assume that, just like how my servants can't use bows yet, they must not be able to use swords until level 25.

Judging from the comparison, it looks like my servant is growing up just fine. I enjoy seeing the results of my labor.

"Wouldn't it be easier for him to strike instead of slash?"

"I probably need to feed him cores. Even if I ignore the issue of weapons, I can't deal with the fact that he doesn't understand any of my orders."

"I haven't got any AI issues at the moment," I say. "The low base stats can be raised by leveling up Secret Art of Necromancy, which I think is the best way to make progress."

"Your servants can't use bows yet, right? But bows are the best choice when I'm in a party with Alf. Well, there's no use crying about it. I'm gonna aim for level 20 for now!"

"I was able to have my servants fight in the second area when my skill level was 1 but their AI level was just over 20—although you should be able to get by as an attacker. The only thing to worry about is having his bones get kicked in. That sent my servant straight into the red zone."

"Considering your buffs, Princess, my servant would definitely just bite the dust."

Since I have my own things I want to test out, now would be the time. I fully equip Unit One and summon him at a raised cost, ordering him to fight a rabbit.

Then I recall him, bringing him back again as the next tier up—a red skeleton at base cost. Once again, he fights a rabbit.

"Oh, he's red now."

"You can summon red skeletons when Secret Art of Necromancy reaches level 10. They cost 200 capacity, though."

"That's a big leap... But I bet they're strong enough to justify it."

"They seem to move better. Maybe it's because their physical abilities go up. But I don't have the capacity right now, since I'm only at 220."

"By the way, do you know what exactly will get you more capacity?"

"I think it depends on the size of the enemy. But their flesh and bones also give parts, so it's hard to make that decision..."

"Yeah, I'm not so sure about those drop rates. I bet we'll have to go past the second area, where the enemies are level 20 and higher. But the other top players say they haven't even seen those drops yet, so maybe it's only necromancers or the undead that get them?"

It's a rate of 1 every 200 enemies or so? That's not insignificant for an MMO. Its use has major limits, though.

What else? I'll give my next summon a double cost with a custom order. The cost doubles with any custom components. Right now, it looks like I can customize four parts of my servant for an 8× cost. For a fully customized skeleton, it's 2× to 8× the cost. Even a 3× cost uses 960 capacity.

Mr. Skelly doesn't have Undying Royalty, so he can't transfer his skills to his servants. That means since his servants can't regenerate automatically either, I imagine he can only summon at night. His current objective is to level up Secret Art of Necromancy during the evening so he can eventually summon them during the day.

I summon Unit Two at the base cost and have him bring over the rabbits Unit One defeated. I stick my dismantling knife in while I chat with Mr. Skelly.

"By the way, Princess. Did you get more race skills once you hit level 20?"

"Yes, they added more options. I took three in total."

"I went with Automatic MP Regen and Special Automatic Regen!"

"Good choices. I also took Life Absorption."

"Yeah, Alf went with that one too. He did Life Absorption and Special Automatic Regen."

"So he ignored Lust for Life as well?"

"Considering this game...it doesn't seem like the kind of thing that'll work very often, right?"

"I agree. I doubt it procs very often, and it doesn't address death penalties either, so it's not the kind of thing you jump to choose. I prefer to save my SP."

"I wanted Magical Opposition too, but hoarding SP seems better."

"That's the lesser form of Magical Resistance, right?"

"It sure is."

"It must be an extra in the magic line of skills. You'll probably get Magical Resistance once you evolve. I have it too, but it's not leveled up much."

"So it'll probably show up when I evolve, but I don't need it right now? Then maybe I shouldn't choose it after all."

There's a chance that extra races learn the higher skills earlier. For people like Mr. Skelly, who evolve after finding a certain item, it's a good idea to take the lowest skills possible first in preparation for their future evolution.

"That reminds me. There was a change to drop rates, but do you know which ones they changed, exactly?"

"You can tell when you turn off Dismantle. Supposedly, there're times where you can't get any meat off of rabbits now. What else...? I guess now with Dismantle, you get the same amounts of meat every time."

"So it's just the meat, then?"

It makes sense that, for drops aside from meat, it takes some fun out of the game to have them spawn at the same rate every time. I suppose that's only natural. For me, it feels like I kill enemies and get meat for cooking as an added bonus. It's much better than nerfed spawn rates for skills involving Gather or Mine.

The second wave of players are out hunting too. I wrap things up with six rabbits and recall my servants.

"Oh, that reminds me," I say. "I got a lead on a place that might have an entrance to the Nether."

"Really? Where, where?"

"It's to the area north of Belstead."

"So the third area in the east?"

"Supposedly there's an unused temple to Stellura there, but it's crawling with undead."

"Oh, that's where it is? I hear it's really dark over there, and even for the third area, it's another grade higher in terms of enemy strength."

"I'm going to go back for a revenge match after I work on my servants some more. After spending that time grinding, I should be around level 30 myself by that point."

"Hmm...there's a real mix there, right? I wonder how they'd act if we showed up as a team."

"I'm curious about that too. Well, I'm sure we'll find out eventually."

The quest never specified that I had to go solo, so I'll see how I feel at the time. For now, I need to focus on raising my levels.

"I think I get the gist of things. I'm gonna head to the dungeon now to level up!"

"Oh, you are? Have fun, then."

I see Mr. Skelly off as he heads to the dungeon. Where should I go next?

I already defeated the bosses in each direction, which basically serves as the game's tutorial, and I unlocked the portals at the towns too. At this point, there should be no limit to where I can go.

Hmm... Ah, I used up a lot of my ribs, didn't I? I should replenish my stock, which means my next stop is Belstead to the east. I'll teleport from the statue at Starting Town.

After I finish my business in Belstead, I exit the town and summon a skeleton and a red skeleton. Unit One, the red skeleton, has a one-handed sword and large shield, while Unit Two, a normal skeleton, can go with a two-handed sword alone. We're hunting piggs and angus today. Banties in the southern forest might be good targets as well. I could also go hunt trolls, since I'd discovered a use for monster stones. But for now, I'm here to secure more ribs.

As I always should, I check to make sure I'm prepared before

I start. I search for one angus and make Unit One and Unit Two attack it. Unit Two is summoned without any additions, so Unit One, the red skeleton, does the brunt of the work. I'm not sure how much aggro he can take from enemies, since my necromancy skill is still first-tier, but it will probably work out, since he's stronger than a simple skeleton.

Hmm...it looks like my minions are capable of hunting. Unit Two is sort of just taking up space, but oh well, that's fine. I feel like they might even be able to fight against enemies linked up in pairs. As for their battle speed, it improves vastly when I step in and attack too. I'm relieved to see that my red skeleton doesn't die, even when targeted.

Now it's time for the true art of hunting. I have meat to secure. I make my servants fight as much as possible, since I want to raise my Secret Art of Necromancy skill.

I think I'll let them hunt for a while so that I can stock up on materials. Once I have all the food I need, I can prioritize gaining capacity and sell my cooking on consignment from time to time. Now that I'm on summer break, I can take my time, play it safe, and maximize my profits.

Piggs now drop two pieces of meat while angus drop four, and it looks like the exact cut is random. That's definitely a decrease compared to before. Piggs used to drop two to four pieces while angus dropped five to seven.

Hmm... Rabbits and wolves only give a capacity of 1, right? While piggs are 3 and angus are 6? They're much better enemies for grinding capacity.

The patch notes said that they were nerfing meat drops, but were there any change to the enemy sizes? That must change the drop tables for meat...right?

Well, I guess the math becomes a lot easier now that they drop the same amount every time. It's only an added benefit of grinding levels, so the value remains in hunting just as it did before.

[That one player] Famous Player Thread #13 [What are they up to now?]

1. Nameless Paparazzi

   This is a thread to discuss famous players in the game.

   Which player has caught your interest?

   The second wave is finally here! Will any of them end up famous too?

   Previous thread: http:// * * * * * * * * *

   >> 980 Next thread's in your hands!

42. Nameless Paparazzi

   Here's a summary of all the famous players for second-wave players to catch up on. Honorifics omitted.

   Cecil: A handsome dual-wielding swordsman. Winner of the martial arts tournament in the solo category. Guildmaster of The Knights of Dawn.

Anastasia: AKA Princess. She's the girl in the gray dress in the official trailer. Her title comes from her race.

Akirina: AKA Rina, the little sister. Runner-up in the solo category during the martial arts tournament. Princess's IRL little sister.

Alfred: AKA Alf. Top 8 in the martial arts tournament. Currently a Dullahan—or in other words, an inhuman.

Honehone: AKA Mr. Skelly. Usually in a party with Alf, sometimes with the princess. Also inhuman.

Kotatsu: Guildmaster of The Critter Empire. Focused on leveling throwing skills.

Lucebarm: Guildmaster of Furry Legion. He's a bear who walks on two legs, and people sometimes call him Mr. Bear.

Musasabi: Guildmaster of NINJA. Hi-yaaaah! His character looks like a joke, but he's actually really strong.

Mead: An elf woman who's one of the top archery players.

Daruma Otoshi: Two-handed hammer player. Has muscle for brains. His IRL player is just some normal dude.

Fairellen: Probably the top player of the fae races. She's a fairy.

Cupid: The girl who discovered the angel races and an info poster.

Clementia: Probably the only plant race player in the game. She and the princess are the rarest races you'll see.

Ertz: A top blacksmith. Dwarf.

Primura: A top carpenter. Bunny girl.

Dentelle: A top needleworker. Human.

Salute: A top chemist. Human.

Nephrite: A top handcrafter. Machinery woman.

Steiner: Leader of the top farming group. He's pretty much always in a party of six.

Studylover: An absolute research freak. But I mean that in a good way. The info he puts out is a huge help.

43. Nameless Paparazzi

Studylover sure gets different treatment...

44. Nameless Paparazzi

He's a really carefree guy...

45 Nameless Paparazzi

I loled at the paths being cleared for the princess, but do all the top famous players get the same treatment?

46. Nameless Paparazzi

I hear they're clearing out space for Cecil too.

47 Nameless Paparazzi

It sounds like people see the inhumans all the time. First-wave players are used to seeing them already, though.

48 Nameless Paparazzi

I wonder what the second-wave players will be like? I'm excited for them.

49 Nameless Paparazzi

Same. With 40,000 new players, I'm sure someone's gonna stick out.

50 Nameless Paparazzi

Let's keep our eyes on them.

I SPEND A FEW DAYS leisurely hunting. It's currently Wednesday morning.

> **[INGREDIENT] ANGUS SIRLOIN**
> Rarity: EP   Quality: C
> A very high-quality cut of meat that you'll be lucky to get from an angus.
> Hard to procure due to the wild nature of the beasts, but their meat is enjoyed by the upper classes.
> Try using it for steak, sukiyaki, or shabu shabu.

I've got real, actual sirloin!

There was even a black angus in the cluster of three I encountered. Once I defeated it...

> **[INGREDIENT] BLACK ANGUS FILET**
> Rarity: EP   Quality: C

> The highest-quality meat that you'll be lucky to get
>   from a black angus.
> Not even royalty are able to enjoy such a rare cut of
>   meat.
> Enjoy it as steak, roast beef, or cutlets.

I even got a filet. A rare drop from a rare spawn. I'll post a screenshot of this and my sirloin on the cooking board.

I also went hunting for banties. I really wish they dropped more than one piece of meat per kill. I now have more feathers than I can use, so maybe I'll turn them into arrows. I'm sure that will help with Alchemy too.

Trolls? I absorbed them all. I prefer the 9 capacity over the tiny chance of a monster stone anyway. The normal drops are nothing but trash.

I'm able to obtain chicken meat as well. For capacity, I'll stick with trolls for now. They take a bit of time to defeat, but it's hard to beat that 9 capacity each.

I also received troll materials due to absorbing them, but it looks like I can't summon one yet. The materials are at level 20, so I must be lacking in skill level.

That said, my skills are leveling up well at the moment.

> **SUPERIOR MAGIC ASSIST**
> Dual Spell
> Cast two of the same spell types at the same time.

DARKNESS MAGIC

Nox Wall

Spawns a wall of darkness that obstructs actions and
causes damage when passed through.

SECRET ART OF NECROMANCY

Forced Conversion

Select a target to convert MP to HP. Available only to
Undead and Immortals.

ALCHEMY

Attribute Control

Transfer the attributes of alchemy cores into other
substances.

This results in a large amount of control over magic
and attribute aptitude in the target substance.

Dual Spell will be a good one to use. The effects are clear and
easy to understand. The MP consumption comes down to the
skill itself and the two individual spells being activated. It uses
more MP than casting one spell at a time, but it's a quick increase
in firepower. I bet it will be a bit difficult to aim two separate
spells at a time, but I'm sure it's something I can get used to.

As for everything else...

Nox Wall, well, it's the common kind of wall-building spell.
It lasts for a decent amount of time. It might be the most powerful kind I have now, but it deals no damage unless someone

actually touches it. So what it comes down to is a race against the clock. Enemies will generally try to avoid this sort of thing. Instead, I can try to make them charge or bump into the wall.

Forced Conversion is probably going to be a priceless treasure. I'm not so sure about what its MP usage is going to be like, but it's the kind of restoration that happens gradually over time, and I can cast it on myself as well. I might be able to use it to convert Mr. Alf's leftover MP, but maybe not so much for Mr. Skelly and myself. Forced Conversion is also less risky than Life Assignment for use on my servants. As usual, the only instantaneous healing power I have is Dark Heal.

Attribute Control is still a mystery to me, but I certainly sense the appeal there. Just off the top of my head, I could transfer an attribute to ingots before I craft them or give a sword an attribute to use in battle. But this still requires research, or at least some help from an expert.

I think I've gathered up enough meat for now. I have 128 pork ribs, ninety-three beef ribs, and 173 rump steaks. I also have 111 pieces of shank meat, but the only problem is my mere eighteen pieces of wolf meat. I've always made jerky with wolf meat. Hmm...what if I made jerky from rump steak? I could charge a little more, I suppose. It also might be fun to sell lumps of roast beef. I can make do with fewer rump steaks.

All right. I'll do some cooking until lunchtime.

I go to the plaza in the center of Belstead and set up my cooking kit.

Today I'm making rump steak, roast beef, and onion soup. That sounds good to me.

I can make jerky and roast beef from recipes, but the onion soup will have to be made by hand. The first step is to create a bouillon.

By the way, bouillon is used for soups, while "fond" is a base for sauces. The one slight difference between them is which ingredients you use to make them.

I undo Inventory Expansion, prepare the meat for jerky and roast beef, place them in the smoker and stone oven, and begin to work on the bouillon.

I prepare the chicken, garlic, onions, and carrots. There're no leeks or celery, so I'll have to skip them this time.

I pour the ingredients into the water I used to boil the chicken and let it stew for a bit. It only takes about five minutes IRL, meaning I can quickly finish up in the game.

I fill my pot with water and add the chicken and vegetables. Once the flames heat it up to about 90°C, I turn it down to a lower heat to let it simmer, where I'm forced to sit and observe for a hellish ten hours (in-game hours, of course). I watch the tick-tocking of Fast Reaction and try to enjoy myself in the meantime. It's important to appreciate the simple things in life when you can.

While I keep an eye on the meats in the smoker and oven, I also remove any scum or extra fat that rises to the top of the pot. This is a very quick process in a video game, which is certainly nice. It almost seems like all they want is for you to remove anything

FREE LIFE FANTASY ONLINE

at all when it appears. I'm sure the quality comes out lower if you skip this step.

My jerky and roast beef are complete, so I collect the food and begin with something else.

> Chef has reached level 15.
> You have acquired the art Magical Expand through Chef.

Oh, look at that. I reached level 15. What did I get? Magical Expand... It's a passive art to increase the satiety of your cooking? I like the sound of that. I only wish it had been around for all that jerky and roast beef I just made!

All right, I'll throw some new meat into my smoker and oven, then cook some onions in a pan with butter. I'll be sure to keep a close eye on them until they caramelize.

After that, I just have to throw in the bouillon I made earlier, let it simmer for a while, and season it to taste. I'll add the chicken I used for the bouillon too. I remove the bones, add the meat, and even include an extra baguette and cheese. Now it's onion gratin soup. Since it's a complex recipe, I'll add it to my Set Menu list.

> **[COOKING] HANDMADE ONION GRATIN SOUP**
> Rarity: NO   Quality: B+
> An onion soup that was made with lots of time and
>   effort.
> Contains a freshly baked baguette, cheese, and even
>   chicken.

> Tastes like a mother's home-cooked meal that will
> warm you from the inside out.
> Satiety +85
> Bonus effects: +5% Agility
> Time duration: 5 hours
> Dish creator: Anastasia

Onion gratin soup results in an Agility buff. Using the Tableware art causes the contents to be condensed, and the "chef" credit has been changed to "dish creator."

It looks like Magical Expand can double things or even multiply them further. Honestly, I feel like I could more than double the prices I've been charging too. What should I do? Cooking prices normally start based on the amount of satiety, then take ingredients and cooking time into account after that. Selling something means you're already confident that it will taste good, meaning taste ultimately isn't a big factor in pricing.

If I simply double the prices, the dishes I sold for 2,200 gold will end up as 4,400, which I multiply by 2.5 again for the B+ rating and buff. That makes it…11,000 gold?! That's way too expensive.

I'm sure the prices will stabilize once more people gain this art, but if I sell my dishes for too little, won't the others not sell at all? I'm sure my creations will sell as soon as I put them up, and there're a lot of new players now, right…? Well, I suppose I'll save up now while I can.

It looks like my new batches of jerky and roast beef are done… My jerky now gives thirty satiety. Jerky's supposed to be simple field rations, but now it's at the same level as my other cooking.

I try out a steak and see that the satiety has gone from thirty-five to seventy. So field rations are increased 150%, while normal cooking is now at 200%? Using Set Menu seems to make it 250%. I'll look into it more later, but for now, I clean up and head off to hand my creations over to consignment.

I price my buffed onion soup at 11,000 gold. The rump steak jerky is 850, while the roast beef is basically a luxury item at this point, right? I'll price it at 1,000 gold. The steak can go for 2,400.

All right. It's time for my lunch.

I relax a little after lunch before logging back in.

I finished up my daily quests this morning, so how shall I spend my afternoon now? I already gathered up quite a bit of meat, so I should be fine in that area. That leaves...fighting trolls to farm more capacity?

I currently have 652 capacity. I've managed to get a lot over the past few days, but it's still not enough. Golems have a base cost of 400, while customized red skeletons cost 600. Fully customizing them would cost me 4,800 capacity.

However, if I take the base stats into account, summoning an improved red skeleton would be better than a fully customized regular skeleton.

My Secret Art of Necromancy will reach level 20 very soon. At that point, I can summon a metal skeleton. Those have a base cost of 400, while a high golem comes out to 800, I believe. Bumping up the size to "large" would be 1,200.

I can summon ants, spiders, and snakes now too, but I don't foresee a situation where I have any use for them. Undead spiders would probably be possible with my skills. I might be able to use them too.

Right now, skeletons are my main force. Once Secret Art of Necromancy is at level 20, I'll probably be able to summon a Unit Three, and I'm hoping to make it a skeleton wolf because of their fast rush attacks.

What else? I'm still eager to go back to the north of Belstead and conquer that area for real this time. Then I can absorb living armor to summon a tank. My plan is to avoid golems, due to both their cost and size.

Skeletons and living armor should both have an upgrade cost of 1,200 capacity. Wolves will be 600 due to their smaller size. With a capacity of 2,000, I could summon three upgraded units together. I need about three times the capacity, then? That doesn't sound so bad if it only means 150 more trolls.

My current options on the table are: raising my level and skills, gathering capacity and materials, or gathering materials for production.

As for art testing, Attribute Control from Alchemy is still on my mind a bit. Assault Pierce isn't something I need to go out of my way to try. It only covers a few wide steps in terms of range, so I won't be able to use it for evasion or anything of the sort.

Royal Stolz turned out to be much more valuable. An icon pops up when you block or dodge, and the more you do it, the higher the number on the icon goes. However, it goes right back down again if you fail a block or dodge. Parry is +1, blocking an attack is +2, and taking damage is −4. It all goes back to zero once you log out. I'm not currently sure how high you can stack it.

All right...I'm going to go to the south, grab some goblin materials, and then move on to trolls to grind for capacity. I can also get banty meat and raise my level while I'm at it.

At this point, I'm thinking I need to absorb new materials once my evolution tree changes. Absorbing a banty unlocked rooster servants for me, while the same went for owls once I absorbed one in the southern region. But that also probably has to do with their different stats compared to skeletons.

I exit the southern gate and head into the forest, slaying and absorbing goblins along the way. Then I return to the town square and teleport to Belstead.

My next stop is the southern forest. I'll absorb any troll I meet and turn banties into chicken meat and feathers. I can use the chicken bones and bouillon for my soups, so I'd like to keep the meat around until I need it. The problem is that banties are small in size, so they don't drop very many items. It's going to take longer than with pork or beef.

I combine the feathers with sticks and stones to turn them into arrows I'll sell on consignment. One combination gives a healthy ten arrows, so I make ten stacks of them for my Secret Art of Necromancy. It's nice to have the free inventory space, even if my servants only get a few of each piece of equipment.

Once I get to the forest, I summon my servants at their base cost. Unit One, a red skeleton, gets a two-handed sword, while Unit Two gets a mace and small shield. Summoning Unit One at a raised cost would have meant I'd have no capacity left to bring in Unit Two as well.

I'll leave the servants in charge of banties. I need to be the one to fight trolls, since the plan is to absorb them.

It's officially hunting season.

Trolls deal wide attacks, so the first step is to parry and stack Royal Stolz. Once I've dodged enough, I move on to my own now-buffed attacks.

I wonder if I should feed my servants more orbs to increase their AI level? I want them to determine some autonomous actions of their own and expand what they're capable of. It would be perfect if they could separate from me a little more and hunt independently, but I'm getting the sense that we can only be a limited distance apart from one another. I just don't know if that's the fault of their AI level or my own skill level.

It sounds like using Tamer allows for once-wild beasts to go hunting for you on their own, but Summoning Spell is better for that sort of thing rather than Secret Art of Necromancy.

I'll give my skeletons some orbs. After all, I can't trade these items away. I give seven of my fifty-seven orbs to Unit One. Eat up now, sonny.

Oh, his AI level went up to 35? Hm...? I see something very specific written there now. They must have added this in the patch.

AI level 1 behaves like a kindergartner, while 10 is an elementary school student. Then it goes up to 20 for a junior high schooler and 30, where I'm at now, for a high schooler.

It also says that once a servant reaches level 30, it links up with other races, performs more actions, and even starts using bows.

You can start asking them to gather supplies for you at level 35. This is where the ability for them to engage in production unlocks. They gain access to the use of magical catalysts as well, including the ability to use darkness magic.

The description also mentions a reduction in the time it takes for servants to adapt to new materials at levels 5, 15, 25, and 35.

The exact values remain a mystery to me, but I think I still want to increase their AI levels now. I may as well push things a little further. I'm sure it won't take all fifty of my cores.

Hmm...yeah, it looks like the cores don't level them up as much now. Just earlier, seven orbs gave Unit One an increase of nine levels, but now it takes twenty cores to level him up to 50. That's only an increase of fifteen levels. I'll stop for now with thirty orbs left.

AI level 40 appears to give servants the intelligence of a college student and allows them to function autonomously. They think and act outside of what you order them to do. This is also when they gain access to magic types outside of Dark Magic. Level 45 allows for complex spells, but since my skill level is too low, that's not on the table yet. I don't have enough skill slots either. It looks like this doesn't matter until Secret Art of Necromancy reaches level 30.

Finally, at AI level 50, they become adults. It sounds like my servants will function just like most residents in the game. This also removes skill restrictions and expands their range of capabilities, meaning I don't have to worry about how to handle them when it comes to skills anymore.

I also learned something new. I actually only intended to feed Unit One nineteen cores to reach level 50, but I decided to add one more just to make it a nice even number. After level 50, the counter hardly went up at all. It feels like just getting my servants to level 50 was like the tutorial section. I'm curious what leveling them up from here on out will be like, but since I'll run out of orbs in no time at all, I think it's best to set the matter aside for a while. I'm now at the point where I don't think my servants will cause me any trouble.

I resummon Unit One and Unit Two just to be safe, and with that, we head back out to hunt.

Hmm...their stats remain unchanged, but their fighting is much more efficient now that they can move better. They don't waste time on pointless steps anymore.

Now that they're capable of more actions, I tell Unit One to take out a banty within my field of view. Unit Two remains as support for Unit One and myself—or rather, he rushes and strikes as he pleases. When I see three enemies together, I'm able to leave them to Units One and Two to divvy up, but I generally make Unit Two prioritize enemies Unit One or I are fighting.

Now I'll raise their efficiency even more. I recall Unit Two and resummon him as a red skeleton wolf with custom materials. Unit One costs me 200 capacity and Unit Two costs me 400, so I'm able to make it work.

I give Unit Two two arms, a two-handed sword, and resummon him. Now that's a shocking sight. He's a dark red skeletal pup with two arms growing out of his back to carry a sword. Since he already has four legs as a wolf, this actually seems rather practical for him? But I can improve that even further. I'll select Sword, Balance Control, and Body Boost for his skills.

Body Boost is a passive stat buff for both Strength and Stamina. The Dexterity and Agility version is called Limb Boost, while the Intelligence and Spirit buff is called Soul Boost. I don't know if the buff they give is as high as it would be if you focused on an individual stat, but since I'm only using this on my servants, it doesn't really matter so much.

For race skills, I stick with the usual Physical Resistance, Life Absorption, Low Undead, and Bone Body. I also grant them my Super HP Regen and Special Automatic Regen. It won't let me change Low Undead and Bone Body, but I suppose that might be natural for skeletons.

All right, Unit Two. Time for you to test out your new toys. In fact, let's have you do lots of testing. I have him hold a two-handed sword...but then again, with this fighting style, a katana might be a better option.

It took a bit of time for him to get used to the new body, but thanks to his high AI level, he gets the hang of it in no time. Maybe I should use cores to get him straight up to level 50? Or at least 30. Anything lower and I'm pretty sure he won't be able to coordinate with other players.

I can still customize his body, right? But if I keep playing around with customization, I'm going to run out of capacity in no time. I'm sure I'll be able to summon metal skeletons soon, so I can't really use customization until I'm at the point where their skills are too high to easily level anymore. What a sad fate.

Summoning a metal skeleton and upgraded armor will be 2,400 capacity altogether. An upgraded metal skeleton dog is 600, so I need 3,000 total.

Customizing the dog alone is 2,400 capacity. I could stop summoning upgraded servants and just customize, but that's 800 capacity too. Adding two arms counts as two-pointed customizing, which quadruples the cost.

Secret Art of Necromancy is useless in the first place without capacity, so for now, I'll continue to absorb trolls until I raise it to level 20.

[What are you up to] Cumulative thread 44 [today?]

1. Resting Adventurer

This is a thread for general posts.

Feel free to write whatever you want.

Just remember that admins will step in if you don't follow the basic rules.

Seriously. They could end up deleting the whole thread, so behave.

Past threads: http:// * * * * * * * * *

>> 980 Take care of the next thread.

455. **Resting Adventurer**

How convenient is that new dungeon?

456. **Resting Adventurer**

You can choose from every region's rabbits and wolves, northern enemies, eastern enemies, western enemies, and southern enemies too.

You can even choose weather: Morning, evening, morning (rain), and evening (rain).

The map is like a condensed version of the real map? That's what I think.

Does that about sum it up?

457. Resting Adventurer

Sounds good. They also say you get an EXP bonus if you go in with a party. It's probably easier on the servers.

458. Resting Adventurer

It's got an EXP bonus, sure, but just like they said, there's really no point for first-wavers. It's just the same enemies you see around Starting Town.

459. Resting Adventurer

But the chefs are actually using it more than you'd think.

460. Resting Adventurer

I guess that makes sense, since you get meat.

461. Resting Adventurer

It's a smaller place and there aren't very many people in it, so it's easy to get drops.

462. Resting Adventurer

Definitely. You've got all regions and the eastern forest.

463. Resting Adventurer

[Breaking News] The princess gave more of her cooking to the consignment seller.

464. Resting Adventurer

No way! I'm gonna buy some!

465. Resting Adventurer

Also, something's up with the prices.

466. Resting Adventurer

...Do you see how expensive it is?

467. Resting Adventurer

It's almost double now...oh? Ooh! I get it! I'm buyin'.

468. Resting Adventurer

Okay, I see now. I'm buying too.

469. Resting Adventurer

What exactly did the princess do?

470. Resting Adventurer

She probably just leveled up Cooking, right?

471. Resting Adventurer

I checked the cooking thread. They say it's from her Magical Expand art.

472. Resting Adventurer

Huh? The princess has arrows too... They must be made with the feathers she got from gathering chicken meat. Poor banties.

473. Resting Adventurer

The princess has Alchemy, right? They work well, but at this price, I doubt she profits much.

474. Resting Adventurer

She probably made them to level up Alchemy. I know she doesn't use arrows.

475. Resting Adventurer

Hang on, how'd you guys find this out so fast?

476. Resting Adventurer

You don't know about favorites?

477. Resting Adventurer

Wait, what's that?

478. Resting Adventurer

Oh, try searching the name Anastasia in the top right.
Look for sellers, not items.

479. Resting Adventurer

Found her.

480. Resting Adventurer

You can see her info if you click her name. You'll figure
out the rest from there.

481. Resting Adventurer

I had no idea this was a thing... tysm

482. Resting Adventurer

How long has this been here?

483. Resting Adventurer

Whoa, this is so handy.

484. Resting Adventurer

H-holy crap. I didn't know so many people never found
this. It was there before the update too.

485. Resting Adventurer

For real? I had no idea. You can check on your favorites
as soon as you select them, and there's even a display
for highlights.

486. Resting Adventurer

The satiety on this cooking is awesome. Hunger meter goes down fast when you're battling.

487. Resting Adventurer

Not as much when you're just hanging out and chatting. I guess it depends what you're up to.

488. Resting Adventurer

The price makes me think her cooking is for first-wavers to buy, but considering those healthy satiety numbers, it actually seems kind of cheap?

489. Resting Adventurer

Going off that satiety...they're cheaper than the time it takes to eat them.

490 Resting Adventurer

Apparently...there's a difference in the satiety boost between field rations, normal cooking, and normal cooking made with Set Menu? She wrote that it still needs confirmation, so we probably need to try it out more times.

491. Resting Adventurer

Her onion gratin soup is so damn good. But it was expensive, since it comes with buffs too... I'm gonna go hunting when I finish eating.

492. Resting Adventurer

What? She was selling that?

493. Resting Adventurer

There were six varieties total. Even the ones selling for 11,000 gold were gone in a flash.

494. Resting Adventurer

Ouch! That's so expensive!

495. Resting Adventurer

It gave 85 satiety and a 5% agility buff for five hours. I was pretty hungry, so this was perfect. But most of all, it's just delicious. It feels like something you would buy from a restaurant.

496. Resting Adventurer

I bought some too, but I can't eat it until later...

497. Resting Adventurer

It's so damn good! You better look forward to it.

THURSDAY

AFTER LUNCH, I return to hunting...but first, I go pick up my consignment profits.

I speak to the receptionist at the trade union and recover what I earned from my buffed onion soup, normal and buffed jerky, roast beef, and the leftover bear soup I had.

It looks like I made about a million gold from all that. The jerky really makes for a nice profit. I give the rest of it to the union. My current gold count is a bit over 4.4 million. That's plenty, since the cost of equipment for my servants has been recovered.

Now it's time to hunt. I leave the union and head for the woods. One more hour and I'll probably have my Secret Art of Necromancy at level 20.

After yesterday's hunting, my base level has reached 24. I also leveled up Radiant Magic to level 10 and learned Lumen Wall along with it. I can already tell this is going to be a priceless treasure in the northern area.

Once I reach the forest, I summon Unit One and Unit Two... and now it's time to ship out.

> Space Magic has reached level 10.
> You have learned Gravitas through Space Magic.

> **GRAVITAS**
> Control a unit's gravity to weaken their movements.
> Gravitational control depends on user's skill level.

Oh! It leveled up—wait...no, that's the wrong one. But what's this? The MP my Inventory Expansion uses went down to only 70% in total. This is a pleasant surprise.

So it looks like I've learned gravity magic. This is probably the kind of thing where you're not supposed to think too hard about the science behind it. Maybe it has something to do with the theory of relativity? Honestly, if you asked if I was curious about it, I would have to say no. I don't demand such scientific accuracy from a video game.

What matters most is the mechanics of the game itself. Does the word "gravity" have a broad or narrow scope? This is the real question, as it greatly changes the meaning of the art. According to the description, it only makes gravity exert twice as much force at its current level.

I wonder if I'll be able to change the direction of gravity once I raise it. I suppose that would mean that anti-gravity exists, in a way. That would hypothetically allow one to fly...but considering the game I'm playing, it would probably rob me of all my MP in the blink of an eye. I'll also need to consider the amount of force and magia needed. One mistake could send me flying into the atmosphere, where I'd burn up to a crisp.

There's no way the game would implement that kind of system and then be lenient with how it can be used. I'll do a little bit of research while I'm out here, starting by determining if this art has any practical uses.

I cast Gravitas on a troll I happen to encounter. It does start to get more sluggish, but it's essentially able to move as it usually would. The MP cost looks relatively small for something from Space Magic, but that's ignoring the fact that this is an ongoing spell. It drains more and more MP the longer I have it activated.

The spell itself isn't so bad, but I'm not going to be using this one. I want my MP to go solely into attacks. I'll probably only use Gravitas if I run into an enemy that's too fast to handle. Maybe once I level it up a bit more, I might be able to bring down any flying enemies.

Secret Art of Necromancy has reached level 20.
You have gained Poison Prod through Secret Art of
  Necromancy.

POISON PROD
Produce a noxious explosion that poisons enemies.

I finally reach level 20 and receive the most unexpected art from it—an attack spell.

An explosion that also poisons enemies? I give it a shot, and while the blast itself doesn't seem very powerful, its visual effect can block line of sight while also dealing ongoing poison damage to an enemy. It activates the same way as other explosion spells. The visual obstruction doesn't seem to affect me or my servants. This actually might be a handy spell to have. I don't know if my vision remains normal because I'm the person who cast it, or maybe because I'm in a party, or maybe my night vision is related somehow? I also want to know why the poison has a strength of 4. Players and enemies have slightly different reactions to status ailments, but this is particularly intense. I just might start opening with this spell in all my battles from here out.

The description didn't mention the strength of the poison... My Dark Aura reached level 30 around Tuesday, which raises the intensity of inflicted ailments to 4 now. It seems like Poison Prod might inflict status ailments based on the intensity the user is capable of. A default level of 4 seems far too overpowered. I'll ask Mr. Skelly to tell me what intensity he gets once he reaches level 20, since I reckon he doesn't have Dark Aura yet.

All right, then. I've achieved my goal of raising Secret Art of Necromancy. I also managed to gather somewhere around 200 pieces of chicken meat, which is more than enough. All the hunting I did over the past few days was worth it. I also have more feathers than I need—so many that turning them into arrows will be a real pain.

My capacity is still under 3,000 as well. I could get to that number in just five more battles, but that'll put me at my goal with nothing extra. I suppose I have no choice. I'll take out five more trolls before heading back.

There we go! I reached my goal of 3,000 capacity, so I'll head back to town...or, maybe the north instead. Before I work on getting to the temple, I want to absorb some phantom knights, then maybe do a little homework.

Suddenly, I run into an enemy I've never seen before. It's even equipped with items. The game shows me that it's called an ogre guard, it's at level 30, and it displays the word "elite" instead of "boss." There's also a stamp that says "apprentice." So it's learning how to be an elite? Is it an elite yet or not? I guess I understand what it's getting at. An ogre studying to be a guard would never be labeled "elite."

I resummon Unit One and Unit Two in their metal forms, deciding to call Unit One with multiplied stats and Unit Two at his base stats but with two customized parts. That comes out to a capacity cost of 2,000, which leaves me with some extra to spare, but I'll hold off on summoning a Unit Three for now.

"Go defeat that guy."

Unit One nods with a *CLACK*, while Unit Two gives me a thumbs up with one of the arms coming out of his back. As always, this is the kind of thing you certainly don't see every day. The main problem is that it's actually pretty cute, despite the wolf being made only from bones. Now that I think about it, it might be a whole lot freakier if it was a normal wolf.

Anyway, putting that aside, this is an ogre "guard," meaning he's equipped with a one-handed sword and a large shield like a

tank. I'm sure his skills fall into the same category. Level 30 should make him weaker than the enemies in the northern area, but now that I've spotted the thing, I figure I may as well fight it.

...Look, mistakes were made. But the base levels in this game are impossible to judge! When it comes to servants, the most important thing is their AI level.

The ogre guard is even doing some simple feints. This is bad. They're impossible to dodge.

My own misstep leads to the ogre landing a slash on me, and once again, I say goodbye to my left arm. That one attack seemed to take out 30% of my health on its own.

The ogre guard's movements are incredibly swift. This must be what makes it an elite, despite its apprentice status. It seems to be clever too. In terms of intellect, that makes the undead from the northern area weaker. What they lack in brains, they make up for in numbers.

Units One and Two deliver their attacks, but I make them retreat after a single blow. It doesn't look as if I'm the only one the ogre is targeting.

Once a troll shows up to join the fight, I leave it in the hands of Unit One.

"Bring out Ironcutter, Unit Two."

I'm ready to wrap things up with these foes, so I order Unit Two to use an art. As he dashes forward, the two-handed sword in his hands begins to glow red, and the Ironcutter connects with the ogre guard as Unit Two flies at it from behind. I retreat back to put some distance between us.

189

Unit Two can really get the job done. That was a completely manual use of an art, wasn't it? While it doesn't hinder movement any, it can be difficult to activate an art, and it might not do much damage. In the end, I see the worth in raising that AI level. But wait... Unit Two? What do you have in your mouth there?

Unit Two's attack caused a large explosion, so I use the opportunity to cast Penetrate. The ogre would just block a head-on collision with its shield. That makes sense. I would do the same, after all.

Once the ogre staggers from Penetrate, I follow up with a delivery of Nox Shot. Unit One joins to fire off Ironcutter, while Unit Two shoots Distance Sword from his position farther away... and it's lights out for the ogre guard.

Now what should I do about these drops? Do I absorb them, or use Dismantle? The materials will consist of ogre parts, I'm sure. To be frank, I assume that Secret Art of Necromancy, unlike Summoning Spell, will result in a different form of skeleton, like usual. Oh well. I'll go ahead and absorb the ogre, regardless.

> You have received ogre materials through Dark Ritual.
> You have earned 9 capacity through Dark Ritual.

Yeah, that's about what I expected.

Now, as for Unit Two... What exactly does he have in his mouth? Ah, that would be my left arm. He went and fetched it for me. Unit Two uses one of his own arms to hold mine up for me, which I accept from him.

But can I even put this thing back where it's supposed to go? ...I see. There's a timer on the arm showing that I have five minutes to put my arm back on my body before it disappears. Dropping the arm unpauses the counter, while picking it up freezes it.

As always, however, the damage to my body lowers my stats. It looks like I can repair my arm within the five-minute time frame without using parts. It will heal fully in another hour and a half...faster than using C-quality parts, I believe.

Let's see... What's next? The arm repair time is pretty inconvenient, even if it's perfectly understandable. My arm feels a bit strange, and my Dexterity dropped on top of that. This will affect Cooking, not to mention any battles I get into.

Hmm...I guess I'll save absorbing the phantom knight for later. For now, I'll tackle my homework and then move on once my damage penalty wears off.

I could work in the game library, but it's 3 p.m. I think I'll use the opportunity to log out and take a break. I can do my homework IRL today, and then it will be time to head to Belstead.

I finish up my homework break and log back in around the time my penalty is supposed to be over. I confirm that the effects wore off and immediately begin to head for the north.

According to the new numbering system added in the update, the former temple is located in area 2-2. Places like 2-1, 2-3, 2-5, and 2-7 are areas with towns like Belstead, and they're numbered in clockwise order starting from the north.

Until now, I thought Starting Town was referred to as the first area due to it being the center of the map, while the area with the temple was called the third area because it was three squares away. But apparently, any place on the border of the first area is the second area, while anything encompassing the second area is the third area. This means that going from the second area, where there are towns, to the third area, where there aren't, means the enemies will get much stronger.

Therefore, the next town must be located on an adjacent map. Or rather…maybe diagonal, instead of adjacent? Even if it's adjacent on the area map, who knows if we'll be able to reach it by walking in a straight line?

Anyway, it's time to go absorb some phantom knights. I've deposited my money already, and my inventory is looking nice and prepared. Even if I die in the process, I will absorb as many phantom knights as I can.

If I reach the point where I can summon a tank, it will be able to take on linked enemies all on its own without any trouble.

I equip Unit One with a steel hammer and large steel shield, summoning him as a metal skeleton at a cost multiplier. For skills, I select Polearm, Defend, Balance Control, and Physical Boost.

Unit Two gets a bronze two-handed hammer and a small steel shield. I summon him as a metal skeleton dog at base cost with two points of customization. I choose the skills of Polearm, Balance Control, Physical Boost, and Footwork for him.

Finally, I assign them both race skills of Physical Resistance,

Life Absorption, Low Undead, and Bone Body, along with my own Super HP Regen and Special Automatic Regen.

Both of their skill levels come out to 20, since they're dependent on my own Secret Art of Necromancy skill. Their Super HP Regen and Special Automatic Regen are the same levels as mine—18 and 12, respectively. Special Automatic Regen at level 18 restores more health than Automatic HP Regen at level 20, so I swapped that one out for Life Absorption and made sure they had Special Automatic Regen slotted in.

Reaching level 20 with Secret Art of Necromancy allowed me four skill slots to use on my servants. The four race skills are by default, so that didn't change. I imagine I'll gain race skill slots as I level the skill up in the future.

With my two dark red, glossy, metallic skeleton servants, I head forward to area 2-2 in the north. Since now seems like a good opportunity, I undo my Inventory Expansion.

Unit Two still needs to get a bit more familiar with these weapons, it seems. I swapped his two-handed sword out for a one-handed hammer and small shield, so I have him practice on the forest wolves we encounter along the way. I absorb the enemies once they're defeated. When Unit Two gets used to his new equipment, it'll be time for the main event.

"Here's the plan, Unit One. I'll take care of the flying skulls in the air, so your job is to watch my back. Armored skeleton wolves should go after me, and I want you to get the jump on them by using your arts when they do. Revenants and forest wolf zombies

FREE LIFE FANTASY ONLINE

will probably target you two, but I don't think they're all that tough. You understand so far, right?"

"Clack."

"As for the linked phantom knights, I'll take on the knights themselves, so you should aim for skeleton enemies. Unit Two can deal with the archers, and Unit One can take out the soldiers. Once they're all defeated, Unit One will watch over the area, and Unit Two can join me in combat. Does that sound good?"

CLACK

"All right. Let's head out."

They probably—no, they *definitely* wouldn't understand all this if they were at a low AI level.

Once a flying skull shows up, I let Unit One watch over the area while the skull and I shoot spells at each other. I'm resistant to its magic, so the fight is no problem for me.

We end up fighting the revenants and forest wolf zombies too, which aren't any trouble either. They don't start out by targeting me, so I take them out easily with an Overspell-charged Lumen Shot.

The problem arises when reinforcements show up while we battle the phantom knight links. We find more as we press forward, so we start heading for the center of the area.

I see an armored skeleton soldier, archer, and a pair of phantom knights up ahead.

"Try and get another angle while I shoot spells at them, Unit Two. Unit One, you're on standby while I build a wall of light."

CLACK

All right. Let's get killin'.

The archers have a wide range of vision, so when they target me, I use Overspell and hit them with Lumen Explosion as soon as they're within range. Then I follow up with Lumen Wall.

Unit Two maneuvers around the wall and uses the blunt attack version of Ironcutter—Armor Break—against the archer's legs from behind.

Unit One stays on guard near me as ordered. These enemy undead don't appear to be the brightest of bulbs. They charge straight at the wall and end up taking massive damage as a result.

The soldier and a phantom knight both head toward me. Before the soldier can reach me, Unit One strikes it with Armor Break from the side.

He goes on to quickly finish up the soldier, who's nearly dead already thanks to my Lumen Explosion and Lumen Wall, and I fire off a Lumen Shot at the knight. That's enough to knock out most of its health. This guy has quite a lot of HP.

From behind the phantom knight attacking me, Unit One offers a hand in the form of a full Armor Break swing. That should finish off the knight.

As for the archer? After Unit Two knocked it over from behind, he grabbed its legs with his teeth, dragged it around the place, and then pounded it with the mace he carries with the customized arms on his back. That was the end of the archer. It's hard not to sympathize with the poor thing.

Hmm...this is going very well. As long as I get the drop on the enemies with an opening spell, we can handle the rest. However,

FREE LIFE FANTASY ONLINE

it still depends on our positioning. The closer we get to the center, the more enemies show up in this area. I still don't think I'll be able to make it to the temple just yet.

> You have gained Living Armor materials through Dark Ritual.
> You have received 3 capacity from Dark Ritual.

Well done, well done. Now I can summon necro-armor. I'll fall back a bit, set up my servants' skills and equipment, and get a lot of hunting done while I'm here.

I've returned to the outskirts of Belstead. Now I need to check on some things.

The new materials I absorbed were for living armor. That's the same sort of body Mr. Alf had before he became a Dullahan. The servant comes with the Armor Body skill instead of something like Bone Body or Decomposing Body.

He'll be resistant to slashing and stabbing attacks, but blunt attacks will do extra damage. This kind of servant seems better than a zombie, although they do move slower in this form. Well, that's a given with something from the tank races. All they need to be able to handle those blunt attacks is a simple shield, after all.

Skeletons move quickly for undead, but they have low Stamina. Zombies are slow, but high in Stamina. I assume the zombies also have extra-effective automatic regen skills.

Tanks have armors and skeletons. Zombies are like air. No,

seriously, they're basically just air, right? Well, there's no need to go out of my way to use them as servants, so I suppose that's fine.

Huh...since Mr. Skelly is currently an undead, maybe he's basically just air too? I'll have to table that question for later.

I move on and change Unit One's equipment, swapping out his large shield with Unit Two's small shield. In turn, Unit Two gets a Zelkova round shield. I'll be summoning Unit Three as necro-armor, and I'll equip him with a one-handed sword and large shield. I can also probably swap out his Polearm skill for Sword to match his weapon, and that should be good.

You may have noticed I don't have enough equipment for this. After this, I'll set some time aside to really plan out how I'm going to equip them.

I don't have enough capacity for a 3× summoning, so I summon Unit One at a 2× multiplier, Unit Two with customizations, and Unit Three at a 3× multiplier. Now we can work on leveling up. The servants themselves are all the same being, so it's nice to be able to let them cooperate with each other unsupervised. If I had to name one problem, it would be that they're still lacking in combat skills despite their high AI level. Players like Mr. Alf or Mr. Skelly are much stronger than these three. Although Mr. Alf and Mr. Skelly are top players, so it's only natural.

Anyway, now that I know the targeting priorities for multiple enemies, the three of us should be fine to come back here another time. It sounds like a great way to grind.

Visually, the necro-armor is a full suit of armor that looks a little worn down with age. I really like how sturdy he appears.

With his steel sword and tower shield, he looks like a force to be reckoned with.

Now it's time to hunt until dinner. I'll have to be careful of my surroundings as we creep into position. Unit Three leads the way while Unit One and I follow, and Unit Two wanders around us.

I take on flying skulls by myself as always. I wonder if a potential Unit Four would be able to use a bow? Tanks sometimes attack as they please, so I suppose I could turn Unit One into an archer instead. Right now, I have no long-distance attacks outside of spells.

All right. Now it's time to bring home the goods.

I don't take as much damage now that I can summon servants, but avoiding so much as a scratch is, of course, impossible.

The problem is with Royal Stolz. Unit Three doesn't have Appeal yet, so he can't draw aggro, leaving it in my hands.

If my servants lose Stamina due to damage, I'll just cast Forced Conversion on them. That should change their little-used MP into HP.

Sure, both my servants and I are creatures of magic, but I think it's fine to whittle away their MP. The leftover MP that it takes to move their bodies can just be thought of as the real MP gauge.

My own restoration is what's causing the bottleneck. The problem lies in how Forced Conversion works. I can use it on myself, but I don't particularly want to lose half of my MP in one shot. It takes 50% of my MP to restore 30% HP. Unlike Life

Assignment, it doesn't stop as soon as you're fully recovered. You could describe it as being in a constant state of regeneration.

I can probably just use Life Assignment to provide my servants with my own HP, then use Forced Conversion to recover damage myself. If only I wasn't a magic attacker. A scarecrow would be more useful than a spellcaster without any MP. I'm sure my servants would be able to power through a little more, but it'd make resource management that much harder.

I'm still trying to reach the former temple in the center of the map, but the further in I go, the more enemies spawn, so I think this destination is still out of reach for the time being. I don't believe I can handle the true strength of the undead—their force in numbers. If they only consisted entirely of zombies, I could pass through undisturbed, but pushing forward any more will just result in death. Instead, I pick a nice spot to stay and hunt.

Also, while I'd been feeling it a bit this whole time, it definitely doesn't feel like light spells are doing 4× damage here. Maybe there's some sort of special effect in this area? Still, even outside of Dark Magic, my spells should have plenty of firepower. Also, I wonder what the deal with this area's strange dim lighting is... not that it poses a problem to me with my night vision. I'll have to leave that question for another time.

Another thing that interests me is how my servants are moving. Though they're supposed to be on the same level as residents, there's still lots of variation between the intelligence of residents themselves. The players are called outsiders, while the residents are simply the NPCs. They can handle one-on-one confrontations, but surrounding them can cause them to panic. Unexpected occurrences tend to disturb them in a similar way. I don't know if that means their AI level is too low or if it's so players can make them join their parties. All I can say for sure is that enemies outrank them, so I can't put my faith in them entirely.

Maybe it makes more sense to summon servants as a solo player but go without them when in a party. I'm certain that Mr. Alf and Mr. Skelly would feel more at ease that way. Being a royalty race gives me the ability to command, and it's not exactly like my skills specialize in giving orders to others.

But partying up may turn out to be difficult—if the others are working overtime at their jobs and I go to sleep at 10 p.m., I'll be asleep by the time they log in. So during summer vacation, I'll have to use the weekdays for production, leaving Saturday and Sunday free. I think I'll just hunt for now.

Eloquent Princess-style Protection has reached level 15. You have gained the art Royal Anti-Magic through Eloquent Princess-style Protection.

ROYAL ANTI-MAGIC
Block and deflect spells. Overwrites Magic Guard and Magic Parry.

So I finally have an anti-magic art? That's going to make my life easier when dealing with the flying skulls.

All right, I'll head back to where I came from, and by then, it should be dinnertime. I'll take out more enemies as I go.

I leave the area with the ancient temple and slowly make my way back to Belstead.

I like the idea of having Unit Three use a one-handed spear instead of his sword. He can deliver little bits of damage over his shield. I also sort of want a two-handed hammer for Unit Two, so maybe I should go buy one from Mr. Ertz. I'll have to test out how he handles a wooden hammer first, though. If I start buying things without picking a style first, it's going to wreak havoc on my wallet. Setting up templates won't be fun, either.

The game service has only been running for a bit over a month now. My skills are nicely leveled, but I'm sure that won't be nearly as easy from here out. I'll have to settle on an objective that isn't just raising my skill levels. If I don't, I might get bored. Then again, both the combat and production systems are plenty of fun, so I'm sure I won't get sick of them. It's just best to have a goal in mind.

But for now, it's time for dinner.

[Another happy day] Cooking Thread 12 [Wifey's cooking tastes best]

This is a thread to post about cooking production.

Talk about cooking here. If it's not cooking, go somewhere else.

Previous thread: http://* * * * * * * * * *

General Production Talk thread: http://* * * * * * *

Attention!

[Boiling Knowledge] and [Stewing Knowledge] exist!

No cooking terrorism allowed!

>> 980 Take on the next thread!

462. Nameless Chef

I really want [Tableware] and [Magical Expand].

463. Nameless Chef

Same...

464. Anastasia

You can make buffed jerky now?

465. Nameless Chef

Ah, I thought so. That didn't work before the patch, right?

466. Nameless Chef

Mine raises regen effects. Not so sure about that one.

467. Nameless Chef

I don't think it looks so bad? The regen amount goes up if you use a regen spell or drink a potion.

468. Nameless Chef

Okay, let's sum up the information everyone's given us.
Strength: Meats, boiled
Dexterity: ??, grilled
Stamina: Grains, ??
Agility: Vegetables, ??
Intelligence: ??, ??
Spirit: ??, stewed
Regen rate: Field rations, ??
That's what we've got so far.

469. Nameless Chef

So there're still a lot of missing pieces. We don't know about frying, steaming, or roasting yet. Restoration is probably smoking, right? Or are field rations just a special case?

470. Nameless Chef

It seems like the buffs are affected by the main ingredi-ent in the dish along with how it was prepared...

471. Anastasia

I'm quite certain that seafood will fit one of those categories, but I haven't tested it myself yet. Another possibility may be fruits for desserts?

472. Nameless Chef

Ah, hang on a second. I have notes from the time I made meunière...

473. Nameless Chef

Is meunière a combination of grilling and seafood?

474. Nameless Chef

Yeah, that's it. It gave me Intelligence and Dexterity.

475. Nameless Chef

If grilling gives Dexterity, then we can probably assume that seafood is what results in Intelligence.

476. Nameless Chef

Let's call seafood Intelligence and leave it there for now. Actually, now that I'm thinking about it, I haven't seen any fruit around...

477. Nameless Chef

Maybe they're growing somewhere outside of the official routes?

478. Nameless Chef

There were raisins in the east, so there's gotta be grapes somewhere too.

479. Anastasia

Yeah, I've always been looking down while gathering things, but never looking up.

480. Nameless Chef

The forest to the east of Starting Town... Did you know you can pick chestnuts there?

481. Anastasia

I never noticed that...

482. Nameless Chef

You can pick castalia in the east. That means chestnut trees. They don't fall, but you'll see them growing up there if you look up.

483. Nameless Chef

So we should walk around with our heads raised?

484. Anastasia

I'll do that. I've been plucking nothing but medicinal herbs and mushrooms this whole time.

485. Nameless Chef

That's right, you're using Alchemy.

Return to the Library

I WRAP SOME THINGS UP, head to bed, and log in the next morning.

My first stop is the library. This world is so detailed that simply fighting all the time would be a waste. I portal back to Starting Town and head to the library.

"Ah! There you are!"

I hear a woman shouting as soon as I spawn in. She must have been waiting for someone to arrive.

"Princess! Wait up!"

Oh, it's me she was after? I don't remember having an appointment with anyone.

"Good day, Princess!"

"Good day. What's the matter?"

"Do you have a little free time right now? I want to give everyone else the time to show up..."

"Excuse me?"

"We've been looking for something to give to you as a thank-you present."

"A thank-you...? Ah, is this about my beauty tips?"

"Yeah, exactly! We have to show our gratitude for these incredible results we're getting."

I recognize these women, so I figured it had to be about the beauty tips. I'm glad to hear they've seen good results. I'll go ahead and accept the gift as offered, since they clearly put some thought into it. Besides, my only plans were to read at the library, so it's not like I don't have free time.

The four women thank me again and tell me the representative for the woman I helped hadn't logged in yet today...or so they thought, until she did log in and tell everyone to gather. They seemed to get that notification as soon as I logged in, but that has to be a coincidence, right? The woman arrives...

"Sorryyy! Were you waiting very long?"

"...Why are you here, Ms. Kotatsu?"

"The other girls told me all about it!" she says with a giggle.

It sounds like she became their representative because I have her added to my friends list.

"We all tried to think of a way to thank you and ended up going for something we think you'll *need* instead of something that's just rare for the sake of being rare."

"Isn't that difficult? Although, I understand why you might be hesitant to surprise me with any rare items."

"Yeah, and you can't use potions because of your race, right? That's how we came up with this."

Ms. Kotatsu waves her hands, and what appears in them is... meat. Ah, I see.

"It's not something rare, you need a lot of it for your cooking, and farming for drops is boring. So we gathered up a whole meat set of rabbit, wolf, pigg, angus, and banty!"

"The cooking board mentioned that boar and bear meat is only for raising the cooking skill, so we didn't include any."

"These are a little expensive, but you can buy them like normal in the game. Since we all chipped in, it wasn't too much for any one person to buy, so don't feel like you can't accept it."

"We'll be really happy if you cook with this meat and sell it on consignment too."

"We don't like those foods you can eat with one hand. We want more cooks to make real meals!"

"Can't you make it yourselves?"

"No way!"

They really did shout that in unison at me.

"What are you going to eat after you leave?"

"Lunchboxes! Booze! Snacks!"

They were like a Greek chorus. "That sounds good, as long as it's not *just* booze and snacks."

"Ha ha ha ha!"

...This is how adult women really live.

"Shall I make something with this gift of meat?"

"Fried chicken!"

"With or without lemon?" I ask.

"With!"

"Without!"

"Either is fine."

"......"

They've silently split up into factions of lemon-lovers and lemon-haters and are now trying to intimidate each other. What exactly are these people doing?

By the way, it was Ms. Kotatsu who was fine with either.

"This is like a comedy skit."

"It's just a coincidence, I'm sure. It's not like we discussed it in advance..."

"This never would have happened if I didn't say anything in the first place."

"I can't believe we all picked fried chicken, like we planned that answer beforehand or something..."

"Well, I was planning on making fried foods in the future, so I have the ingredients for it," I said. "But I don't have any lemons, and I'm not going to make it if it's going to cause fights."

That snaps them out of their fighting moods. I probably would have lost control over the situation if I hadn't warned them.

I move a bit more out of the way and set up my cooking kit. I know what I have to make.

Let's see... They brought me pure oil, virgin elulu and elunta oils, and about fifty pieces of each kind of meat. Oh, they even made sure to include pork intestines and butter.

One bottle of virgin oil alone costs 3,000 gold, so I'm definitely going to indulge with this. It's a game, after all! The usage limit on the oil comes down to the number of times used, not the amount of the liquid itself, so it seems perfect for deep-frying.

I think I'll need one pot for frying and one for regular cooking. I pour the virgin oil into the first pot and fill the other with
water.

I split up the banty meat into chicken for bouillon and the
rest for frying. Then I prepare the vegetables for the bouillon.

I go with B-quality water, then add in an egg and scramble it
up. I use Cooling on the egg and water batter, along with the flour
itself. Then I add the cooled flour and mix it together a little.

I scoop the batter into the oil with my chopsticks and give it a
temperature check.

"Not quite ready yet."

I work on the bouillon while I wait for the oil to get hot
enough. I can use this for more onion soup in the future.

I occasionally skim the foam off the top, and I check the oil's
temperature again. I pour in a little of the batter and since it immediately floats back to the surface, that means it's ready. I mustn't
forget to chill the batter either, or it will turn out too gummy.

"There, that's probably good enough."

"I'm so excited, I'm drooling."

"We're in a video game, though."

"I wish I had booze to drink with this..."

"I want to start off with a nice glass already."

"I know, right?!"

I coat the chicken meat in the batter and plunge it into the
pot with a sizzle.

"I just love this sound."

"Me too!"

"I never get to fry things at home."

"You never cook anything though, right?"

"Heh heh!"

The women certainly are chatty. I can hardly bring myself to look at them. But they're in good spirits, by the sound of it.

"You're so good at that. You'll make a great wife!"

"You sound like a creepy old man."

"What's wrong with pointing out a good cook?!"

Is it possible these women are already drunk?

As soon as that thought crosses my mind, Ms. Kotatsu steps in. "You guys have been drinking already, haven't you?"

"Nope, I'm sober."

"Seriously?"

They're surprisingly worked up for being sober. I'll leave them to Ms. Kotatsu. I have cooking to do.

I keep my eye on the oil and remove the chicken once it's nice and brown, replacing it with a new piece. I love how the pop-up tells me the state of the oil at all times. Right now, its status still says "great."

If only I had other ingredients like shrimp. I wonder if they would be mad if I fried up medicinal herbs I picked and told them they were fried wild vegetables. I use Laundry to clean up the herbs before tossing them in. I'm pretty sure Ms. Kotatsu did a double take at that. *Shh. You didn't see anything.*

Unlike the chicken, the veggies fry up right away. They really look like the real thing.

"Whoa, are those wild veggies?! I'm taking those!"

"Hey! No fair!"

"...Wh-what are these? Fine, if you want them so much, take them."

"Whaaat...?"

Those are some sour faces they're making. Busted. "Ah, they don't work, do they?"

"They taste like grass. It's like eating a leaf."

"The princess sneakily threw them in... Those are medicinal herbs, right?"

"I don't think I'll be able to pass them off as wild veggies, will I?"

Next, I take out a zoomishroom.

"Woo-hoo!"

"I think I'm done adventuring. What say we just focus on eating instead?"

"We thought these might work, since they're used in potions..."

"But isn't that why you included medicinal herbs too?"

"They're edible, they're edible."

"Really, they're edible!"

"More like homicidal."

"*You all* should be the ones eating them if they're so edible!"

"Would you like them roasted? Or fried?"

I end up making both kinds. I present the women with fried zoomishrooms and zoomishroom skewers.

"Oh... Oh? These actually work."

"Yeah, surprisingly..."

"For real...? I'll just have the normal fried chicken."

"Not fair!"

"So unfair!"

After that, I fry some cheese and give tonkatsu a try too. That brings the oil's condition from great down to average, then all the way down to bad, so I wrap things up. Pouring the oil down the sink causes it to dissolve into polygons and disappear, making cleanup incredibly easy.

The bouillon I made results in a perfect onion gratin soup.

"Can you believe we bought her a gift, but she ends up using it to feed us delicious foods?"

"Seriously!"

"It's so crispy and yummy!"

"Your gifts really helped me, so there's no issue there."

This fried chicken really *is* delicious. I might be able to sell it if I put three or four pieces on a skewer. As far as profits go, I should really focus solely on jerky, but it's boring to make the same thing over and over again.

I would also like to try making dry-cured ham, since it's so hard to make in real life. But I only have pork ribs, so I should probably use beef instead—the rump steaks with less fat.

Then, four men approach our group.

"Oh, hey there, ladies! Wanna come party with us?"

If I remember correctly, dry-cured ham is made by cold smoking. I don't think it will require any different seasonings than what I use for jerky. The biggest problem will be managing the delicate balance of temperature. Dry-cured ham is made without exposing it to direct heat, so in real life, sanitizing the meat is the biggest hurdle.

For now, I start by dissolving salt and sugar in water to make a brine. The meat will take some prep work too.

"Wh-what? Why're you ignoring us, ladies?!"

"Huh? What?" they all responded in unison.

I assumed they were ignoring them intentionally, but they were actually too absorbed in food to hear anything, huh?

Ah, but Ms. Kotatsu was definitely doing it on purpose. To react is to lose in these sorts of situations.

The four men who approached us are clearly second-wavers, although their equipment doesn't look like the kind beginners wear.

"Let's go hunting! We'll teach you how it's done!"

"Mph!"

I understand how the girls feel, but I wish they wouldn't choke on their food and spit it out everywhere. Let's see...I just need to let this sit for a day, then drain the water. Some time manipulation should do the trick.

All of us ladies here are first-wavers, after all, with Ms. Kotatsu and I being top players. Aren't these other four women highly ranked as well? I see they're holding steel weapons. Steel is currently the strongest material you can use, so I'm sure they were far from cheap.

Looks like the meat's finished resting. I add some black pepper and garlic to the brine I made earlier to let the meat marinate. Again, I rely on the handy tool of time manipulation. It looks like it'd takes a whole week otherwise.

"I doubt you can teach us anything. Can you bother someone else?"

"We're first-wavers, so we probably hunt in different areas."

The ladies nod their heads as they eat. They're clearly more interested in food than men. I'm sure that's only more apparent since we're in a game right now.

"F-first-wavers...? Th-then could we ask you for some advice?"

This hurts to watch, but I understand the response. I just wish I couldn't see the anxiety in their eyes.

All right, that's probably enough salt-pickling for now. I appreciate the extra-fast MP regeneration I get for being in the center of town. Now I soak the meat in water for a few hours to remove the extra salt.

The four men look to be around the age of college students. These women are old enough to drink, at the very least, but they're also total gamers. They pursue what's fun for them—they don't let others tell them what to do. The impression I got from speaking with them is that they're also not the types to appreciate flattery. In fact, they're probably very annoyed to have their dinner interrupted. I can see the dead-eyed looks on their faces. *Come on, boys. Read the room!*

Aside from the four other women, Ms. Kotatsu and I are wearing fully made-to-order equipment.

A single glance at us should tell them that we have enough money to deck ourselves out like this. But I'm sure that sort of thing is hard for beginners to tell, due to a lack of information about the equipment and item economy.

By the way, Ms. Kotatsu is a cat beastwoman with brown hair, yellow eyes, and a pair of hot pants that expose her white legs.

She's a bit shorter and slimmer than me and runs a guild called The Critter Empire: a place not specifically for furries but for people who simply love things like cat ears, tails, and animals.

The next task is to work out how to repeat the process of drying and smoking this meat, since I can't tell how dry it is. Maybe I can use Humidity Control for this.

"Hitting on girls and refusing to leave them alone is cause for a warning!"

"Oh, hey there, Ms. Kuon!"

"Hello everyone. I'm a GM."

She's got a big smile on her face, although the men have totally frozen up.

"These things have been coming up recently since the new update brought in a lot of new players. This game isn't a dating app, guys!" She turns toward us. "We added a sexual harassment report button to the GM call feature, so if someone refuses to leave you alone, please feel free to contact us with that."

"Oh, that's right. Did they change how the GM call works?"

"People really just skim through those patch notes, huh? Please tell your friends, both male and female. Sexual harassment reports take top priority, so you'll be assigned a GM to handle it instead of an AI."

With that, Ms. Kuon sends the men away with a cry of "Shoo, shoo!" The men really seemed persistent, despite being rejected. Ms. Kuon tells us that they're patrolling for a while, since all the new players were just added to the game, and any severe violations they catch will have the player sent to a punishment room.

The four men from earlier weren't breaking any particular rules, so the situation ended with them being shooed away.

"Ah, and thanks for the beauty tips. A GM can't give you a present, of course, so this is all I can do to express my gratitude. Feel free to call for me if any strange people try to cause trouble for you. From a management perspective, we'd be feeling a huge loss if famous players quit the game over something so silly."

"No one's tried any funny business with me yet. But you know about my beauty tips too, Ms. Kuon?"

"As a woman, I can't help but be curious as well!"

Well, that's perfectly fine with me.

I end up using Humidity Control on my ham to remove some of the water, then I keep an eye on the temperature as I cool the smoker.

"I'm going to go patrol another area now."

"See ya!" The ladies continue their Greek choir impression.

What a dramatic send-off.

I smoke the ham over and over again, making sure to observe the dryness each time. The worst-case scenario would be having to repeat this process for two weeks. After two hours of smoking, I string the ham up, dry it, smoke it again, and then dry it again. After a bit of time to rest, the dry-cured ham is finally ready.

> **[COOKING] HANDMADE DRY-CURED RUMP HAM**
> Rarity: NO   Quality: B–
> Smoked meat made with careful precision over a long period of time.

> Enjoy the delicious flavor in thin-cut strips.
> Satiety +30
> Chef: Anastasia

Hmph. Only B–? My Humidity Control really must be the problem. I should work out a better way to dry out foods.

This dish contains as many servings as roast beef. I cut up some thin strips and serve them to the others.

"Here's my newest creation."

"Dry-cured ham!"

"This is what you were working on?!"

Since we're inside a game, the servings I gave them disappear as soon as they start eating. With that, it's time to go our separate ways. I'll use the rest of my time playing in the library as planned.

"Welcome, Miss."

"It's nice to see you again. Do you have books that contain global maps or world information?"

"We sure do. What grade of books are you looking for?"

"I don't mind if they're broad or don't go into too much detail."

The librarian shows me to the books I'm looking for.

I'm sure I wouldn't understand any high-level books about this world. I still don't even know what countries exist or where they're located.

I accept the books from the librarian, take a seat at a table, and begin to read. The result is a newfound comprehension of this world's geography.

The continent we're currently on consists of four large countries, with Starting Town located in the center of the continent.

The kingdom to the northeast is called Kradahl—a land of dwarves who produce an abundance of metal goods.

To the northwest is the Enchanted Tiaren Kingdom. They're known for the production of spells and potions, which is why they also grow magic plants. It's occupied by elves.

The east consists of the kingdom of Nearence, where they farm and raise livestock. It's also where this world's main church is located.

Finally, there's the Chrichston Kingdom to the west. My book doesn't give me much information about the country's exports, but that one resident once told me that they grow tea leaves there.

You can also set sail from Imbamunte in the south to reach yet another continent. There, you'll find the large, militarized empire of Dinait—home to a grand fighting arena that is always a source of much local activity.

The southern continent is the biggest one, and supposedly it's also home to most of the smaller countries. In other words, the continent we're currently on appears to be a peaceful place.

Other towns exist in all four cardinal directions from Starting Town. These five, including Starting Town itself, are regarded as the Malcarant Principality by the other four countries. The book also states that each land has established trade routes.

In other words, once you go past the second area that we're currently able to reach, you'll land in one of those four countries.

There once was a war over control for Starting Town, but the period of strife came to an end when no ground was gained. I understand why any other country would want it. It has a port town and exists in the middle of four great lands, after all. While Starting Town was never taken by another country, they didn't leave the conflict unscathed.

Eventually, they proposed a compromise: Starting Town would never become part of their own nations, but neither would it belong to any others, and that's been the case ever since. Any of the four countries who attempt to conquer the area will immediately become the enemy of the other three, as well as the enemy of Starting Town itself.

In a way, I can see why the war ended so quickly. All of these countries have their own unique exports. Chrichston to the west would have it particularly hard.

Making an enemy of the eastern region would mean a sharp decline in food supply. Making an enemy of the northeast would mean a loss of metal—or in other words, weapons. The northwest can't be antagonized without a loss of potions. Starting Town itself, as the scene of the war, would result in a fatal loss of salt. But the biggest obstacle, according to the book, was the interference of monsters. It was a disadvantageous battle to fight on all ends.

The four countries declared the five towns independent, including Starting Town in the center, and forbade anyone from meddling in their affairs. As a result, Starting Town now provides them with critical supplies of salt for cheap.

The town is probably so huge because it includes trade routes for four separate countries, not to mention that it's also the place where we all start out. So the noble's mansion to the northwest must belong to the Malcarant family, who governs the region around the town.

As for the empire to the south...there isn't very much information about it in these books. All I can conclude for sure is that they're engaged in wars, although I'm not sure whether that's something we players can meddle in at all.

For now, I'm satisfied that I've learned the names of the countries in this world.

The nobility system here doesn't seem different from what I know. Royalty are at the very top, followed by titled nobles: duke, marquess, earl, viscount, baron, etc. Each country rules differently on whether or not those titles are hereditary or not, like knights, for example.

I may be royalty as far as my race goes, but my actual position in society is no different from a commoner. I'm assuming that might change once I reach the Nether...but I'll find out for myself eventually, so I may as well put that on hold for now.

I still have a bit of time left. I remember that there are picture books and tales of legends here too, so I'll read those next. I already read Volume One, so I'll move on to Volume Two.

The gods, who were too powerful to directly affect things on this planet, gave birth to spirits.
These planet-born spirits cultivated the earth in place of the gods.

After countless years, they produced the living creatures that the gods desired.

The gods returned to their own realm and continued to watch over the planet.

So the spirits exist as proxies for the gods. At this point in time, I should probably avoid antagonizing them.

Let's see...there are four volumes in total. That leaves two more.

Creall, the supreme deity, granted the other three pillars their own unique roles to prevent conflict.

At the bottom, the energetic goddess Sigrdrífa was given the role of overseeing battles and victory.

Haventhys, the calm and gentle middle pillar, was given the domains of love, growth, nature, and rest.

At the top was Stellura, with all remaining roles granted to her, no matter how painful they may be.

Those were the domains of life and death, contracts, and judgment.

A god with control over life and death must travel to a place outside the realm of the gods.

Stellura made this decision by determining that the supreme deity should not be the one in charge of this work, and so she chose to head elsewhere.

Creall granted her the title of second-in-command. With it came the ultimate powers of rule over time, space, and fate.

Though they aren't something she can always use, Stellura's powers of time and space allow her to travel back to the realm of the gods.

Who knows? Perhaps the four pillars are gathered at this very moment to enjoy a cup of tea together.

I see...

To be honest, my knowledge from real life made me worry about what the origin of Stellura was referencing, but she doesn't particularly seem to be evil in this game. It sounds like she gets along well with the other gods. But that's only if this picture book is the final volume in the series!

The official story of this world is that Creall and Stellura's powers are what allowed us outsiders to come to this world in the first place, so I'm sure we'll be all right.

Anyway, it's time for bed. I return the books to their shelves and decide to check with the librarian.

"Do the illustrated books of legend end at Volume Four?"

"Correct. Even the churches won't have anything more than that."

"Oh, is that right?"

"You'll only find the original books that were copied to make the language less difficult, but the actual content isn't any different. You wouldn't want them to not line up now, would you?"

"Yes...I guess that's true. I wonder if the gods still get along to this day."

"Who can say? At the very least, I doubt they're fighting right now. I'm sure we'd see the effects of that here if they were."

"Nothing's happening, which must mean they're at peace."

"That's the idea."

Now that someone else has verified that conclusion, it's time for me to take my leave.

I stretch at the inn, log out, stretch in real life, and head to bed.

[What are you up to] Cumulative thread 45 [today?]

1. Resting Adventurer

This is a thread for general posts.

Feel free to write whatever you want.

Just remember that admins will step in if you don't

follow the most basic rules.

Seriously. They could end up deleting the whole thread,

so don't be naughty.

Past threads: http://＊＊＊＊＊＊＊＊＊＊

>> 980 Take care of the next thread.

528. Resting Adventurer

Hey, what's up with the paths being cleared whenever

Princess is around?

529. Resting Adventurer

Yeah, I was wondering about that too. I don't get it.

530. Resting Adventurer

I don't get it either, but it looks like it's the second-wavers doing it for some reason?

531. Resting Adventurer

I like it. It's easier to get around when you just creep behind the princess.

532. Resting Adventurer

Are you a stalker?

533. Resting Adventurer

Hell no! What stalker would be strolling along directly behind their victim in broad daylight?!

534. Resting Adventurer

I get it. It's nice to cruise along those open paths. I just don't get why it's happening.

535. Resting Adventurer

Well, Princess is famous, you know? That's probably why, right?

536. Resting Adventurer

She's gorgeous, and she's wearing that dress too.

537. Resting Adventurer

Maybe everyone's too scared to ask for a handshake? Like she's way out of their league?

538. Resting Adventurer

But the princess is so friendly.

539. Resting Adventurer

She's not all about frills either. Remember how she would chop meat with her rapier?

540. Primura

She says that rapier is nice and sharp, actually.

541. Salute

Princess is rougher around the edges when she's cooking just because of how good she is at it. All of her movements are at optimal efficiency. Does that make sense? You can't multitask like that unless you've cooked a lot...

542. Resting Adventurer

Multitasking during cooking is way harder the more recipes you know!

543. Resting Adventurer

Now that I think of it, I remember how she was baking bread from scratch while also cooking soup and sausages during the tournament.

544. Salute

I think her brain is good at processing that sort of thing, but who knows? Hmph, my break is over.

545. Primura

I'm on summer break!

546. Salute

Damn youuu!

547. Resting Adventurer

Good luck with your homework!

548. Primura

I did it this morning! I tested out the in-game homework!

549. Resting Adventurer

Oh, how was that new feature?

550. Primura

You select your homework files, and they appear in the game with a pen! I'll bet it's like how people feel when they go to a café to work or study!

551. Resting Adventurer

Ah, I see. If there's anything in there you don't understand, go ask one of the grown-ups around you.

552. Resting Adventurer

I feel like I wouldn't be able to help even if she asked me.

553. Resting Adventurer

Same.

554. Resting Adventurer

What would Primura be working on right now?

555. Resting Adventurer

I don't remember anything about schoolwork anymore.

556. Primura

Simultaneous equations! Linear functions! Chemical reaction equations!

557. Resting Adventurer

Oh yeah, I remember those! Is that with the periodic table of elements? You've gotta find a way to memorize that!

558. Resting Adventurer

"Happy Henry Likes Beer but Could Not Obtain Food,"
right? How does he survive on just beer?

559. Resting Adventurer

That's so nostalgic! And who says he survives?

560. Resting Adventurer

Nooo!

561. Resting Adventurer

Such is the harsh reality of life.

562. Resting Adventurer

No mercy.

563. Resting Adventurer

But with that mnemonic, you still have to memorize the
first nine elements on the table in general, since it only
tells you the order.

564. Resting Adventurer

I guess they assume that much is easy for students.

565. Resting Adventurer

Henry can never obtain food or else you'll lose nitrogen
from the list.

566. Resting Adventurer

Exactly.

567. Resting Adventurer

Aside from students working hard on their homework,
what's the guild situation looking like?

568. Resting Adventurer

The famous players who made guilds are Cecil, Kotatsu, Lucebarm, and Musasabi.

569. Resting Adventurer

They've already formed guilds?

570. Resting Adventurer

Cecil: The Knights of Dawn

Kotatsu: The Critter Empire

Lucebarm: Furry Legion

Musasabi: NINJA

That's the list.

571. Resting Adventurer

NINJA made me lol, but there's no way to describe those guys other than NINJAs. Lowercase just doesn't do it.

572. Resting Adventurer

Hi-yaaah!

573. Resting Adventurer

Kuh-chaw!

574. Resting Adventurer

Aren't Kotatsu and Lucebarm going for the same thing there?

575. Resting Adventurer

No, there's a difference.

576. Resting Adventurer

Are you a second-waver or something? They're nothing alike.

577. Resting Adventurer

If you just like cute critters, like dogs and cats and little animals, then you go to Kotatsu's Critter Empire. Thinking cat ears are cute is low on the scale of furry-ness.

578. Resting Adventurer

If you REALLY like animals—if you're a furry, basically— then you go to Lucebarm's Furry Legion. That's where you go if you want your entire face to be a cat face, not just your ears.

579. Resting Adventurer

I see... You have to know exactly what gets someone going or else you'll start a war with them.

580. Resting Adventurer

Exactly!

581. Resting Adventurer

If you want to join either one, you go and interview with them and check them out. You can go to one of the two guilds that way.

582. Resting Adventurer

Good for them, differentiating like that!

583. Resting Adventurer

As for NINJA...I don't think I need any more details about that one. What about the knight guild?

584. Resting Adventurer

With a top player as the guildmaster, it's super strict.

But not about player skill or equipment, just for your character as a person.

585. Resting Adventurer

Well sure, it's an online game. Of course they care about that.

586. Resting Adventurer

You want everyone to have a good time, after all. But supposedly they'll even let second-wavers in as long as they clear that one requirement.

587. Resting Adventurer

The only other thing is that they're looking for people who want to conquer new areas. They'll probably be really into events and stuff, right?

588. Resting Adventurer

Exactly. To put it simply, they only want good people who are highly motivated to play. Top players (lol) and conquerors (lol) won't make it in on that alone. But real life takes priority, so don't worry about that part. They're not a guild who will kick you out for being busy IRL.

589. Resting Adventurer

In other words, we should be prepared to represent a super famous guild if we want to join...

590. Resting Adventurer

That's probably true.

591. Resting Adventurer

What's old man Ertz going to do for a guild? Make one for production or something?

592. Resting Adventurer

Who knows? I think I remember there being something about forming partnerships between guilds, so I'm sure he'll end up making one.

593. Resting Adventurer

What do partnerships do?

594. Resting Adventurer

I don't know any details!

595. Cecil

Guild partnerships seem to be a way of combining guild quests and arranging orders.

For example, if Ertz's guild partnered with mine, we would be able to put in orders to his whole guild.

Here's an outline...

1. Make a list of items you want them to craft, along with a proposed cost and deadline.

2. Their guild sends back an adjusted cost and deadline.

3. You go back and forth a few times until the details are settled, then it becomes a contract.

4. Once you select the materials, they're purchased with the other guild's budget, then sent over to them.

5. The other guild selects the items they've crafted, you send the money, and the deal is complete.

That's what I've got from it so far. I think it's going to be a great feature.

596. Resting Adventurer

Oh look, it's Cecil. This stuff looks pretty helpful.

597. Cecil

I'll bet it becomes a valuable system.

Although, as you'd expect with management, they did write "Transportation time depends on distance between guilds."

They also give you options to shorten transportation time as part of expansions you can add to your guild house.

598. Resting Adventurer

Uh...uh-huh... Ah! (I see.)

599. Cecil

Partnered guilds, especially production guilds, are probably going to run into trouble if they're too far apart.

8

Friday

Alchemy...basic recipes...magic stones...hmm, I see. Magic clay, is it? This is clearly an interim material, but what could it be used for? I think I'll head to Ms. Meghan's store, since I want to ask her about Attribute Control from Alchemy.

I leave the inn and make my way to the general store.

"Good afternoon."

"Oh, look who's back. Are you here for shopping? Or Alchemy?"

"Alchemy today."

"I see. Ask away, then."

I start by telling her that my Alchemy skill reached level 10. This was the result of making lots of arrows from banty feathers.

"So you learned Golem Training, did you?"

"I just haven't tested it yet, since I have my necromancy skill."

"It's better to feed magic stones to your necromancy servants instead of a golem."

She explains that if I was only using golems, it would be all right, but since I summon servants, I should prioritize giving them stones. The tricky part of necromancy servants is the capacity—in other words, flesh and bones. If that isn't a problem for you, you choose necromancy. If it *is* a problem, then golems are the way to go.

Ms. Meghan also explains that researchers, who struggle to secure flesh and bones, usually work with golems, since they only require stones.

"So what's on your mind?"

"I would like to know about Attribute Control and magic clay. I've been giving my servants any magic stone I find, so it's hard to use them for any experiments."

"Hmm, I see. Attribute Control is usually used once you get your hands on an elemental stone. I don't think you'll find anyone with them around here... Oh, how did finding an entrance to the Nether go?"

"Ms. Luciana told me what she knew. Thank you for telling me about her."

"Did she say it's to the northeast?"

"Yes. I took a look at the area, but there're a lot of undead, so I don't think I can reach the entrance yet."

"They must be mid-tier undead, right?"

"Yes, around level 30."

"That means you're getting dark stones?"

Stones that come from enemies of a certain attribute share that element. Attribute Control is what allows you to transfer that element to another item. However, physical items come with different levels of magia reception. It comes down to how well magia can pass through and be stored in the item, and if it isn't suitable for such a force, it will break on contact, unable to contain the energy.

"As for magic clay, you can use it with Golem Training, Doll Creation or Handicraft."

"It makes sense for dolls and golems, but why Handicraft?"

"It's clay, so you make dishes with it. I'd bet only royalty or nobles use it, though, since it costs so much."

"I see. So dishes fall under Handicraft."

"Now that I think of it, you have Cooking, right?"

"I do."

"And you use Tableware on dishes with magical effects?"

"That's right."

"Hmm...if you're able to, you should try using magic clay to craft some crockery."

Items with magical effects are generally stored in other magical items. This prevents them from degrading, and depending on the item, it might even boost their magical effects.

Messing with them further can also end up requiring the use of a special environment, she explains.

"To make something with magic, you need magical materials, a magical environment, and an experienced crafter. If you want to guarantee good results, you'll need all three of those."

"A magical environment...?"

"They're for the most experienced crafters, so they cost a pretty penny."

"You mean an advanced production kit?"

"That or an environment. The environment will make you more efficient, of course."

A kit or an environment. "Environment" must refer to housing. After all, our production kits are portable.

"There's more than one kind of magic clay too. Be sure to adjust the dirt based on whatever you're using it for. A golem needs durability, while a doll needs more magia optimization. Crockery needs beauty. You can look for these things yourselves."

"Dolls need magia optimization?"

"Doll Magic originates from the golems, allowing you to see from the point of view of objects you move with magic strings. Dolls are generally made from wood. I'm sure you understand why. It's because wood is used as a magical catalyst."

Wood is durable and remains stable when in contact with magia. It also grows everywhere, so it's relatively cheap. Pretty much all you need to do to wood is whittle it down to make it usable. Magic clay is easy to process, but it requires other things like magic stones and slime gel, which makes it cost more.

The Log skill helps with wood, but to make magic clay, you need to obtain dirt via Gather and craft the clay itself with Alchemy. It's not very forgiving on your SP.

Well, this is still an MMO, so I may as well just buy it instead... but can I even find someone who sells magic clay?

Alchemy isn't exactly a popular skill right now. The biggest reason for that would be that you can only reach a maximum quality of C when crafting things with it. Is there really no way to get around that?

"That reminds me. Is it possible to alchemize things that are higher than C quality?"

"Hmm...wait right there a moment."

She heads to the back and returns with a book in hand.

"Read this...then this, then this."

I look at the pages she shows me and see the words "Alchemy circle expansion cores: 1–3."

"You can process magic stones as cores and surround them in the alchemy circle to strengthen it. This will let you make higher-quality items. But this is secret information I'm passing on to you as my student. Don't go telling anyone else about this."

"So if someone wants to know about it, I should tell them to take on a teacher."

"An alchemist can do nothing without becoming a student. How else will they craft the fruits of their labor?"

The student receives the secret knowledge from the teacher, casts an alchemy circle, and strengthens it by enclosing magic stones that have undergone special processing. This should remove the quality limit of C on my items. Three cores should make B, A, and S quality available.

But the main problem is that I don't have enough magic stones on hand for this process. The strengthening requires medium, large, and enormous stones. Not that I've ever even seen an enormous magic stone before.

"I've been absorbing all enemies lately, so I don't have any stones. Is there any chance that orbs will do the trick?"

"...Orbs?"

"These."

"Where...where did you get these?"

"My ring creates them from excess magia."

"I knew the equipment you have on seemed unique. Anyway, you should keep quiet about this. Also...you haven't had the gods try to start anything with you, right?"

"Why do you ask?"

"Where did you get that equipment?"

"In the catacombs to the northeast."

"Northeast...inheritance from the past. An undead with a black-and-white inheritance... I see. Very well."

She takes my orbs and heads to the back. It sounds like they won't work as a replacement for enormous stones.

Still, is there some sort of meaning to my clothes beyond being equipment? The color, maybe? I remember that quite a while ago, I heard about the best colors we're supposed to wear. Ms. Meghan mentioned black and white along with the gods, which must be something that has to do with the church. Since Ms. Meghan suggested I keep quiet about this, the only person I can ask is Ms. Luciana.

I don't see the need to ask her about my equipment, but what about the colors I'm wearing? We outsiders don't have such customs.

Ms. Meghan returns while I'm still pondering these questions. "Here, take these."

[TOOL] ALCHEMY EXPANSION CORE 1

A physical ball representing the secret knowledge passed down from master to pupil.

Activate by placing inside an alchemy circle to increase item quality limit by 1 rank.

[TOOL] ALCHEMY EXPANSION CORE 2

A physical ball representing the secret knowledge passed down from master to pupil.

Activate by placing inside an alchemy circle to increase item quality limit by 1 rank.

You have fulfilled special requirements, unlocking an extra art for Alchemy: Alchemy Expansion Ex1.

You have fulfilled special requirements, unlocking an extra art for Alchemy: Alchemy Expansion Ex2.

Alchemy expansion cores aren't something you can give away, even as a teacher's student, as the mention of "secret information" implies. Any normal student would head to their teacher for such an item in the first place. That's where their personality and skills can be evaluated. But that's not enough on its own either. Of course, a pupil is going to be on their best behavior in front of a teacher. Anyone would understand this much. The teacher has to ask the townspeople about their student's reputation as well, bringing the game mechanic of affinity into the mix.

This is where wrongdoers will get a glimpse of hell. The method and speed at which a resident comes to be fond of you is different for everyone, and boosting your reputation with one person does nothing for how the entire town sees you. This is a pretty difficult mechanic. That one person can influence others to some extent, but that depends on their personality too. The best strategy is probably to get the old ladies who run the street stalls on your side. I'm sure there are other ways to do it that don't involve Alchemy.

"Come bring me an enormous-sized magic stone once you've got one. That will let you craft S-quality items. Of course, that's only if you do the process right."

"The quality of an Alchemy product depends on the quality of the materials, right?"

"That's generally how it goes. The other vital element is Magia Control. The rest is up to you."

"...Magia Control?"

"Alchemy allows you to produce things by manipulating magia. What do you expect to happen if you go and waste that magia?"

"I see. That makes sense. I'll pay attention to that from here on out."

"Having an environment is important too. Those portable kinds can only do so much."

"You mean I need a home of my own?"

"If you want to get serious, securing an environment is the first step. The results you see will be totally different if you manage to do that."

From the perspective of the residents, those who take up production must be in it to make a living, so they need a good place to do it: an environment of their very own. Their success in production is highly dependent on it. Be it for Alchemy or Blacksmithing, an environment is just another one of your tools for production, making it absolutely essential to the process. Securing one for yourself is probably a huge factor in how your future plays out from then on. Ms. Meghan tells me that environments are very expensive, meaning most students generally borrow their teacher's.

But in the end, this is all from the perspective of those residents who need to make a living. It makes sense when you think about it, and I can tell the developers included this to feel more realistic.

My teacher is Ms. Meghan. I assume she's quite the veteran in the art of Alchemy, judging by her age, so she can probably craft S-quality items, right? Although the ones she sells in her shop are usually around C.

"Ah, that's right. You're immortal, so any potion you make won't work on you."

"That's correct."

"You can sell C-quality potions at my grandson's shop—the one I pointed out to you before—but for anything else, bring them to the adventurers' union."

"Oh, they buy those at the union?"

"They sell any consumable for adventurer, as long as the item's C+ quality at the very least. That's why they'll buy them from certain people too."

Isn't Appraisal supposed to be a rare skill to the residents? They must not purchase items unless they're from trusted crafters. I've also just learned that Ms. Meghan's grandson was the one running that pharmacy next to the union.

C-quality items can be described as average quality, which means shops will take them if you're able to make them. Apparently, crafting B quality is all it takes for people to regard you as quite the skilled producer. We outsiders can mass-produce B quality, but that must be like a special buff for the main characters you often see in single-player RPGs. There still haven't been any reports of A quality yet.

But anyway, C+ quality alone, not to mention B-level items, go for quite a lot more money. Of course, the prices go up with each increase in quality, but it's hard to get your hands on anything higher than C+ in the first place. Apparently, that's why the adventurers' union sells high-quality goods as a means of supporting its members. The "C rank or higher" limit on which members can buy from them is probably because the items are so pricey, lower-ranking union members probably won't be able to buy much at all.

Ms. Salute sells the items at her stand for quite a nice price too. It's definitely not possible to stock up on those. Maybe that's because the residents have things like rent and food expenses to pay that the game mostly leaves out?

The best way to save up money is consignment, but selling to the union can help raise affinity. Affinity doesn't seem like something to treat lightly, so I'll make my money from cooking, along with selling any potions I make to the union.

Oh, I should ask about clothing colors while I'm at it.

"Does the color of clothing have meaning here?"

"Sure, to some degree. But you're not banned from wearing any color in particular."

She explains that this is usually a matter that the clergy are concerned with. In other words, the colors of the gods are red and green, blue and yellow, and white and black. They use gold for accents, but everyone generally avoids bright colors. This way, you can immediately tell which god the clergyman is devoted to just by the color of his robes.

"Black-and-white robes with gold embroidery are the colors of the supreme deity and his second-in-command. Not even clergymen wear those colors. The more peculiar colors would be iridescent ones."

Ms. Meghan says that you have to be pretty brave to wear the colors of the supreme deity and their second-in-command. It's not a forbidden act, so you won't be punished for it—you'll just experience the painful stares of everyone around you, judging whether or not you're a suitable person to wear those colors.

It must be because they really feel the presence of the gods.

"You're undead, meaning you follow Stellura. It's not a strange sight to see you wearing black-and-white clothes. But things aren't easy for the undead if Stellura decides to abandon them, so be sure you're living righteously."

I pause to think. "Because she holds the faces of contracts and judgment?"

"Exactly. I'm sure you lie, so lie for the sake of others, not yourself. She'll let it slide in those cases."

"I see. I'm just realizing that I probably shouldn't say things like 'I swear to God' without being careful, huh?"

"It would be best if you didn't. You definitely don't want to say 'I swear to Stellura;' that's the gravest of them all. If she takes that as a contract and you end up breaking it, monsters will come and get you."

"Don't tell me... The outer ones?"

"Indeed. Do you have influence with outsiders? If so, be sure to tell them about this."

In real-life terms, I would be coming face-to-face with hell, wouldn't I? Ms. Meghan says the church teaches about this too, but how many people really go out of their way to attend church? It would probably be more amusing to keep this information from my fellow players, but I'll go ahead and clue them in. It feels safer to be accurate about what I say...but it's also not my fault if some people choose to test out the effects of a broken promise to see what happens.

"Don't get in the way of the executors. They'll kill you without a second thought."

"Very well. If I help anyone, it should be the executors, right?"

"Doesn't matter if you do. They'll still erase you. Not even outsiders can get away with slighting them."

We outsiders came to this world thanks to Creall, the supreme deity, and Stellura, the second-in-command, right? While the executors are under Stellura's jurisdiction... Yeah, I see why that wouldn't work.

I've been here for quite a while now, so I should probably head out. As soon as that thought crosses my mind, though, the door swings open and a man rushes into the shop.

"Granny!"

"What is it? You're so loud."

"I've got the materials, but I can't craft them all in time! Help me out!"

Ah, it's the grandson from the shop next to the union. I saw him while I was delivering my potions.

"...Fine, then. If you have the time, help us out and I'll watch over you."

"I'm curious about Magia Control and that sort of thing, so I'd like to watch," I say.

"Oh, you're the one who brought all those potions, right?"

"That's me. I can't use them, personally."

"She just became my student not too long ago. C'mon, let's get going."

"Huh?! You never told me you got a student!"

"Sure I did, just now."

"You're kidding..."

Despite his confusion, the grandson carried in the materials from the front, left us a list, and returned to his own shop.

"We'll be crafting C-quality items, since these are going up for sale, but this won't be a waste of time."

"I'm ready to try crafting. I'll focus on the magia I'm using too."

"Every item has an optimal amount. It's something you just have to memorize."

Ms. Meghan watches on as I create the beginner's HP potions, HP potions, MP potions, anti-emetics, and other such potions from the list. It's my first time crafting restoration potions that treat status ailments. With boosts from Ms. Meghan's instructions and the environment I'm crafting in, they come out at C quality. It appears that herbs are used for treating status ailments. I start by extracting components from the herbs to later combine with distilled water.

"Focus your attention as you pour in magia. It's all about quantity, speed, and timing. You don't want the energy to escape the alchemy circle, so make sure you're controlling it and add a fixed amount to the item."

"This is where Magia Trace comes in handy."

I can see magia already anyway, so I focus my attention on its presence.

I release magia into the empty alchemy circle and observe it closely. Sending it in all at once causes it to leak out of the lines of the circle, while raising the speed sends it flying out of the curves. In other words, the alchemy circle itself is like a waterway for energy.

During compounding, I place the materials down and release magia, which gathers in the materials. With fixed amounts of energy, those materials start to dissolve in the magia, filling up the circle and gathering in the middle to form a completed product. It's a mysterious process, but I have no complaints in that regard. Alchemists are truly amazing.

Hmm...I understand how magia flows. Now I just need to observe how much magia is needed, or possibly even memorize it.

"You're High Undead, right? So isn't there no point in you having Magia Trace?"

"My race does already allow me to see magia, yes. I don't need to use the spell."

"Convenient, huh? Your precision is looking good. Keep going just like that."

I still have a lot to make. The materials provided are helping to level up Alchemy, which is a delicious reward in itself. It's sort of like how food tastes best when it's purchased on someone else's dime. Anyway, I'll remain silent as I craft on.

I don't want the quality to turn out too high, so I save the expansion cores for later and craft potion after potion. This is probably plenty good enough, since I'm practicing Magia Control. The act of crafting makes me feel like I'm learning everything I need.

> Superior Magic Assist has reached level 15.
> Superior Magic Assist art Dual Spell has grown stronger.

Oh? Dual Spell became Triple Spell, and now it looks like I can cast three at a time. I bet those numbers will keep going up for a while.

Let's see, the next potion to make is...huh? Cold medicine, stomach medicine, digestive support, and energy boosts? Wow, they even have hangover cures and medicine for pregnant women.

> **[RECOVERY] COLD MEDICINE**
> Rarity: NO   Quality: C
> Flavored medicine.
> Promotes the healing of infectious diseases.

...I see. It's flavored medicine. I guess it would be stranger for this *not* to exist, but it's not something that matters to players. In other words, it has nothing to do with gameplay. I like this sort of thing. I bet crafting these will help raise my affinity with the residents.

It looks like cold medicine is made from olives, turmeric, basil, and cinnamon. I see... So those are the kinds of things these potions consist of. I continue to craft while still asking for tips from my teacher.

> Appraisal has reached level 30. You earn 2 SP.

Oh, and now Appraisal is finally up there too. I used it a whole lot during this session, after all. Alchemy and Superior Magic Assist also went up three and two levels, respectively.

I like how this "environment" thing works. This must be the kind of production environment that's set up for housing. It makes magia easier to release and control when doing Alchemy. Ms. Meghan's environment is a pretty top-notch one too, by the looks of it.

"That went a lot faster with the two of us. Anyway, I can't leave the shop empty, so the potions are in your hands."

"Very well. I'll be taking my leave, then."

"Work hard out there."

I take the potions we diligently crafted, exit the shop, and head to the grandson's store next to the union.

I was ignoring it until now, but these potions are stored in a magic bag, aren't they? Maybe it's easier to call it an infinity bag, since it has extra space inside? Or an inventory bag, since it's just like how a player's inventory works.

But this bag isn't like the pouch I wear on my belt. To describe it in simple terms, it's a pouch-shaped inventory shortcut. It has a bit of extra space to it, but the inventory slots are the same.

Some people will probably find that feature convenient, while others will wish it linked to their inventory. In my current situation, I wouldn't be able to carry all these potions unless it was like this.

But that brings up a problem. If bags like these exist, I'm probably able to craft them. Space Magic and Needlework will clearly be necessities for such an item. As far as Alchemy goes, I'll most likely need those secret cores too. What else...? There's also Enchant Magic, so maybe an advanced spell from that line? I would love to have one of these, but I can tell crafting one is beyond my skill level at the moment. Just the secret cores alone have to be passed down from master to student.

I walk through town, observing the bag as I go, until I arrive at the pharmacy and head straight inside.

"Good day. I have a delivery of potions for you."

"That gray dress... You must be Granny Meghan's student? Go on through to the back of the store."

A woman I don't recognize is manning the store. Perhaps she's the grandson's wife? Regardless, I head to the back area.

"That was fast! Thanks for the help!"

"It was no trouble. I learned a lot."

"I'm so impressed that you became Granny's student. She's one of the top alchemists in this area, but she's been famous for never taking on students."

"Is that right? She's the one who brought it up to me and everything..."

"Really?! How strange... Yep, these all look great."

The woman was checking over the potions as we spoke. It sounds like there aren't any issues with them. Ms. Meghan and I checked them too, so it's not like I was worried in the first place.

"I bet these will sell out fast."

"You already sold the other potions I delivered?"

"I sure did. They were gone in an instant... Can other outsiders not make potions themselves?"

"It's a tedious process, so it's not very popular right now. I'm sure some of the new outsiders will take up potion crafting, but it might take some time before they're producing anything usable."

"It's a great time to make profits, but I wish it was just a little less hectic."

Good luck to you, I thought. *I know it'll be tough, but the second-wavers should be able to start making their own potions here soon.*

All right, I've dropped off the potions, and now seems like as good a time as any for lunch. I log out for the time being.

I take off the VR console and go to the living room. My sister rushes in while I'm starting to prepare lunch.

"Oh! Sis!"

"Hm?"

"Information about the second official event just came out!"

She tells me that the official site was updated a little earlier. I'll have to check this out for myself.

It looks like the second event, *"Good Ol' Summertime Camping,"* will take place on the fourth Saturday of August.

"Wow, camping?"

"It's gonna be survival camping!"

Let's see... *"What would you bring to a deserted island?"*

"I see. There're restrictions on the items you can take."

"Of course. That's what makes it survival!"

You can take one type of equipment in each category. This means you'll need to work together with other players to survive on the monster-ridden desert island. Player killing isn't banned, but it will probably just end up sealing your own fate in a situation like this.

"It says you can get knocked out one time, and if it happens again, you're sent back to the normal area."

"They're changing the time perception to make it last eight days. The EXP is gonna be delicious!"

Sleeping in the game is a requirement to reduce mental fatigue.

A lack of sleep will result in penalties like a reduction in stats. I'm sorry to say that even though those who play as races like the undead don't need any sleep and take no penalties, the person playing the game still needs sleep. Gamers need to remember to rest.

Our characters have to eat too, of course. The survival event means gathering your own ingredients for food, unless you're one of the races that doesn't need to eat.

"Well, I do have to sleep...so yeah."

"The lack of a need for sleep was always a way to add flavor to the game. The same goes for eating."

"Full-dive technology creates a need to consider how tired players might get."

The normal servers only speed up time inside the game, but there's no change to the physical time you experience. That would cause all sorts of problems. Just think of the physical fatigue the players would experience from gaming nonstop...or rather, their mental and emotional fatigue would be more affected. Their heads would certainly be aching.

You're able to log out during the event, but they suggest refraining from constant logouts. After the fourth time, you'll have to wait some time before logging in again, so that's when you should be ready. Finish up eating and using the bathroom beforehand.

"Do you think your mind gets confused if you're constantly logging in and out?"

"Brains are surprisingly dumb when it comes to this sort of thing. But you'll still be able to take phone calls and send emails through the VR console, so the only reasons to log out are to use the bathroom and to eat."

There's battling, production, gathering, and exploring. We can spend our time on the event island however we like. We can also take any items we acquire back with us.

We'll still be allowed to unlock skills during the event, but our individual scores will be lowered. That could be a big problem for gathering and production skills. The exact rules are a secret, but they suggest trying to figure it out for ourselves by reading the event synopsis.

Anyone participating in the event will have to sign up in advance. The option opens tomorrow at midnight. We're told to be sure to register before we forget. Our equipment and items on hand will be recorded as soon as we register.

The boat to the event area leaves ten minutes before the event begins. Once it starts, the boat will drift to the coast of a deserted island, but if you form a party first, you will all end up at the same place.

The notes also say there are no safe zones on the island. Management really just slips these things in there, don't they?

So we can only bring in one variety of each item from the outside? I'm really going to have to give this some thought.

"What are you gonna bring with you, Sis?"

"Hmm...definitely my cooking and alchemy kits," I respond. "I don't know about Gathering tools, since you have to choose one. I wouldn't need any of it if I was going on my own, though."

"Right, your race means you don't need food or potions. The undead are so overpowered in this event!"

"But I still need to sleep."

"I guess..."

"Maybe we'll need rope and stuff?"

"For knives, we'll already have our swords, and we can make water and fire with spells. Hmm...maybe potions are more important than I thought."

"I think a pickaxe would be best."

"For ores? Hmm, but...ah! Materials to repair equipment! But in that case..."

I don't need equipment repairs, food, or potions. What I'll need if I end up in a party with Mr. Alf and Mr. Skelly is a pickaxe. The problem is Mr. Alf has to bring his large shield, leaving him not many other options.

But as far as points go, it's definitely best to have my cooking and alchemy kits with me, right? I can't imagine many players will have those. The biggest obstacle of all is probably going to be the number of gatherers compared to the number of crafters.

"Alchemy seems like a good option for a deserted island. But since the monsters will probably drop meat, maybe I can smoke them... No, I doubt I'll have enough salt or sugar."

"Personally, I want to bring potions."

As for wheat, barley, and radishes, it sounds like we'll be able to find those if we search the island. We're also allowed to farm, and the harvesting speed for crops is increased. They even say the island will have fruit trees.

This is quite the pickle.

"I've got to go with the alchemy kit. As long as one other person has a cooking kit, I can help out, but alchemy kits can only be used by their owners..."

"Ah...that's true. I think I'll go with a pickaxe."

I should probably read my Alchemy recipes again before the event starts. I'll also pick up any items I'll need on the island.

Since I have the website up anyway, I may as well post on the BBS while I'm here. I share a warning that *they* will appear if you don't behave how you're supposed to...and also that even though they're free to test it out, I'm not responsible for whatever happens to them.

"Is this for real, Sis?"

"I'm not going to try it, so I don't know for sure, but I don't see why she would lie to me."

"Someone will just have to put their life on the line."

"I doubt that will go well for them. But sooner or later, I'm sure someone will go for it," I predict.

"Please don't die, research team! If we lose you..."

"Next week: The research team perishes."

"I bet we'll be hearing about it any minute now."

"By the way, Stellura is the goddess of reincarnation."

"Oh, is that right? Wow, that sounds scary... Ah, there it is." My sister points out a message. "'Tragic news: The outer ones are scary. You'll die. I died. Forgive me; I'll never do it again. It's a trauma-inducing machine.' They're so damn reckless..."

"They knock you out in one hit, then come back for more while you're waiting to respawn...?"

"I thought you were supposed to be invulnerable at that point... Whoa, he got his body torn up too? His sanity must be at an all-time low."

"Then he respawned with all his money gone and his skill levels lowered..."

"There are skill level penalties?!"

It sounds like they have their own special death penalties as well. This is a lot worse than I expected.

...The outer one was a big gray toad with tentacles coming out of its head?

"Hmm...? Wait, it's a Moon-beast! The super sadistic frog torturer!"

"Maybe he was lucky that he escaped with only a torn-up body," I respond.

"Oh, another brave hero died. What was it this time...? 'A bluish dog-like haze getting bigger and smaller attacked me with some sort of ball thing.' Does this person speak Japanese?"

"Hmm... An evil, bluish, hazy dog that transforms?"

"Ah! The pup trinity!"

"Right! The Hounds of Tindalos!"

"It coils around you to administer ptomaine poisoning...at 4% HP a second?!"

261

"It licked his body to deal damage? This poor man..."

"It kept licking him once his HP was gone. He couldn't even fight, and it didn't stop until his body was gone..."

"How weird is this game? 'The person being attacked gets it the worst, but anyone who witnesses the attack is also in for a bad time.'"

"Stellura is based off of Yog-Sothoth, right? But they've got Tindalos too. Shouldn't they be enemies?"

"The 'Tindalos' story comes from a different world, so it seems like things are different here."

"We can probably just think of the outer ones as Lovecraftian stuff. The one who grants them a home must be Stellura, since she's Yog-Sothoth."

Judging by her roles, she doesn't appear to be evil. I don't want to know if she is indiscriminately violent or not, but right now it appears like she only hunted down the people who broke their contracts. Well, I'll just choose not to think about what the witnesses went through.

People seem to agree that Stellura is Yog-Sothoth, but the other gods don't have any obvious correspondences. Fertility in Lovecraftian stories would be Shub-Niggurath, but I haven't heard any information about that sort of thing. Who knows about the other two pillars?

Anyway, I now know that Moon-beasts and Tindalos hounds exist in the game, although it's still unclear if players can become them or not. Couldn't they be evolutions of frogs or dogs? Well, the Hounds of Tindalos only look like dogs to people, but I think their true form is undefined. Oh well. It doesn't matter. Time for me to jump back into the game. I finish my lunch, rest for a bit, and then log back in.

I want to change up my equipment before the second event... but we can only bring in one of each piece, right? In other words, crafting beforehand won't do me any good. I'll go hunting for Alchemy recipes instead.

What recipes would be useful in a survival situation...? Probably stuff like bottles, potions, arrows, and shovels. Actually, I remember how to make a shovel. You combine wood with stone or ingots. I can also craft a pot or a pickaxe. Ignoring the higher-cost recipes, this Alchemy thing really comes in handy.

All right, now what else should I do? I suppose it's either exploring or leveling up. No more crafting for today, since I already spent my morning on it. For now, I'll go on a walk around town.

"Oh, hi there, Princess. Here for some shopping? Or just out on a stroll?"

"Good day. I'm just getting a walk in. But I do need a refill on some supplies."

"Coming right up!"

Here at the older woman's vegetable stall, I replace the onions and garlic that I used in cooking. By the way, she's probably somewhere around fifty years old.

"Incidentally, I heard something about the outer ones showing up. Did you make it out okay?"

"That was just a couple of outsiders being silly, so please don't worry about it."

"Is that right? Just be careful. You don't want to get wrapped up in that kind of thing."

"You can get wrapped up in it?"

"It depends. You'll usually be fine, but it depends on what exact promise was broken. There once was a nation that insulted Stellura, and it ended up being destroyed entirely in a single night by monsters led by three women."

"Three women...?"

"One was an elderly woman, one was middle-aged, and one was a young girl."

I remember something about that. Hmm...what was it again? Let's see...

"Oh, that's right. The church called them 'Our Ladies of Sorrow.'"

Right, the three mothers. If they're here too, of course the country would end up ruined.

The three mothers were Mater Lachrymarum, Mater Suspiriorum, and Mater Tenebrarum. Though they resembled normal humans, considering the other legends of Lovecraftian lore that are in this game, they must be incredibly strong. They just respawn unless you kill all three simultaneously, and when they're together, they combine all their stats to share a total sum. Not only can they each control animals, but they'll inflict you with status ailments that affect your hearing, speech, and vision. I'm sure they can also summon all holy races and command them.

I don't know how accurately they've been recreated in this world, but if they showed up now, I doubt any player would make it out alive.

The Medium sure is chaotic. There must be fans of the series working for Future Software, but they probably couldn't let such entities dominate the game. That must be why they made the Medium to fit with the rest of this world. I imagine it's a pretty big place too.

These monsters aren't here to destroy the world, since they act as messengers of the gods. That said, they aren't allies either. They just don't generally meddle in our affairs. The one exception, of course, is when they come to deliver judgment for breaking a contract.

I wish I could learn a little more about the story surrounding Stellura. I don't know about the Medium, of course, but I'll probably end up dealing with the Nether and Abyss myself in the future.

There are probably maps associated with other legends too, but I haven't come across any information on that subject yet.

I suppose I'll wander around a little more. Chatting with the residents is a great way to learn new things.

"Oh, out for a stroll, Princess?"

"Yes, I am. Good day."

"The weather today's looking perfect for a nice walk!"

All the residents really like talking to me.

"Ah, hey, Miss!" a group of four children called out in unison.

"Good afternoon. Are you heading out to play?"

"Yeah!"

"I see. Be safe out there."

"You got it!"

They sure are lively. A little too energetic, perhaps. The AI is impressive in ways like that.

Just then, I notice an old woman pressing a hand against her lower back and wincing in pain.

"Is something the matter, Granny?"

"I was trying to get to church, but I think I threw my back out."

"Oh dear... Can I use a healing spell on you?"

"That will only make the pain go away temporarily."

"I see. I don't have Holy Magic myself..."

"Not many do. Don't you worry about a thing like that."

My Strength stat is very low, so I probably can't carry her on my back. Hm...I'll try something else instead.

"I have an idea about how to carry you. Please wait just one moment."

"Oh, is that right?"

I'll summon Unit One as a skeleton ogre with the custom role of fighter, add up the stats...oh, he costs 2,400 to summon? I have 3,100 capacity at the moment, so that works fine. I'll give him Sturdy, Balance Control, Strength Boost, and Footwork. Since we're going to a church, purification resistance is a must-have too.

"All right. Come to me, skeleton ogre fighter."

"O-oh? So you're a necromancer? You don't see that every day."

"Do you know how to give a piggyback ride, Unit One?"

CLACK

"Hmm...maybe I should give it a try for myself first."

I make Unit One turn his back to me and crouch down. I climb on and tell him to stand. Unit One is a skeleton, so there're plenty of parts to grab hold of. That was an unexpected benefit of this whole plan. He wobbles a little, but it's an acceptable amount. Balance Control and Footwork are really getting the job done.

But I can tell that this isn't the sort of thing to walk around freely with. What idiot chose an ogre for a job like this? He's over two meters tall. It's more like standing on his back than being carried.

I decide to keep the same skills and summon him again as a metal skeleton fighter at a 3× multiplier. This comes out to a total cost of 2,400, just like the ogre. That size difference is a major factor.

I hop on his back again and can tell that a metal skeleton is the way to go. Now it's time for the real trial. I jump off, make him lift the old woman up onto his back, and begin to walk.

"Oh, I like the feel of this," the old woman says. "Are you sure I can take him to a church?"

"I made him resistant to purification, so it should be all right."

"Wow, you're clever. I heard purification resistance is a hard skill to give."

Well, all I did was copy my own skill for Unit One. It's a lesser-known trick of the trade.

While the sight of an old granny on the back of a metal skeleton is a little alarming, what other choice did I have? I doubt I could carry her myself. Unit One is certainly stronger than me.

Unit One pulls her legs around his pelvis, and she reaches forward to hold onto his ribs. All I have to do is follow them from behind, right? I'm sure he won't drop her or anything.

"Wait there a moment, Unit One."

CLACK

I summon a skeleton rabbit with the same skills as Unit One and send him toward the church first. He reaches the entrance and hops up onto two legs.

"It looks safe to me. Let's head inside."

As we approach the church, one of its workers rushes outside.

"Undead?!" he shouts.

Oh no! Run away, Unit Two!

"Hey! Get back here!"

Unit Two hides behind my legs.

"Oh? What's this?"

"I'm sorry. He's with me."

"I see. You're a necromancer, then? That's a huge relief."

"I've brought a woman with an injured back. Where should I bring her?"

"Is that right? Come this way, please."

With that, Unit One and I are led to a spot away from the chapel. It looks to be a medical treatment room or something of the sort. Unit One sets her down, completing our journey.

"You really did me a favor."

"I'm happy to help. Please take care now."

Now where should I go next...? Oh look, it's Ms. Luciana.

"My, my. If it isn't Ms. Anastasia!"

"Good day, Ms. Luciana."

"Hello there. How are things going with finding the Nether entrance?"

"It's still going to take some more time. The undead in that area are incredibly strong."

"It would be much easier if you had Holy Magic...but it's not very convenient for an immortal to use herself. Please don't overdo it out there."

"I'm going to train a bit more before trying again."

Now that I think of it, which god is Ms. Luciana devoted to? Her robes are dark in color, but a closer look tells me they're actually navy blue with gold embroidery.

"Is something wrong?"

"Ms. Meghan just taught me about clothing colors."

"Ah, I see. My robes don't represent anyone in particular. I suppose I would say they're for all the gods, if I had to. People like me generally dress in navy and white."

All of the robes worn by the clergy are of the same design. Only the colors appear to be altered, while the stitching color represents their rank.

She explains that the order goes red, green, gray, and then to gold. These are the colors of the gods' hair, as well as the order they were born in. The red color of Sigrdrífa represents a newcomer, while Creall's gold color signifies a master.

"I see. So if you're devoted to a god, you show it with the color of your cloth."

"Exactly. It's a way of sobering the devotee."

"Since you have gold thread, you must be a master, right?"

"Hee hee hee! Well, I *am* an old woman. I'm a veteran of the church at this point."

She's very smiley and pleasant, but the faces of the red-threaded people around us appear to be twitching. Even the gray threads are putting on strained smiles.

"Your clothes have a slightly different design, Ms. Luciana."

"Oh, so you caught that, did you? Clergy don't openly reveal their personal ranks, as they're all servants of the gods. But that doesn't mean there aren't certain times where we need people to know who we are. The thread color is one way of showing that, but if you look even closer, the designs aren't exactly the same either."

I imagine these clothes are all made by hand with unique designs, meaning they must be for the elites of the church. More fashion-conscious people will probably spot these differences in design.

"As archbishop, I run things in this whole area."

"You mean not just at this church but the entire area? I see. You're even higher up than I expected."

"People usually act differently around me once I tell them. I find it better to keep that fact quiet and blend in with the others."

"Then allow me to reveal something as well. I said that I was undead, but my race is actually that of the Immortal Princess."

"Hang on just a moment. That would mean... But why are you here? Ah, that's right, you're an outsider... Stellura? Is that really an acceptable god for an outsider?"

Oh, I've really confused Ms. Luciana. The others in the room look pale too. *I promise not to eat you! I may be a meat-eater, but I'm no cannibal...*

"Excuse me. You're Ms. Anastasia, right?" one of the onlookers asked.

"Yes."

"You mentioned how you were searching for an entrance to the Nether. Are you here because you're an outsider?"

"That's correct."

"You hear that?" Ms. Luciana calls out. "Calm down, everyone. I forbid you from disclosing this information. Understood?"

Everyone is nodding their heads violently.

This is a much more dramatic turn of events than I expected. I'd like to learn a little more about the situation. Maybe my prediction about my home being the Evernight Castle in the Nether was correct after all? If that's the case, I understand why people are confused about my presence here.

"Hmm...does Meghan know about this?"

"I've only told her that I'm High Undead."

"I see... Let's relocate, shall we?"

We head from the garden to a nice room inside the church.

"All right, first of all... How much do you know about immortals and the outer ones?"

"I've only read the book *Stellura and the Darklight Races*," I reply.

"Is that right? So you know that the Nether and the Abyss are the realms of immortals, while the Medium is home to the outer ones?"

"I do."

"Those beings hardly ever leave their realms, aside from a few exceptions. The outer ones arrive when someone breaks a contract with Stellura. Immortals come when there are...let's say 'problems regarding souls.'"

"Does that mean, since I'm out here, that something has gone wrong?"

"That's right. The other issue is your race being 'princess.' Do you know about the ruling class?"

"Like the outer one?"

"They belong to a different category. The ruling class refers to any individual with command skills, even among monsters."

That would apply to the general I saw during the world quest, but I don't think I've seen anyone else like that.

"The existence of the ruling class is a threat to us, and royalty sit at their very top. These are individuals referred to as kings, queens, princes, and princesses. As you would imagine, their command abilities are on a much different level. One kind you see comparatively often are goblin kings."

Goblins are so low level that even a newbie F- or E-ranked adventurer could beat them one on one, as long as they've got the gear. But that's only when the goblins don't have backup. A goblin under command of a general would be much more difficult for a newbie to defeat. As for one under the command of a king? They would have no chance.

In other words, any individual with a royal title is a target for immediate extermination. They're simply too dangerous.

The number of people they're capable of leading, not to mention the ability to raise their army's stats, makes them leagues ahead of other commanders. The second problem is the other ruling classes who tend to gather around royalty.

Goblins are generally very weak, so even under a king's command, they're unlikely to overrun a town, although said town may not be left unscathed.

Naturally, the more powerful the monster, the more damage they're able to deal. Anyone who spots a royal is supposed to immediately run to the adventurers' union so that a hunting party can be formed. Ms. Luciana explains that depending on the situation, word may even be passed on to the military as well.

"Undead royals are seen as particularly dangerous. The undead may not be very intelligent, so they're not a problem on their own, but their base stats are high, and they possess plenty of unique skills. They also come in great numbers. With the birth of an undead ruler comes a terrible display of true power amongst their group and is cause for the nearby armies and clergymen to become fully mobilized."

I pause to process all the new information. "What about the immortal ruling class?" I finally ask.

"They're different from the undead ruling class, of course. Immortals generally live in different environments, since they control the worlds the rest of us go to after death. We don't call them the 'ruling class.' The stories passed down over the years refer to the royalty of the Nether as Nemeseia. We treat them on the same level as royalty from any large country, but since they influence our afterlives, they're far more important to us than any earthly royal."

I may be a princess, but immortals aren't inherently the enemies of mankind. So I'll be seen not as being part of the ruling class...but as a royal in my own right? Apparently, my influence is also greater than that of any king.

"But immortal members of royalty are supposed to be in the Evernight Castle, ruling over the Nether and Abyss. I just don't understand why you're out here with us."

"I may be an outsider, but you think me being here is causing problems regardless?"

"I do. I said you should do it anyway, but I think heading to the Nether sooner rather than later would be the best option after all. Royals aren't born every day, and they may be feeling your absence."

In human terms, any family of the king would be considered royalty, but it sounds like monster royalty isn't yet understood. They only come into existence suddenly—sometimes a few years apart, or sometimes hundreds. Ms. Luciana tells me that managing such a system is difficult.

She also explains that members of the ruling class outside of royalty are born here and there too. They exist to gather monsters under them, so if they're spotted too late, major wars become inevitable. I believe that must be what happened during the world quest.

It sounds like two members of royalty belonging to the same race have never been discovered at the same time. I wonder if the Evernight Castle is missing its master? But since players are outsiders, this must be an exception to the rule.

By the way, I also learned that aside from undead, the wolf rulers can cause quite a lot of trouble. Imagine an army of wolves being led by a commander. You get it, don't you?

"I hope to make it there within two months, going by this world's time."

"Hee hee hee! Please just make it there before I die."

"I think I can promise that. Try to live another forty years, okay?"

She kind of sounds halfway serious, though. Is she really that worried about an afterlife without a leader?

Well, I won't ask her about that. I decide to change topics. "So royals can make other people stronger? I have two royal command skills of my own, so I guess I know that's true already. There are probably command skills that can be used to give orders, depending on the situation. I understand why that would make goblins a lot more powerful."

"Wow! Might I ask you about your skills' effects?"

"I don't know the exact numbers, but they change depending on skill level. Privilege raises all stats, while Command boosts all stats and makes you more intelligent too. Royalty gets the boost of all stats...and depending on the scenario, we can share the skills we possess as well."

"Three skills that raise all stats and an intelligence boost alone would be enough of a threat. But you even share skills too?"

"Right now, it only works on my servants, but I'm also able to give them my own race skills."

It's not unusual for a game to treat monsters and players differently. I also can't deny the possibility that enemies may be able to grant skills to those of the same race under their command as well.

"I see. I'll have to share this information with the adventurers' union. Thank you very much."

"Of course."

We chat a bit more before I take my leave.

In the end, I learned that princesses are members of royalty among the ruling class. Being immortal on top of that was the problem. It's perfectly normal to run into generals and kings for enemies in other games, but this particular game seems to give those titles much more weight.

To put it simply, they were at first scared to learn that I was a princess, then relieved to learn that I was immortal, only to think about it some more and realize that's not much relief at all, frightening them even further.

In real-life terms, it would be like meeting someone only to learn shortly after that he's the king of Hell. Wow. Okay, I'm sorry for what I did. I won't be revealing my race so easily from here on out. I doubt it will bring me anything but trouble. I've learned some useful information today.

For now, I decide I'll go back to the temple area after the second official event. It sounds like immortals really need to prioritize reaching the Nether. I'm glad I have a real goal in this game now.

I wonder what that goal would be for the other races? Well, I don't exactly have any way of finding that out.

"Aaah! Princess!"

That voice from above? Yes, it had to be Ms. Fairellen.

"Good day. Do you need something from me?" I asked.

"Take a look at this!"

> **[MATERIAL] FAIRY NECTAR**
> Rarity: EP   Quality : C
> A flower's nectar made using a fairy's unique magic.
> As delicious as it is, its small quantity makes it
>   incredibly rare.
> Each fairy can choose whether or not to give you
>   nectar. Try befriending a fairy if you run into one.

"Wow, you made this?"

"I was trying it out, but it's impossible to harvest. I need a field full of flowers!"

She shows me a potion bottle half-full of vibrant, beautiful nectar. It's glowing a little bit too. She tells me that she spent an hour flying around to collect this much, meaning the process is a huge pain without a flower field.

She also tells me that she already sold a bottle to a resident trader as a test, and it made her a lot of money. The nectar has a rarity of Epic, after all. Judging by the description, I'm sure there's no other way of getting this stuff.

"The quality seems like it depends on the status of the flowers. It's really hard to make!"

"That sounds like a fairy version of honey. Have you already tried some?"

"Yeah, it was delicious. I'm gathering it up so I can drink it. Oh, you can have that bottle."

"Are you sure?" I ask.

"Of course! But I'd be even happier if you used it to make some kind of sweet treat!"

"Hmm...I haven't gotten around to making sweets yet."

"You could probably just lap it up too, but that's no fun, you know?"

"All right...I'll try to come up with something."

"Looking forward to it!"

With that, she flies away. She's sure having fun up there in the sky.

As for me, I'll continue my walk a little more, then go grinding...the inevitable fate of all RPG gamers.

[May you carve new roads] Comprehensive Thread 34
   [As you walk]
   1. Passing Conqueror
   This is a thread for comprehensive strategies.
   Fill it with anything that has to do with conquering new
   grounds.
   Past threads: http://✳ ✳ ✳ ✳ ✳ ✳ ✳ ✳ ✳
   >> 980 Take care of the next thread.

692. Passing Conqueror
   How's progress on the third area looking?
693. Passing Conqueror
   Slow but steady, I think...
694. Passing Conqueror
   It still looks like it's going to take some time to get
   through.

695. Passing Conqueror

But it actually looks like the official route to the neigh-
boring town...or maybe the "next" town, I guess, is going
to be easier than we first thought.

696. Passing Conqueror

By official route, you mean the actual roads, right?

697. Passing Conqueror

Yeah. You know how they use carriages in this game's
world? Those routes are the ones the traders take,
meaning they're relatively safe and the enemies aren't
that strong.

698. Passing Conqueror

In other words, leaving those official routes means
you'll run into enemies that are a lot tougher.

699. Passing Conqueror

So following the roads is super safe?

700. Passing Conqueror

Yeah, I think we can assume that.

701. Passing Conqueror

Both adventurers and traders can use those routes, so
we should probably ask at the union.

702. Passing Conqueror

What should we look out for if we go that way right
now?

703. Passing Conqueror

Right now, we're focused on the undead area to the
north of Belstead, and the ocean.

704. Passing Conqueror

Right. The undead area in the north is pretty tough, but the ocean's even worse.

705 Passing Conqueror

The ocean? Where everyone's buying a boat, sailing out, and running into hell?

706 Passing Conqueror

You'll die and lose your boat at the same time. It's a mess. Those boats aren't cheap.

707. Passing Conqueror

We humans can't battle in the ocean... If you just want to fight, then the undead area would be better.

708. Passing Conqueror

Dying on your boat is the best option. Some of the enemies might drag you into the water, and tanks just sink straight to the bottom.

709. Passing Conqueror

You get to experience drowning. Although they don't make it that realistic, of course.

710. Passing Conqueror

It's hard to tell who they added an area like that for. Although I'm kind of relieved the devs did make it, since it seems like their sort of thing.

711. Passing Conqueror

What happens there?

712. Passing Conqueror

The same as above ground. If you stop breathing, an

FREE LIFE FANTASY ONLINE

oxygen meter appears, and once it runs out, your HP
drains until you die.

713. Passing Conqueror

...That's exactly it. You can see it above ground too.

714. Passing Conqueror

Unlike other games, you can stop breathing anywhere
in the world.

715. Passing Conqueror

So you're saying we should pick up sniper rifles?

716. Passing Conqueror

You mean like when you hold your breath to ADS?
I get it.

717. Passing Conqueror

I get the joke, but no one's talking about snipers.

718. Passing Conqueror

There're no guns in this game?

719. Passing Conqueror

Does it make sense to bring guns into a world of
swords, bows, and magic?

720. Passing Conqueror

But there're still machinery people in the game.

721. Passing Conqueror

True! I bet we'll get guns soon. I won't complain as long
as they're balanced.

722. Passing Conqueror

Ignoring the guns for now, has anyone else been seeing
traveling traders lately? Or at least since the update.

723. Passing Conqueror
Yeah, I see them walking along the roads with their resident guards.

724. Passing Conqueror
It feels even more realistic now. I wonder if they're showing up now because we defeated the bosses in each direction.

725. Passing Conqueror
Until yesterday, there used to be escort mission events, but you usually had to be rank C or higher to take them, right?

726. Passing Conqueror
C or higher for escort missions, yeah. They actually gave pretty nice rewards.

727. Passing Conqueror
That was because they took so long to complete. I was told that people have to be that strong because it's irresponsible to let you guard someone unless you have the proven character and skills for it. That made sense to me.

728. Passing Conqueror
Hard to disagree with that. The official routes seem the same as always, but it's really bad when you go to the areas outside those.

729. Passing Conqueror
That must be why no one lives there and there're no towns. Those lands belong to the monsters.

730. Passing Conqueror
I'll probably start venturing outside the official routes soon.

731. Passing Conqueror
Traveling off the beaten path is something every adventurer has to do!

732. Passing Conqueror
I'm not going near that ocean though.

733. Passing Conqueror
Let's have the Nixies deal with it for us.

734. Passing Conqueror
The fairy race water dwellers? But I bet water's their strongest skill. Not having any type advantages has gotta be rough.

735. Passing Conqueror
Well, I'm sure they have a skill of some kind. Like underwater breathing.

736. Passing Conqueror
I want those movement restrictions gone too.
It's too hard to fight in that state...

737. Passing Conqueror
First things first, we've got to unlock the portals in every town.

738. Passing Conqueror
But we don't even know the names of the countries, much less the royal capital city.

739. Passing Conqueror

Yeah, me neither. Do you think residents will tell us if we ask?

740. Passing Conqueror

They may be commoners, but I'm sure they'll know the names of the countries... Right?

741. Passing Conqueror

I hope so...

742. Passing Conqueror

Can we talk about the new numbers added to the area map?

743. Passing Conqueror

And how, going off the numbering system, the place with all the undead is still only the second area?

744. Passing Conqueror

This.

745. Passing Conqueror

That one spot is on a different level!

746. Passing Conqueror

The enemies there are usually pushing level 40. Seeing third-area enemies in the second area must mean something.

747. Passing Conqueror

How about you go check it out for us?

748. Passing Conqueror

Thanks, but no thanks.

Saturday

All right, time for me to log in. It's Saturday at 1 p.m., and it's also afternoon inside the game. I arrive in Starting Town's town square. I spent the whole morning reading leisurely in the library.

What should I do today? My Appraisal is at level 30 now. I decide to check over my equipment. I'm sure it will have more to tell me.

APPRAISAL LV. 10

 DEF: △

 MDEF: △

 Applicable Skills: Light Armor

APPRAISAL LV. 20

 HP Regen Boost: Minor

 MP Regen Boost: Minor

APPRAISAL LV. 30

 New power will be unlocked each time the player
  receives divine protection.

 Complete defense against specific special attacks.

So the dress I have equipped in my torso slot really must have something to do with the gods after all. If I can't strengthen the item in the same way I can an armor, how often am I going to receive this divine protection? I wish I could see the future here... This probably isn't the sort of thing that happens regularly, right? I don't want my equipment to remain weak unless I go out of my way to do things that involve the gods. This makes me excited about what reward I'll get from Ms. Luciana's quest.

As for divine protection...I probably need to pray in a church, don't I? This may be a game, but just praying for the gods' help seems a little too simple. I doubt I'll get anything just from having my brain waves checked.

If you asked me if I believe in gods and spirits in real life, I would say that they very well may exist. They just don't affect our world in any palpable way, so it would be more accurate to say that I don't care whether they exist or not. That's why I'd sum it up with an answer of "I suppose they're probably real, right?"

Basically, I don't believe that they *don't* exist, so I'm able to go to places like temples and shrines with the appropriate attitude.

But that's really it... Maybe I should really get into the spirit of RP and pray with an innocent mind? The whole reason I'm in this world is supposed to be thanks to Creall's permission and Stellura's powers. I suppose I could give a proper prayer of gratitude for that fact alone.

The vague "complete defense against specific special attacks" remark is now attached to all of my armor. I want to find out more about what it does, but there's currently no way to do so.

For now, I head straight to the chapel.

It's somewhat occupied, since it's the afternoon, but I go in and pray in front of the Stellura statue.

Nothing seems to happen. Well, it would be too easy if all it took was one prayer to get a blessing.

Now what should I do today... Hmm? My Instinct is acting up. The corner of the statue's base is turning somewhat hazy. The smoke thickens and pools to create a dog-like figure... Is that you, pup trinity?

```
LORD OF TINDALOS    LV 100
Attribute: ?
Weakness: ?
Resistance: ?
Genus: Outer one
Species: Ruling race
Status: Normal
```

So the boss showed up? I can't see any of its stats. My Danger Sense isn't activating, and Instinct isn't showing its weaknesses either.

The Lord of Tindalos appears to be changing in shape and size every second. I'll try not to give it too much thought, since that's what he's originally supposed to do. Unless I want to end up getting my head checked, I'll just accept it. Ha ha ha...

The beast begins to circle around me. I wonder why he's here. Danger Sense isn't picking anything up, and I never made any

FREE LIFE FANTASY ONLINE

contracts with the gods in the first place. He stops moving around and steps in front of me. As soon as our eyes meet, Danger Sense activates!

I feel a light blow to the right side of my skirt, along with the sound of metal colliding against metal. By the time my hand reaches my rapier, I've already been hit with the attack. I didn't even see it coming... But that must be the power of a level 100 boss. It appears that the Lord of Tindalos attacks with his tongue.

"So you really did receive that equipment from Master? If not, you wouldn't still be standing there."

He spoke! No, wait, I was already told that we would be able to communicate. This must be what "complete defense against special attacks" means... I wonder if he'll answer questions.

"Who...is your master?"

"The goddess Stellura," the beast replies.

"So this equipment really does have something to do with Stellura?"

"It does. But it has lost much of its power."

"Then...do I need to return it?"

"No. The equipment chooses its owner. If you are able to wear it, then you already deserve it."

Hmm...I see. Is that why I had to get skewered to death so many times at first? To be honest, this equipment is pretty dangerous stuff.

But when I explain that, the beast tells me that I'm mistaken. The weapon was simply protecting its owner. Straying from the correct path there means you're seen as an intruder.

As long as the owner is alive and healthy, no one aside from them will be able to touch the equipment. In other words, when I lean my rapier against something, no one else will be able to make contact with it, even though the weapon is right there in front of them.

"Hm, so you're an immortal? An inexperienced, yet certain ruler. Set out in search of the first gate to the Medium inside of the Nether."

"So there's a way to access the Medium from the Nether?"

"Fulfill your role. Never forget your gratitude. That will lead you down the right path."

"My role...?" I ask, confused.

"Start by unifying the Nether. It is in a state of distress. Hurry and save them."

It sounds like my race has a role to play. Regardless of whether it's a main story or side story, it's nice to have a story playing out.

"My advice? Don't acquire any more attribute spells. Also, study up on languages."

"In other words...keep the spells I have right now? And why languages?"

"Follow Stellura's example. Deal only in light and dark. As for the languages, you'll need them later."

So it's fine if I have light and dark spells. Does that mean radiant, holy, darkness, shadow, and the combined space spells are safe? But nothing from other attributes? That must be because the other gods rule over fire, wind, water, and earth... I see. Well, I wasn't planning on choosing those anytime soon anyway.

The one problem is that he's telling me to level up Linguistics. Does that mean I have to grind by reading books at the library? I intended to do that in the first place, but now I really need to set some time aside.

"Wait, why'd you come here in the first place?"

"Just to see."

I pause. "See me?"

"Yes. I sensed a prayer from a unique individual, so I came to check."

"I...see."

"I shall go now. Persist diligently, fated one."

With that, he fades away from a dog shape into a sort of haze, gets absorbed by the corner again, and disappears. I guess he just wanted to have a chat before he left. He came to check on me... and that's that?

"He seemed like a good guy."

"Ms. Anastasia...what did you do?"

Ms. Luciana approaches me, massaging her temples for some reason. All I did was pray! It's not my fault.

"I just said a prayer, and for some reason, the Lord of Tindalos showed up."

"One from the ruling race wouldn't come here for something so simple..."

"I think it was a problem with my race. He said he just wanted to come check me out."

"Ah...I see. Well, it doesn't look like any trouble has come from it, right?"

"Exactly. No trouble. He already left and everything."

"It looks like he dialed back his aura." Ms. Luciana turns back to the others in the church. "No one has collapsed, have they?"

"No, Lady Luciana."

"Very well. Back to work, everyone."

At Ms. Luciana's orders, the church occupants return to normal business. I suddenly remember that I'm here at the chapel in the middle of the day. *I'm sorry for the commotion, everyone.*

All righty then. The unexpected conversations put me a bit off schedule, but since I'm on summer break, I still have lots of time available. I even got some very helpful information that will probably relate to my future evolution, so I'm happy with how things turned out...aside from how scary that thing was.

To sum it all up...when it comes to elemental spells, I've got to stick with the ones that are related to Stellura. I also need to level up Linguistics at the library to make my future objectives easier to achieve. The goal is to get to the Nether, then look for the first gate that will lead me to the Medium. That's everything I learned.

Now...what should I do first? Hmm...maybe hunting? Yeah, hunting with some reading in between. I want to reach the Nether before I hit level 30, since that's when I might evolve again. In fact, it'll probably be easier to grind levels during the second event.

"Oh, hey there, Princess! Lovely weather today, huh? I can feel my skin roasting in the sun. Oh wait, I don't have any skin! Ah ha ha ha!"

"Good day, Mr. Skelly. Was that an undead joke?"

I'll have you know that my automatic regen skills are more than enough to keep my HP bar full right now. A parasol just reduces the experience you gain for those skills, so in all honesty, it's a hard choice whether or not to use one.

"Are you up for some hunting, Princess? How about eastern Belstead? We might be able to reach the next town."

"You want to push into the east while we hunt?"

"I heard that there're horse monsters not too far in!"

"I see. I would love to absorb one of those."

"Right? Alf should log in soon, so we're gonna go hunting as soon as he gets here."

I would certainly love a horse. I was planning on spending my summer weekends playing in a party in the first place, and since I have no other urgent business at the moment, this is the perfect opportunity.

"What are your plans for the event, Mr. Skelly?"

"I'm gonna participate, obviously! Alf and I are going together. What about you?"

"Can I join you?"

"Sure thing, sure thing!"

"It's probably going to be hard to get around with different races for this second event."

"Agreed. Did you pick what you're bringing yet, Princess?"

"My alchemy kit. It's going to give me the widest range of use."

...Wait. Mr. Skelly has an alchemy kit too, right? What's the point of bringing the same item as other party members? I doubt he has alchemy expansion cores, but if we really need an item with good quality, we can go to the respective crafters for help.

"Why don't I go with my alchemy kit and you take your cooking kit?" he suggested. "Not that any of us eat..."

"Hmm...that might be a better plan."

Mr. Alf just logged in. They were planning to meet up in Belstead, so we head to the statue and teleport away.

"Hey, it's the princess!"

"Mr. Skelly told me you two are going east."

"We sure are. Take the lead for us, all right?"

I invite Mr. Alf and Mr. Skelly into my party, then the three of us head to the union to pick up some hunting quests. From there, it's off to the east. Taking these quests now and again is important if we want to increase our rank at the union.

"What are you taking to the event, Mr. Alf?"

"I still haven't made up my mind yet. If we can only take one 'variety,' that presumably means one inventory slot. Outside of potions, we probably can't bring more than one weapon in, unless it's the kind that stacks."

"Yeah, that makes sense. I think you're right about that."

"It would be crazy enough if there were no quantity restrictions on that one category of weapon you choose, but to be honest, who has the money for that?"

"One weapon alone can cost around 200,000 gold. It sounds like the event story is that we've been set adrift, so they're going to explain it as: 'You were lucky enough to have one variety of item on you in addition to your equipment.'"

"There's no way they'll let your weapon break if you don't repair it, right? For eight days, you can maybe repair two or three times. I doubt we can use gold there, so if we have to search for ores, maybe a pickaxe is the way to go."

"Another problem is whether or not we'll be able to meet up with Mr. Ertz and the others..."

"Can't we make sure we end up in the same place if we form a raid party? Actually, that probably won't work. I'm guessing that'd still have us end up in totally different places. Our only option might be to put in a ton of effort so we can link up with them along the way."

"Isn't that part of the 'set adrift' story too?"

We discuss the event while simultaneously killing enemies, pressing forward to our destination. It's only piggs and angus when you're this close to a town, and I'm all too used to killing those.

The other two tell me that they heard that since the way to the next town is along a road, we likely won't get lost on the way. Technically, it's only trodden dirt, but a road is a road. The brown line going through the plains leaves no room for us to wander astray.

"The enemies should start changing up around here."

"King slimes and army horses, with accel hawks up in the sky."

"That reminds me. What are slimes like in this world?"

"Slimes are always so different, depending on what game you're playing!"

"There was a slime player on the inhuman forum who wrote up some information."

I suppose I should go look for that, since we'll probably be fighting them very soon.

> **VISCOUS BODY**
> Physical resistance.
> Magic damage multiplier: 4×
> Super HP regen through water.

Which means that if we're battling slimes, the only ineffective spells will be anything in Water Magic. Their physical resistance is at about 80%.

"This seems like one of the scarier creatures to face in the game."

"I won't be able to help you at all. Take care of them for me!"

"Supposedly, they're hard as hell to beat if you fight them in the rain."

"Ah, I see. So the weather is a factor too. How interesting."

Mr. Alf will be in charge of army horses, since he's already riding a horse. Meanwhile, Mr. Skelly and I will take care of the king slimes and accel hawks.

We keep walking forward. In the other areas, we would have reached a forest by now. Here, the plains continue to stretch out before us, with different enemies spawning along the way.

"...It's like they tried to cartoon-ify a slime and failed."

"I see what you mean."

They aren't round like the slimes in a certain other game. These slimes are more like a gel unable to maintain its circular shape, slithering along the ground to move. It's like gravity is almost too much for them to bear. The king slimes are about the size of a person, and they move even slower than zombies.

Mr. Skelly and I manage to take it out with one lance shot each. That quadruple damage multiplier is tragic.

"Hey, I didn't get anything!"

"They say the only things they drop are slime gels."

Slime gels are materials for Alchemy. I believe you get magia water—an ingredient for magic clay—if you combine slime gel, purified water, and magic stones.

But what matters most right now is getting those horse components. I feel like once Mr. Skelly and I hunt and absorb two of them, we'll be able to get to the town in the third area.

Having a Dullahan's horse fight an army horse doesn't feel fair... Then again, neither of them are human, so maybe the rules don't apply.

The enemies here in the east range from levels 24 to 28. To be honest, I probably wouldn't lose to any of them even if I were on my own, since they're at the appropriate level for me. By the way, Mr. Skelly is level 26 right now, which puts him two levels above me.

"Hmm...I guess they're stronger than angus, at least?"

"Looks like they headbutt, stomp with their front legs, and kick with their back legs."

These may be at higher levels than the angus and have a more aggressive AI, but in their current state, they're little more than air to us.

They dash forward, turn on their front legs, and kick with their back legs. I bet that would hurt...but only if they manage to hit you, of course.

Mr. Skelly absorbs the first horse.

"There're lots of slimes around here, but not so many horses, by the look of things."

"Probably because they're the strongest enemies here."

"I do appreciate whoever cleared the skies for us a little."

"Same."

There're quite a lot of accel hawks flying around here. It's a pain to deal with them when they swoop down on you from above. But Mr. Alf is usually the one they target, perhaps because he's highest up on his horse, so they're not too much of a bother for Mr. Skelly and me.

Mr. Skelly hasn't summoned a horse, since I haven't found one of my own yet. However, I have something I can test. I wait until an accel hawk swoops down at me...

"Gravitas."

Using Gravitas from Space Magic, I double gravity for the accel hawk. The forces pulling it toward the ground increase, or perhaps I could say that I've just doubled its weight.

I don't know if this art is more effective against flying types, but as soon as I cast Gravitas on the hawk, it loses control and plunges into the ground. Mr. Alf's horse gives it a good stomp to finish it off.

"What was that?"

"That would be Space Magic. It increases a target's gravity."

"Ah, I get it."

"What's the magia efficiency like?"

"Hmm... If you're shooting at things in the air with precision, then this is the one to use. But that's only if every hit is a guaranteed knockdown, like we just saw."

"That would make things easier. Why don't we do a little challenge to test it out?"

"Sounds good to me."

"I'm down!"

Mr. Skelly takes the slimes, I target the accel hawks, and Mr. Alf takes the army horses. We'll help each other whenever we're not wrapped up in something, of course, but this is the plan for when we're fighting multiple enemies.

Gravitas works by selecting an individual target. This makes aiming extremely easy. It's simple enough to drag enemies into a coordinate point-type attack like the Explosion spells, but surrounding an individual enemy with them uses up lots of magia. These flying types don't have much Stamina or defense, so all you have to do is shoot them down.

"I'm curious about the slimes' attack patterns, but I doubt any brave heroes have tested that out yet."

"Ha ha ha ha... Of course someone's tested it."

"They shoot out at you like a whip, wrap around you, and start to digest you."

"Ah..."

"Apparently, you die a few seconds after you're absorbed. It must be the type of attack you can't escape from once you're in it."

"The southern coatls could get you in their mouths without killing you, but it was instant death as soon as they swallowed."

I didn't know about those attacks, but it's pretty common to see instant death moves like that in games. Well, it's certainly better than being slowly digested inside a monster's stomach.

"Sadly, it sounds like men's dreams don't come true during those attacks! Ha ha ha ha!"

"Yeah, I'm not surprised they're not the pervy kinds of slimes that only dissolve clothes."

"The slimes that only eat minerals and fibers? I could see those existing, but this is an all-ages game, after all."

"So would you call king slimes omnivores?"

"Actually, according to the adventurer residents, they only dissolve flesh and leave behind all the equipment."

"Ah, so they're just the gross kind of slimes. That's worse than the tentacles in the south."

"Well, it's for all ages..."

So the slimes are actually carnivores? I can imagine them saying, "No, that's not it!" But even if they were the pervy kind of slimes, it wouldn't be fair for them to only affect women and not men. Gender doesn't matter if their diet is strictly equipment. But how would they react to people like Mr. Skelly and Mr. Alf, who are just bones and armor...? Yeah, I'm going to stop thinking about that.

"You always walk around completely naked, Mr. Skelly. Are we sure that's allowed?"

"Nooo, don't peek!"

"Who the hell gets turned on by bones...? Actually, there're almost definitely people like that, and I don't want to know about them."

"It's a big world, after all!"

"Hey, look, there's a horse."

We don't run into enemy fights very often, probably because this is a trading route. The slimes are usually easy to ignore, the army horses are pretty rare, and the accel hawks don't show up that often unless you stray from the path. Even though traders hire guards, the trading routes would be functionally useless if it were that common to get attacked here.

Mr. Alf kited an army horse and accel hawk toward us.

I shoot down the accel hawk with Gravitas as it's diving, at which point Mr. Skelly steps in with Shadow Bind from Shadow Magic. Black arms crawl out from the shadows to keep the hawk pinned to the ground.

Mr. Skelly works on the army horse after that, while I approach the struggling accel hawk and slice into its head with my rapier. Between that hit and the fall damage, it's enough to finish the enemy off. Then I move on to the army horse to take it out as well.

"Okay, go ahead and absorb it."

"Right."

> You have received horse materials through Dark Ritual.
> You have earned 6 capacity through Dark Ritual.

As for the accel hawk, it's dismantling time. But all I end up with are feathers for arrows.

These horses will probably work best with skills meant for traveling. I set up a horse with Legs, Footwork, Balance Control, and Agility Boost, then swap out Life Absorption for Swift Foot in race skills. That will allow me to raise my Agility, while also giving me a speed bonus whenever I ride the horse.

I can summon a horse, a battle horse, or an army horse, and I think I'll go with a 4× multiplier since they're only medium in size. The cost for an army horse is 800 capacity, so I'll summon one and see what it's like to travel by horseback.

"Okay, Unit One. You're a horse now. Let me...actually, can I even ride you?"

"Ah... What's that seat thing called again?"

"A saddle."

"Right, yeah. You probably need one."

My skeleton army horse consists of nothing but bones. He has no flesh at all. Maybe I have to summon him as a zombie?

"Why don't you try getting on him? It's a game, you know, so maybe it's not as hopeless as it looks."

"I guess you might be right."

Despite this horse seeming impossible to ride, he's still undead—a magical being—so maybe common sense doesn't apply.

By the way, Mr. Alf is riding an armored horse with no reins or saddle at all.

"Oh, looks like it might work."

"I think so. I just probably can't fight like this."

"You'll want the Horseback skill for that. It helps with both stabilization and combat when you're on a horse."

Since my horse is made of bones, I don't jostle too much. It's easy to hold on to his bones to stabilize myself...but I also can't really hold a weapon in this position.

Mr. Alf explains that Horseback helps to both fight and stay upright on a horse, so maybe if I raise that skill, I won't have to hold on to the horse like this anymore. That would make fighting possible.

"I use a staff, so I can probably do one-handed attacks once I'm more used to this. But I can tell that my movement's restricted."

"My weapon is one-handed too, but do I need to make the horse take Horseback skill?" I ask.

"It's probably worth trying that out."

I don't have Horseback unlocked yet, so we'll just have to keep clip-clopping along like this. Mr. Alf and Mr. Skelly are riding beside me.

To recap, our party currently consists of: a headless armor riding a headless horse; a skeleton riding a skeleton horse; and me, in a dress, riding a skeleton horse. We must look terrible.

Right now, I feel more like I'm squatting on a moving horse than riding it. I don't look very elegant like this. My character's reputation might even take a hit. I need to do something about this, and fast.

We should be in a different area by now, but our surroundings look the same as ever. Surrounding us is the same peaceful field as before. The only difference is a bit of a slant to the elevation.

"The enemies here are rabbits and wolves?"

"The higher tiers of their races."

"And they're traveling in packs?"

"They sure are. They must be linked."

The rabbits don't seem to be spawning as frequently. The enemies I see are fear rabbits and gray wolves, and they're all somewhere around level 30 and above. Fear rabbits have a dark red tint to their fur, while gray wolves are exactly what they sound like.

"Are the rabbits supposed to be scarier? Fear is a status ailment you see in lots of games."

"But why rabbits?"

"Maybe it's natural selection. These could be the rabbits who survived all the overhunting."

"Ah..."

Well, the rabbits in this game are very delicious.

Setting that aside, it's time to head for the center of this map. Our priority is to unlock the portal at the town.

"Wait, what? There's something else here. Is that...an ostrich?"

"Technically it's called an avestruz, but yeah, that's an ostrich, all right."

Avestruz start at level 30 and are ostriches with sharp beaks and strong legs—whoa, one's coming our way!

"It's targeting us!"

"Make a run for it!"

Thus begins a race between horses and ostrich. Both, of course, are monsters.

Mr. Skelly is a bit faster when we're running at full speed, followed by me, and then Mr. Alf trailing behind. Maybe that's because of the difference in our weights? Mr. Skelly's just bones, while I'm a zombie wearing a pretty heavy dress.

Maybe I would have been even faster if I summoned Unit One at a 3× multiplier.

"This ostrich is fast! Talk about scary!"

A group of undead being chased by a charging avestruz who never moves his head even slightly... If anyone saw us like this, I bet they would laugh.

But Mr. Alf? He's a lump of metal atop an armored horse fleeing an ostrich. That's pretty crazy on its own. I may have buffs, but this horse is still really going for it.

Maybe undead are actually the most capable types of horses? They don't have the concept of stamina, right? So can they run at top speed at all times? The only problem is how it looks. But such is the fate of all inhumans...particularly the undead.

The avestruz seems to stop targeting us once the town comes into view. He just didn't know when to quit.

> You have fulfilled special requirements. Horseback is now unlocked.

Oh, it looks like I got the skill I needed. I'll try it out later. I doubt giving it to my horse will make much of a difference...but I understand the necessity. These creatures are going to be vital from here on out.

"Is this the stamina difference we're seeing?"

"It's slow, but we *are* going up a hill right now..."

"Do you think we could have escaped without your buffs, Princess?"

"There's no way I would have made it out, at least."

We were lower in level than the avestruz, after all. The fourth area will be filled with level 40 and higher enemies, so we won't be going there anytime soon.

For now, we head toward the town.

"St-stop!"

"Of course."

I figured the gatekeeper would stop us. Talking to him is my role in the group. I recall my horse—it might freak him out otherwise.

"Huh...? You're a necromancer?"

"We're immortal outsiders."

"A skeleton and..."

"That would be a Dullahan. I'm a zombie, personally."

"You too?! Huh...do you have an adventurer's card?"

"Of course. Here you go."

"Let me see... All right, everything checks out. Welcome to Barberek!"

"Where can we find the adventurers' union?"

"It's to the south of the town square."

"Thank you."

He lets us in after checking our adventurer's cards. It appears that regardless of whether you're an outsider or a resident, it makes no difference so long as you have your union card.

We'll sightsee later. Our first task is to unlock the portal.

> The portal to Barberek has been opened.
> You can set this location as your respawn point.

I reject the option to set my spawn point, and with that, the mission is accomplished.

"They've really got a color scheme going here, huh?"

It feels like they tried to make all their buildings with as much white material as possible. Looking around, it's nothing but white, white, white. This had to be intentional. Of course, time has taken its toll on the buildings, so they've not been able to maintain their pure ashen look.

"Isn't that because this country is home to the main church? That's the only reason I can think of."

This town is in the kingdom of Nearence, a thriving economy of agriculture. It's said to be home to the main church.

"What should we do now that we're here? We could split up, or we could go hunting again."

"Hmm...why not hunt, since we're all together?"

"Yeah, for sure. It'll be easier to explore when we're by ourselves."

"Then let's head to the union, report our quests, and ask for information about the area."

I can hunt for food ingredients on my own some other time.

Just as we were told, we spot the building with a sword and shield on its sign to the south of the town square. That would

FREE LIFE FANTASY ONLINE

be the adventurers' union, all right. We'll head there... Oh, someone's selling grapes? This town must be where the raisins in Belstead came from.

But I stop myself from getting distracted and enter the union. I then approach the woman at the front desk. I'll start by reporting on my quests.

"Could you tell me about the monsters in this area? Aside from the western ones."

"Of course. Wait just one moment."

She stands up and quickly returns with some documents in hand.

First, I learn about the regions surrounding the town. These enemies are the same fear rabbits, gray wolves, and avestruz we saw before.

When fear rabbits run low on stamina, their fur stands on end and they become enraged. When that happens, those with a low Spirit stat will be inflicted with the fear ailment. They must be resistant to Spirit attacks, but that doesn't exactly concern us either way.

Gray wolves are wolves that gather in packs of three, something one should take into account.

"Avestruz are generally peaceful, but they chase after anything that moves fast, thinking it to be a fellow avestruz. But when they realize you're not one of them, they will immediately attack. Please be careful around them, since they're hard to outrun. Watch out for their kicks too."

"Those damn birds have terrible eyesight."

"Ah ha ha ha! Think it chased us because we were on horses?"

"Sounds like it. If you run on your own two feet, it might be a fifty-fifty chance. Those birds are the enemy of all traveling traders."

Now that I think about it, the avestruz really picked up speed along the way. We were only able to outrun it because we gained speed too.

Even more annoyingly, they react to anyone they spot running, and even though they have bad eyesight and seem to think they're seeing a fellow avestruz, they're fast enough to catch up to get a closer look. And once they see you, they get upset? Yeah, that's quite the bother.

I won't mention anything about the woman calling them "damn birds."

"We have bounties for their extermination, so we hope you'll take care of them."

"Is there an easy way to defeat them?"

"Taking out their legs will do the trick. They just roll to the ground awkwardly."

"Their legs...?"

"They're thicker at the base, so you have to hit them at their ankles. Fortunately, their meat doesn't taste too bad."

Look at that grin on the receptionist's face. Again, I won't comment on it.

But the meat isn't bad, huh? I appreciate that information, even if hunting them will probably be a huge headache.

It would probably be easier if I was able to fight horseback. I could block leg attacks that way, and perhaps block rabbits and wolves to some extent too. Running all over the place would get annoying in a fight, so I'll have to prioritize getting the avestruz to stop first. Once it's still, I'll go for the legs and watch out for kicks.

To the north and south are forests, while to the east is more plains. But the northern forest is quite sparse, since it's at the foot of a mountain, while the southern forest seems more dense. The eastern plains are much like the western ones we came through.

To the north are murder plants, raptors, and schlaf owls.

Murder plants are of the plant race; they're able to use their roots to move about and fight using their vines as whips. Raptors sound like what you would expect from the name. They walk on two legs and have tiny arms and large heads. They belong to the raptor genus, so I guess they're not actually dinosaurs? Finally, schlaf owls sit in trees and lull anyone who passes underneath to sleep. Then they attack their slumbering enemies.

To the east are pigg monks, angus chargers, and glome hawks.

The piggs will have the Brawler skill, it sounds like. Angus chargers use a strong charging attack. Glome hawks fly at you like lightning bolts.

Finally, the south apparently only has trolls and ogres, but those trolls come in the forms of barbarians and crushers, and the ogres are soldiers, grapplers, guards, and thieves.

The enemy levels in the north and south range from 34 to 37. The eastern ones are 35-39, which means we'll have to stick to hunting the level 30-34 enemies that are closer to the town. This really puts the difficulty of the area around the former temple into perspective.

"If we go by levels, then we should stick by the town, but we're also familiar with the eastern enemies, right?"

"That's true. Since we're in a party, I think we can take 35 to 39..."

"I can picture the cows and birds, but what do you think a pigg monk looks like?"

The enemies in the temple area were level 30 at the lowest and 38 at the highest. However, I had the advantages of quadrupled light damage there and the reduced damage from Undying Royalty. There won't be anything so convenient up ahead. I wonder how we'll fare. Will we be able to defeat the animals with all their stamina?

"For now, let's go with the area around town and check out the east without taking any quests for it."

"Okay!"

We leave the receptionist and head to the quest board, where we select hunting quests for fear rabbits, gray wolves, and avestruz. Then we exit the union.

Now it's time to do some hunting until dinner.

A fear rabbit's attack patterns seem to be the same as the rabbits near Starting Town. Fear rabbits are much higher in level, so they're stronger, but that doesn't mean they're any more difficult to defeat. They get angry and inflict fear when their stamina was at or below the halfway mark, but that's their one unique move. And us immortals remain unaffected by it, to boot. In other words, they're the same as normal rabbits as far as we're concerned.

FREE LIFE FANTASY ONLINE

Next up were the gray wolves. They're a little bigger than normal, their fur is gray, and they gather in packs of three. Mr. Alf took on two of them while I cleaned up the third. Once we got used to teaming up like that, they were no different than normal wolves either. Mr. Skelly used Shadow Bind to take down one of the wolves Mr. Alf was handling, then helped beat up another. Finally, he took out the one he'd bound, followed by the final wolf that I'd already nearly killed on my own.

These enemies drop meat, along with fear rabbit horns and gray wolf claws.

Next up is the avestruz. Just as the receptionist explained, they don't approach us when we walk around normally, so we make sure to finish up our fear rabbit and gray wolf quests first.

"All right, now it's time for some ostriches."

"I'll start by testing out Horseback."

"Let's see, let's see..."

First, I assign a servant with Horseback, and then it's time to see how this works...with Mr. Skelly's help, of course. I'm in a dress, after all.

"What do you think?"

"Yeah, this changes things. It's easier now!"

"That's good to hear."

So I don't need to go out of my way to choose Horseback for myself. The skill might have less of an effect if I don't have it equipped, but right now I have no interest in researching that far.

Now it's time to summon a 3× army horse. I ask Unit One to sit down so I can climb on.

"I see. You're right, this is completely different. I think I can fight on horseback like this."

"I knew it!"

"Since Mr. Alf is the slowest, shall we go in triangle formation?"

"Okay!"

"Got it."

Now we just need to head toward the area with avestruz, and when they start chasing us, we'll lead them to an empty area to fight. That sounds good to me.

Mr. Skelly and I ride parallel to each other with some space in between us, while Mr. Alf follows a bit farther behind, allowing us to form a triangle. Once we pass by an avestruz, it starts to chase us. It even speeds up once it gets pretty close. Yeah, we definitely pissed it off.

Mr. Skelly and I fire off spells while the avestruz tries to peck at Mr. Alf.

"Hmm...? Nox Wall!"

Mr. Skelly places a Nox Wall in between Mr. Alf and the avestruz, causing the bird to run right into it. I see. This is much more efficient than trying to hit it with spells. Mr. Skelly and I take turns placing walls until the avestruz is finally dead.

"This seems like the easiest way to do it, right?"

"I think so."

"I don't mind as long as I'm only getting pecked. What say we gather some meat now?"

"Hmm...I want to absorb one first. We should be able to get ostrich materials."

"I bet they're totally different in skeleton form."

"Ah, sure thing."

> You have received avestruz materials through Dark Ritual.
> You have earned 6 capacity through Dark Ritual.

It looks like they're the same medium size as the horses.

Mr. Skelly goes on to absorb the next ostrich we kill.

In this party, our rules are that we take turns dismantling enemies we killed, and anything you gain from that belongs to you alone. That means that when your turn is up, you're free to choose between dismantling and absorbing as you please. If something rare ever turns up, I'm sure we would discuss it amongst ourselves, but we generally just dismantle unless it looks like the materials will be extra good. The exception would be if we ran into a dragon.

We all have different equipment and required stats, so we don't try to take things from each other. Accessories are really the only equipment slots I have open in the first place.

> Players Ertz and Dentelle have unlocked "Sub-weapon system."
> See the help menu for more information.

> New information has been added about Faded Pouch of Protection.

"Ooh?!"

"Oh man!"

"What's this? Let's check the help menu and see."

ABOUT THE SUB-WEAPON SYSTEM

This is a means of using a secondary weapon. You'll probably be familiar with this kind of mechanic, which allows you to quickly switch between weapons without opening your inventory.

If you have an item equipped that allows you to maintain a secondary weapon, this system will be available to you. However, this mechanic is different from many other games.

Your sub-weapon will be taken outside of your inventory just like your main weapon, so you will be required to consider the size and storage location of this equipment in advance.

I see. It's a system for switching weapons. Now what was that about my pouch?

APPRAISAL LV. 10
> DEF: △
> MDEF: △
> Storage Expansion: Minor (10)

APPRAISAL LV. 20
> Carry Limit: 2
> Capacity Available: Average

APPRAISAL LV. 30

New power will be unlocked each time the player
receives divine protection.
Complete defense against specific special attacks.

It looks like it lets me maintain more things now. Without those options, I probably wouldn't be able to keep another weapon on me.

I guess since it's a full-dive VR game, they want you to think about where you'll attach your weapon. Won't that be hard on short people, though?

"That was always inconvenient. But now it'll be easier to swap to my mace."

"I won't use this at all, since I've only got one staff."

I take my dismantling knife out of my inventory and place it next to my rapier. It never let me hang two weapons there before. I'm not sure if the knife counts as a weapon or if you can hang things outside of weapons there too. Probably the latter.

"Is that your dismantling knife?"

"That's right. This makes things easier."

"You only use the one rapier, don't you, Princess? The dismantling knife is a good choice. I think I'll do that too."

"Are belts for storing specific items?"

"That's what my belt does. Once you get Appraisal to level 20, you can see how many slots it lets you hang things from, as well as how much it can hold."

"Let me see..."

It looks like they both just have one hanging slot, and the storage level is minor. So they can only hang on to that one main weapon. They'll need to make use of the new equipment that I'm guessing Mr. Ertz and Mr. Dentelle developed.

"I definitely want to get that before the event starts."

"I can probably put if off until later."

Mr. Alf immediately begins to contact Mr. Ertz and Mr. Dentelle.

I should ask them for more ring accessories myself.

Armor consists of eight different slots: head, upper torso, lower torso, waist, arms, legs, back, and cloak.

This new mechanic is probably an upgrade to the waist category, since it adds slots on both the right and left for a weapon and a secondary weapon.

The equipment system feels like a mix between real life and typical game systems.

There are also fourteen accessory slots: neck, ears, wrists, ankles, and each of your fingers. But you can't stack more than one necklace, and you can't put multiple rings on one finger either. That makes ten rings in total. That's quite a lot of slots, but I'm sure it costs a lot to fill them all.

"All right, shall we get going again?"

This time, we start by making the avestruz run into the wall. Since the wall is a continuous spell, and you can only activate one at a time, the older wall disappears as soon as you cast a new one.

"Ah, I'll do the next one!"

"There're two of them pecking at me..."

321

"But you seem fine, though?"

"I guess I'll get by."

"As for the walls...can they only take two enemies at once?"

"I don't think they can handle three. There's no way of knowing if all three will charge at the same angle."

Two of the ostriches are running after Mr. Alf, but one wall can take care of them both. Three ostriches would be too wide for the wall. Who knows if the third ostrich will stay in line? I suppose we'll be fine as long as they keep following from behind.

"I think it will work if they follow single file, instead of running parallel?"

"Ah, I get it. It would be perfect if they run into the wall one at a time like that."

It feels so nice to go galloping through the fields of grass on horseback...even if that peaceful scene is being interrupted by a herd of ostriches chasing us from behind. Will we really be able to keep ahead of them? There are no enemies that chase after you around Starting Town.

In any case, you've got to make them take the bait right away, or else the road to dismantling is long and hard. Yes, I'm quite the idiot.

> Darkness Magic has reached level 15.
> You have acquired Nox Magic Missile through Darkness
>   Magic.

"They're only dropping meat."

"Same for me."

"I only got meat too."

"...I guess the drop rate is good for hunting?"

"Agreed. I don't hate this, though. I get to level up my defense skills and Riding at the same time."

I'm also leveling up both my light and dark spells, so I'm not all that upset by the outcome.

"Mr. Skelly, do you have Magic Missile?"

"Yeah, I've got MagiMiss!"

"I just learned it. How does it work?"

"Well...it staggers enemies like how arrow spells do. They shoot out like balls, trace targets pretty well, have the same force as ball spells, and use an amount of MP somewhere between balls and lances."

"Ah, so it's antiair."

"You should start with Dual Spell, then go for MagiMiss. Since you've got Gravitas, you might end up running low on MP."

"It sounds like this will work for enemies I can't take down with Gravitas."

"Most likely, yeah. It also works on fast ground enemies too."

I can probably just memorize it based on the "missile" in the name—a guided projectile spell.

We continue to move forward since we're near the eastern region. The enemies here change to pigg monks, angus chargers, and glome hawks.

"These piggs seem pretty normal, don't they?"

"Yeah...I think so. The angus have bigger horns, I think."

"Such lovely horns! The birds…well, I can't see them very well."

I end up dismounting my horse to fight a pigg monk. Let's see how much these sad piggies have changed.

Once Mr. Alf attacks one, the pigg starts to wag its tail, walks forward, stands up on its back legs, and assumes a fighting stance.

"Hmm? Whoa!"

It steps forward and delivers a straight punch, but Mr. Alf blocks it. That pigg may be cute, but the sound it made when it collided with the shield was anything but.

This feels a lot like the Eastern boss—the Fighting Bear. In other words, a real fight is about to break out.

Mr. Alf begins to fight back.

"Think he'll die if he fights alone?"

"I don't like that these piggs look exactly like the normal ones…"

"Let's help out!"

"Oh, that was fast."

I attack the pigg monk with a spell as he dishes out punches, kicks, and even spin kicks.

It seems to have quite a lot of stamina. We keep attacking for a while, until I gather magia in my hand…and send my attack art's red light from my hands to the pigg. That's when Danger Sense activates. The red line appears to show an incoming punch.

I use Royal Counter to block it, so the pigg monk goes back to attacking Mr. Alf.

"Oh?"

"So it doesn't just target whoever's built the most aggro?"

"I'm glad he didn't come for me!"

I follow up with another attack to finish off the pigg monk. The drops are the same as in Belstead.

"Yikes, he was tough..."

"What a strong pigg..."

Next up on the list is an angus charger. However...

"...All of them are linked?"

"Even the pigg was kinda tough... Think we should stop?"

"Good idea. Killing them will be hard enough, but think about how much time it will take."

"Why don't we hunt ostriches?"

"Yeah, let's do that."

We head closer to town for some avestruz hunting. We run by any we spot, bait them to chase, kill them, dismount the horses, and dismantle. Then we get back on our horses, look for more ostriches, bait them, and hunt them.

We also battle any fear rabbits and gray wolves that happen to be nearby while dismantling the ostriches.

> Rapier has reached level 15.
> You have acquired Regenerate through Rapier.

Wow...Regenerate deals six attacks at once? It doesn't mention relying on Agility or anything. I'll have to try it out to get a feel for it.

"Could you bait some rabbits for me, Mr. Alf? I want to test out an art."

"You got it."

"Want me to use Bind?" Mr. Skelly asks.

"Yes, that would be great."

"Okay!"

Mr. Alf immediately baits a fear rabbit, Mr. Skelly binds it, and I make use of the Regenerate art.

I focus on using my skill and hold the glowing red rapier to my chest. At that moment, six attacks go flying forward at an impressive speed. That wasn't linked to my Agility at all. I could never move so fast. It also seemed to activate my royal movement assistance.

"Wow!"

"You're like a knight."

"It's as powerful as attacking up close. The problem is that the attacks seem to land in random spots."

My rapier is meant to be targeted at an enemy's weak spot, which gives it a power boost when you successfully land a hit there. I'll try it in manual mode next. It will take some getting used to, but I bet that's the best way to utilize it.

I do my best to trace the same movement I did with the semi-automatic version. I bring my blade to my chest like a knight and raise the tip upward. Then I take a step forward with my right foot and plunge the blade forward.

"I see... So if you get good with this art, you can probably land six stabs in the same spot."

I ended up shooting a dozen times, but that was because I had missed the weak spot with some of them. The three of us defeat the rabbits together.

This is a useful attack. I'll practice with it next time I'm solo. Being able to stab an enemy in their weak spot six times is much more powerful than any spell. I can use Break Parry to mess with an enemy's balance, then kill them instantly with Regenerate. Of course, that's assuming the enemy isn't undead.

After hunting ostriches for a while, Mr. Skelly suddenly asks me something.

"By the way, Princess... You're a total roleplayer, aren't you?"

"Where did that question come from?"

"Ah, from the inhuman forum?"

"Exactly!"

Apparently, this was a topic of discussion on the inhuman board. Most players who choose inhuman races either really love their race of choice, or they're really into roleplaying. They said that even if the player is interested in a more unusual gaming experience, they wouldn't keep playing if they didn't love any of the inhuman races.

Mr. Alf and Mr. Skelly appear to be from that first category. They just really love armor and skeletons. They knew those were the choices for them if they wanted to be something other than human. That's why they wanted to hear my thoughts on the subject.

"I see. I'm just the curious type, myself. It came down to either a zombie or a sexy radish for me, so I ended up going with zombie, since it still has a human form. If I made a new character now, I doubt I'd get the kind of head start I did with this one."

"That's true. It's also a waste to get there after putting work into your character."

"Exactly. Since I already evolved into this race, I'm happy sticking with it. I wouldn't call myself a roleplayer. It's not like I was aiming to become this race anyway."

"I see!"

"The way you move and talk really made me think you were roleplaying."

I feel like I had the same conversation with Ms. Primura. I think I was with Mr. Ertz and the other crafters at that time.

"I have the royal movement assist setting turned on, which is why I move the way I do. As for my speech...it has to do with my real-life circumstances, but this is my natural manner of speaking."

My mom is Japanese and my dad is British, making my sister and I both mixed race. After I was born, Dad started learning Japanese from Mom along with me, so I grew up hearing Japanese in a very polite, default manner of speech, like it comes from a translation.

"Well, back when I was in kindergarten, my little sister threw a fit. She would cry that she hated how I spoke. Tomo and Sugu even agreed with her. They all said it was like I was speaking to them as strangers."

"Ah...yeah, kids pretty much never talk like that."

"Because of that, when I was with my family or close friends, I tried to imitate how they spoke. I'm able to do that with them naturally now, but you can think of those two groups as the exception to how I normally speak."

"Now I see why your sister sounds so fluent in English during her streams!"

"We speak English at home sometimes too. It's quite the mix."

Mom also told me that it's natural for people to speak formally once they're adults, so it's not something I need to work on correcting.

"Although, I suppose I don't need to deny that I fall into the roleplaying category. I've always let myself be taken by the flow of the story during quests and events."

"That's right; you were a leader during the defensive war!"

Mr. Noah also assumed that I was a natural RPer when he suggested I become a VR actress. I could get really into roleplaying for that too. Perhaps the one issue is that people already think I'm roleplaying, even though everything aside from the movement assist is me being my normal self.

"Since you're a princess, I feel like you should be a little more commanding when you talk."

"Ah...I suppose that's true."

"People think you're roleplaying as a gentle and sweet kind of princess character."

"That's the situation on the BBS."

"I see. Well, I'm fine with that, and I don't see a need to correct anybody. It *is* something I think about from time to time."

"Role-playing only when it's fun for you... There're lots of people like that!"

I'm not a hardcore roleplayer at all right now. I simply get into character a little bit when the time, place, and mood feel right.

"Speaking of RP, I heard that people figured out occupations!"

"Yeah, that's right!"

"Huh? Occupations?" I ask.

"Check the help menu. You'll find it there."

"Oh, I see the 'new' mark on one category."

ABOUT OCCUPATIONS

Occupations are jobs that players may take.

Players who take on a job will have "Occupation" and "Title" added to their stats.

Each occupation will come with certain quests, but it will also require a more careful managing of relationships with residents.

Occupations may be particularly suited to roleplayers. If you're interested in finding new ways to enjoy this world, consider the option of employment.

EX:

Occupation: Clergy	Title: Priest
Occupation: Adventurer	Title: C rank

   * Union members can toggle display via Options.

Occupation: Craftsman	Title: Blacksmith

"I see... So it's that sort of thing."

"Right now, we have 'occupation quests' and 'titles,' but no occupation skills yet. Apparently, occupations are basically like normal work, especially with the quests. All you get as a reward is money."

"Doesn't that make it more suited toward roleplayers?"

"Supposedly those 'titles' come with pretty nice effects, but that's it. You also get to go to special areas for those in your field."

So it's for people who want new ways to enjoy this world. I see. Some people may genuinely want that sort of life. It's all about what interests you, and since it doesn't provide incredible effects or skills, it isn't something you absolutely have to pursue. I wonder if anything will change once I go to the Nether... I'll look forward to it.

All the three of us are doing now is galloping around on our horses while we build walls, so we're able to talk and hunt at the same time.

> Your race level has increased.
> Radiant Magic has reached level 15.
> You have gained Lumen Magic Missile through Radiant Magic.

Ah, just hit level 25 as well.

Oh, and Undying Royalty is level 30 now. This allows me to give one extra skill to my servants, so I'll make sure to give them all some sort of purification resistance.

Secret Art of Necromancy is one level away from 25, which will allow the servants to have even more skills.

Everything else needs a bit more work. The next art I learn should be from Space Magic.

FREE LIFE FANTASY ONLINE

As we continue to lead ostriches into walls and scatter the wolves and rabbits that appear while we're dismantling, eventually it becomes dinnertime, so we decide to head back to town.

We return to the union, receive our quest rewards, and part ways.

"Great work today."

"See you!"

"See you two later."

After dinner, I'll explore Barberek and search for more food ingredients.

Now it's 9 p.m., which is also nighttime in the game. Until bedtime, I must go on a journey in search of food. I'll head straight to the shops.

What am I after today? Oh, they have adzuki beans and soybeans, along with apples, peaches, and grapes. The peaches are called persias, the grapes are called milveden-nearence, and the apples are simply apples. They also have fermentation barrels.

For now, I'll buy some soybeans. Perhaps I need a fermentation barrel too, even if it's a bit expensive...? Since it's made of wood, maybe I can ask for Ms. Primura's help before I buy one.

There are so many kinds of wine here too.

"Are you a traveler?"

"Yes, I'm an outsider."

"I see. The kingdom of Nearence is famous for our wine, made from milveden-nearence, which bears the name of this land. You may eat these or use them for wine. Most of what we sell are in some way related to wine."

I see. So that's why the wall is stocked with so many wine bottles. They appear to have four types of red wine and two types of white. However, my drink of choice is black tea. It's not as if I'm old enough to drink IRL in the first place.

They even sell celery and broccoli. Hmm...for now, I'll stick to soybeans, apples, and persias.

I consider it pretty urgent to make soy sauce and miso soup. Wine seems fun to make too, but I won't be able to drink it myself.

[STORAGE] PORTABLE VEGETABLE STORAGE (GREAT)

Rarity: RA   Quality: C   Price: 60,000

A portable box to hold vegetables for cooking.

It can hold up to thirty varieties.

This is an appealing item too. It holds ten more varieties of vegetable, for a total of thirty. The price is 60,000 gold. I bet there's a version of this for meat storage too. However, there's no rush to buy one right now.

What looks even better to me is...

[STORAGE] PORTABLE SPICE RACK (LARGE)

Rarity: RA   Quality: C   Price: 23,000

A small portable shelf to store spices used in cooking.

It can hold up to forty-five varieties.

Finally, this is what I've always—wait, what's with this price? Huh? It's so expensive... Ah, but it stores more than the vegetable version, so considering my inventory, I have no choice but to buy it. Yeah, that's it. Farewell, my beloved money!

The soybeans have a use limit, so I buy ten of those, as well as ten apples and persias. I then head to the trade union, withdraw money, purchase the Portable Spice Rack (Large), and exit the shop.

As soon as I reach the town square, I add the rack to my cooking kit, open it up, position the shelf, and store my spices away while I'm at it. It even holds flour? That's convenient. It won't hold my eggs or fruit, though.

I wonder if I'll be able to find fruit storage. It has to exist somewhere.

Ah...this was worth the 23,000 gold. Now I have forty-two more inventory slots remaining. All that dire inventory management feels as if it were a dream.

Now it's like I'm using Inventory Expansion from Space Magic as a means to level up the skill and nothing more. By the way, I turn that off whenever I'm in a party. Managing such a restricted amount of MP is no fun.

I pack up my cooking kit, wander the city a little longer with the time I have left, and then log out once more.

Epilogue

Good morning. It's Sunday. The big event starts next week. It's been a week since the second-wave players joined, and I'm sure they're starting to get used to the game. I'll also bet they're scrambling all over the place because there're so many things to do.

Meanwhile, I'm at the in-game library to do some reading. I like to read IRL fairy tales, but I also like books that contain information about this game—FLFO.

One example of in-game info is the difference between golems, machinery, and dolls. Golems are the ones who prioritize certain functions, while dolls prioritize appearing human. Armor races who are capable of communication are called machinery.

Since dolls must appear human, those that don't match that description can usually be regarded as a golem.

Armor races are beings made from metal armor that was clearly crafted by a person. They're usually spotted in dungeons and attack by firing spells at you. In other words, anything you would refer to as a "robot" is part of the armor race in this game.

The ones that specifically coexist with other races are called machinery.

I'm not sure if the things written in this book would be considered "common knowledge" in this world, but if not, then that really changes things. There are cookbooks and the like that contain recipes guaranteed to have in-game uses, but maybe for books like this, I should just interpret it as someone's opinion? Who knows how the game wants to mislead us.

I could have relied on it more if the author was listed as Future Software or something, but this name looks like it could belong to any normal resident. It could just be flavor text. Unless I can corroborate the information in here, I shouldn't just accept it as fact.

Maybe I can go to the townspeople and pose the information I've learned in this book as small talk. While I'm here, I could also look for books from other authors, but it's hard to tell what I'm going to get from the titles alone. Yeah, I'm going to ask around town instead.

The adventurers' union will probably be a better source of information than the town grannies this time. I can just picture the old women laughing off my questions with a "Who knows?" But adventurers have probably witnessed things like this with their own two eyes, especially the veterans with their many types of equipment. I doubt that a newbie would have a lot to tell me.

Oh, look at that. Tomo's messaging me.

"Hi, it's me."

"Oh, it's you? I didn't realize... No, that's not how whisper chat works."

"I'm just killing time... Like a student does..."

"I can just tell you're up to something dumb... But that doesn't matter. I wanted to ask you about the beach."

"Yeah?"

"Our equipment—or rather, our swimsuits—are almost ready. When do you wanna go?"

He's talking about the trip he mentioned at school. I remember him saying he would ask Mr. Dentelle to make them, since he gathered the materials already.

"I'm playing solo right now, so I'm available any time."

"Okay. I'm free again on Wednesday. Does that work?"

"Wednesday afternoon?"

"I guess that works."

"Got it."

I finish my conversation with Tomo and go back to my books.

Having lost my concentration and not being in the mood anymore, I leave the library and go for a walk around town.

Oh...! It's that penguin! I'm glad to see he hasn't changed. I can practically hear the sound effects of how he walks from here... He's a player wearing a penguin onesie and carrying a two-handed steel sword. In the game's current state, just carrying that weapon alone is quite a display of status. You can tell he must be in the top percentage of players. Oops, I just lost sight of him in the crowd.

Oh, that girl's got the right idea. She's wearing chain mail under her leather armor. Her gloves and shoes are leather too. She's even got a cape. I spot her lance, round shield, and a mace at her hip as well. She reminds me of a mercenary who values substance over style, which I think she made work in this world. But of course, as a girl, she's not covering her head with a helmet!

She must do most of her fighting with the lance and shield, but when she's up against an enemy who can resist lance attacks, she switches to that mace to go for blunt attacks. With her shield, she can be an off-tank, but I'm guessing she's an attacker, since her main defense is said large shield.

Ah, and off she goes somewhere else.

The event will be here soon, and everyone's hustling and bustling around. I'm no exception.

Now that I got my reading in, it's time to get serious too.

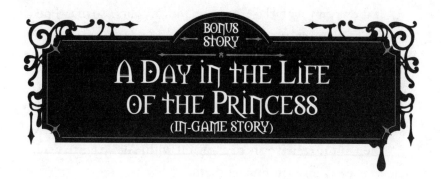

A DAY IN THE LIFE OF THE PRINCESS
(IN-GAME STORY)

"OH, PRINCESS!"

Ah, it's one of the first-wave female players who, along with Ms. Kotatsu, gifted me those cooking ingredients.

"What is it?"

"Um, do you know a way to stand that will make me look more beautiful?"

"I do, of course...but setting the game aside, it definitely won't be any fun IRL."

She stares at me for a moment. "For real?"

"Maintaining good posture requires a lot of muscles."

It's pretty painful if your muscles aren't trained for it. In other words, the simple act of standing becomes a workout... which might sound good, but to put it another way, you need to start with some amount of muscle unless you want to embarrass yourself...

"If you don't have a little muscle already, you'll be trembling, and it'll be obvious that you're forcing it."

"I see what you mean..."

It shows on your facial expression too, of course, so the whole thing is just hard to watch. But the biggest requirement is to have some confidence in yourself. Without that, you'll never be able to stand tall and proud.

The next requirement is to know yourself. In this case, that would mean knowing the advantages of your own body. For me, my chest is the easiest part to show off with. All I have to do is move in a way that accentuates that.

"The problem is that you can never be naked, of course, which means your clothes will play a big role in it too."

"So…I have to find both the clothes and posture that work for me? Just one won't be enough on its own?"

"I won't say it's pointless to perfect just one, but you can maximize your own charms by working on both."

It's not a bad thing to present the most flattering version of yourself. It's far more preferable compared to not bothering at all. The only problem is in *how* you present yourself.

"Men aren't a woman's enemy. A woman's enemy is other women. You must be careful not to make your efforts too obvious, or else you'll make them hate you."

"That's so true."

With that, I teach her tricks she can use that won't lead to her overexerting herself.

"…Like this?"

"To be honest, anything more than that will be too obvious, so there's really no other way to go about it…"

"Is that right?"

"I'm talking about things like a model's strut."

"Ah, I see, I see."

"You can get by with roleplaying in a video game, but it's not so simple in real life."

A woman's appeal is in her curves. What models do is stand in a way that maximizes that appeal.

"But what models do best in the first place is posing, not just standing," I explain.

"Ah..."

"Photographs determine which direction you're going to be looked at from. Please try to focus on maintaining nice posture instead of how you're standing now."

"Would I be shaking IRL if I did this?"

"Maybe, if you don't stand like this normally. It's also harder to keep that posture for very long."

"But it won't do me any good unless I make it a habit, right? Hmph. Are my party members here yet?"

"Are you going hunting now?"

"Yeah. Thanks, Princess!"

"Of course. I think I'll do some hunting myself."

I say goodbye to the first-wave woman and head out to hunt as well.

AFTERWORD

GOOD MORNING? Good afternoon? Good evening?
Since I don't know which to choose, I'll greet you with a "hello." I'm Akisuzu Nenohi. What a handy word. But what time is it really...?

I want to sincerely thank you for purchasing Volume Three of this series.

This book was quite a struggle. Unlike the web version, the print version comes with a fearsome enemy of letters and lines... also known as a page count. This foe was most strong indeed.

Unless you're starting this book at the afterword, you will probably understand that this volume was like a "bridging" book. Actually, if you think about it realistically, these sorts of things do happen in video games. You spend lots of time grinding...be it hunting, gathering, or crafting.

As a VR video game, there are certain things you absolutely need to include. The world they play in is still essentially at the tutorial level for beginners. That's why the quests are going to occur a bit later.

I also improved the BBS chapters. I think they read a bit better now. Although, all I did was indent the text portions. That was about the limit of my capabilities.

I hope that this was a bit easier for you to read.

All right, as for Volume Four... I'll probably be able to fill an entire book with the official event. Or rather, copying and pasting those sections from the web version may be enough to fill the next book on their own... That's where I'm at currently. Copying and pasting it really surprised me. Editing the BBS chapters will probably cut it down quite a bit, but apparently, I have 455 pages already. I really wrote a lot about that part of the story.

I would like to change some parts, since it's no fun to release a book that's exactly the same as the web version, but I'm currently struck by how much space I'll have to work with before I even start.

Please pray that I manage to fill up—no, please pray that I manage to safely release Volume Four next. Let's start with that.

Anyway, I'd like this book's page count to mostly consist of the story instead of the afterword, so for now, I'll say...until next time.

—AKISUZU NENOHI, 2019

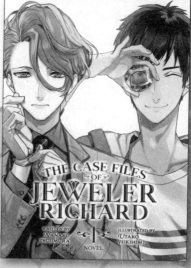